Royal REPLACEMENT

LOVE IN LAANDIA
SWEET ROYAL ROMANCE

HOLLY KERR

Also By Holly Kerr

Royal Rumble

Royal Retelling

Royal Rising

Royal Reluctance

Royal Rebel

Royal Replacement

The Love in Laandia spinoffs:

Coffee Break with the Billionaire

Babysitting the Grumpy Billionaire (coming soon!)

plus

Suitor Science series

Love & Alliteration series

Don't series

Charlotte Dodd series

Royal Replacement

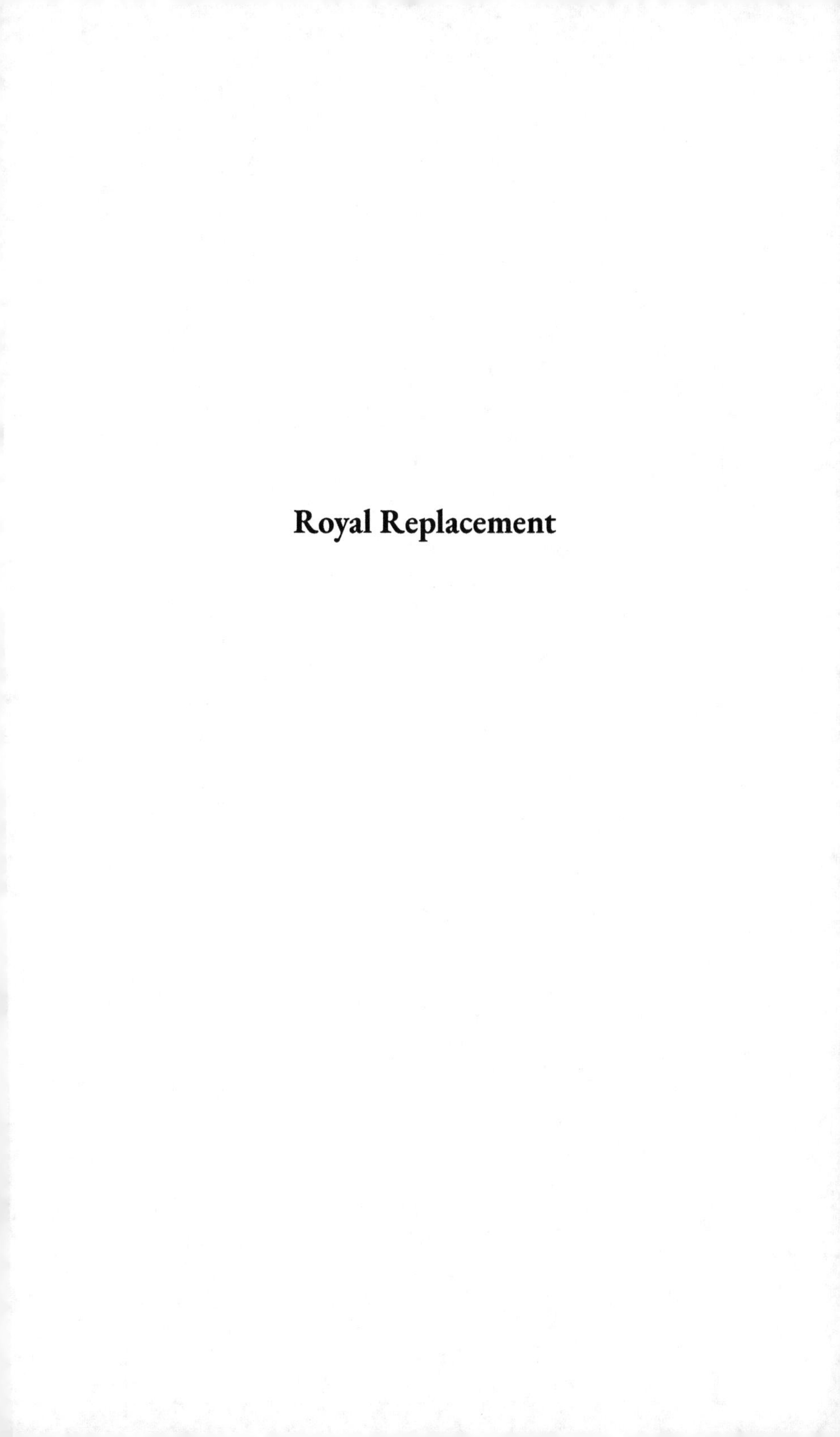

Dedication

To all my readers who wanted more Love in Laandia.

xo

Prologue

O NCE UPON A TIME, a girl caught a boy cheating off her math test.

"Stop looking at my paper," I hiss at Spencer Laz.

First year of high school. First math test. First time I've ever spoken to Spencer.

I know who he is, of course.

He's from the castle—not part of the royal family but as close as he can get because his father, Duncan Laz, is both best friend and chief advisor of the king Laandia. He's the Ned Stark to Robert Baratheon. The companion to the Doctor. Jarvis to Tony Stark.

He was also the bass player for Kräftig heavy metal band, which he founded with King Magnus. But I know him more from the covers of the romance novels I steal from my mother's bookshelf to read.

Duncan is too old for me to even contemplate his attractiveness, even though he's the ultimate definition of a silver fox. But his son?

Spencer has just gotten back from his foray into British private school, leaving him with a hint of an accent that is both pretentious and oddly sexy.

I never imagined thinking Spencer is sexy, but the years away have treated him well. He's grown into his height—and his hair. Most of the male population at Battle Harbour High School sport a too-short haircut, outdated mullet, or even the more outdated Justin Bieber haircut, but Spencer's dark hair already has my fingers itching to run through the messy waves.

Not that I would ever do that. Not that he would ever want me to.

His time away has made Spencer just a little more polished. A little more sophisticated.

But that doesn't mean I'm letting him cheat off my test.

"I'm not looking at your paper," Spencer whispers back at me. The corners of his mouth curve up like he's amused at my accusation.

Even with the hint of a smile, I'm not amused. "What are you looking at then?"

Spencer cocks his head and stares at me.

I stare back.

He widens his eyes, like I should know what he's looking at.

I have no idea—

Oh.

Spencer gives me a little half-smile and turns his attention back to his test.

Oh.

Now I'm distracted since for the rest of the test, I spend more energy trying to figure out if Spencer is *really* looking at me rather than trying to solve the equations for x.

I solve that problem because Spencer makes it clear he's *still* looking at me. Throwing little glances at me, quick enough that he doesn't meet my gaze but each time his lips curve up slightly in a way that makes me desperate to see his whole smile.

After the test is over and collected, I gather my bag and my wits, because I'm going to have to talk to him.

"How'd you do?" Spencer asks, slinging his knapsack over his shoulder. His dark green polo shirt brings out the green tints in his eyes.

I shouldn't know there are green tints anywhere near his eyes.

"I should have looked at your paper," I admit, which isn't exactly letting him know that he distracted me, but comes close enough.

Spencer finally smiles—a real, full smile complete with lips and teeth—and produces a flurry of butterflies in my stomach. "Not sure it would have done any good."

He's a year ahead of me and but something about his boarding school education didn't equate to the Laandian education system, so he's stuck in my grade nine math class, along with Prince Bo. Spencer and Bo have been best friends forever.

Before I can respond about the test or the possibility of cheating, Spencer juts his chin to where Prince Bo leans on Hettie's desk. "They seem to be getting pretty friendly."

I turn in time to see Hettie smile up at Prince Bo like he's the second coming of Harry Styles, and the butterflies crumple mid-flight.

Hettie Crow has been *my* best friend since we were born.

Literally: we were born nine hours apart, and our mothers shared a hospital room. They stayed friends over the years, despite the many differences in their lives.

The main one being Hettie's mom was the exhausted mother of six, soon-to-be-seven kids, with a husband who spent weeks at sea with his fishing boat, and my mom was a new mom, still living in the haze of being a newlywed, with a dentist husband who doted on her.

Not to mention that there are certain challenges that come with being part of the Crow family in Battle Harbour.

But the two women stayed friends, and Hettie and I became best friends. Until Hettie's mother vanished in the middle of the night.

She left Hettie and the rest of her family without a word or a note or a reason—just ran away. After that, my mother became something of a fairy godmother to Hettie, and I became her protector, looking out for her as much as I could. Hettie was different from the rest of her family—soft and sweet and gentle—the consensus was she needed help so she wouldn't get pulled down into the quagmire of her family.

Since then, Hettie's been my ride or die.

Which is why on the second day of school, when Hettie mentioned how she liked Prince Bo's smile, and how much cuter he got over the summer, I immediately shut down the half-baked crush I'd been nurturing for the prince for years.

It wasn't difficult—Prince Bo is *Prince Bo*, and I'm Abigail Locke. I talk loudly, and too much, and I'm pretty good at soccer. There's no comparison: Hettie is delicately pretty, great with kids, and the nicest person I've ever met.

And the first weeks of high school haven't been easy for her.

They found Hettie's grandmother living on the streets in nearby Mary's Harbour, her brother got arrested, and she never got invited to Clare Digman's start of school slumber party, where apparently, they tried honey mead, and Dina Lapierre drank so much that she threw up in Mrs. Digman's garden.

My loyalty prevented me from going, but I still heard all about it.

Hettie needs a win.

Hettie deserves to find her prince, and if it's literal, even better. I would never compete with her.

Besides, Prince Bo never smiled at me like he does at Hettie.

"I think we're past the *seem*," I point out, holding my bag like it's a shield preventing the last residue of infatuation for Bo to seep out of the compartment of my heart where I shoved it down deep.

With a quick glance back at me, Hettie allows Bo to escort her out of the math class.

He carries her bag along with his own.

They make a cute couple. Yes, they do.

"Yeah." Spencer watches them leave, a rueful half-smile starting at the corner of his mouth. Does he think they make a good couple? Do they have his approval if they were to start dating?

If he says anything negative about Hettie, I will show him the reason I'm the star centre of the soccer team this year.

I stand awkwardly at my desk because I get the feeling he has more to say. Or maybe, I just hope he does.

And it better be nothing about Hettie.

"I just thought," Spencer begins and my heart gives a leap like I've scored the winning goal. "If they're... you know... then maybe we..." He pauses. He may sound tongue-tied, but he looks as confident as his father posing on the cover of a romance novel. "You know."

Is he saying what I think he's saying?

I'm not exactly sure what he's saying.

But whatever he's trying to say, it sends a fluttering thrill through me, knocking out whatever was left of my crush on the prince. Because Spencer Laz is Spencer Laz and every girl in Battle Harbour has been in a tither since he got back into town.

And I think he's saying that he wants me?

Maybe?

"Do you do everything Prince Bo does?" I ask instead of leaping into his arms with a whooping, *yes, please, yes* that almost every female in school—and some of the males— would undoubtedly respond with.

My response surprises him.

It surprises me too.

"Well, no," he admits.

"And I don't do everything Hettie does, so is there a reason that you think we... *you know*. Should do everything they are doing?"

I have no idea what they're doing. I know Hettie likes Bo, and a blind person could tell Prince Bo is into her, too. They like each other, and they text and talk, but there's been no actual date yet. Or talk about a relationship.

I would be fine starting something like that with Spencer.

But... is it wrong to think Spencer isn't great at this? That maybe he's going about it in the wrong way?

I want Spencer to give me... *more*.

My little heart, with its steady diet of romance novels for the past two years, wants a declaration of *like*. As in, he likes me.

Or at least a declaration that he hasn't stopped thinking about me since he blew past me on his way to the principal's office the first day of school.

"I don't know," Spencer continues without a clue of where my head is thinking. Or how my heart is beating. "It might be convenient."

Convenient.

The thrill is there, but it's not flowing as much. In fact, it kind of stalls because *it might be convenient* is not what anyone hopes to hear.

1

Abigail

"YOU REALLY DON'T LIKE Spencer anymore?"

The name sends a stutter through my chest, so strong that I'm at a loss how to answer. Because it's complicated. I like Spencer—I'll always like him.

Love him.

But I don't *like* him. For a few reasons. And I don't like him in *that way*.

I've thought of that day in math class so many times, wondering if I made the right decision. Wondering if I'd jumped at the chance back then, if things would be different for me now.

Things would definitely be different—I wouldn't be on the verge of a panic attack hours before I'm about to make my entrance as The Suitorette.

I would never have had the opportunity to be The Suitorette.

And it's a little ironic that it's Hettie's daughter that's asking me about my feelings for Spencer, because it was always Hettie who wanted to know what I felt about him.

If I liked him. If I love him.

If I think we'll be able to get back to being friends.

I think so—eventually. And I think I'm doing a pretty good job moving past, moving on; so much that the heart hasn't done the stuttering for a while. I've been able to hear the name *Spencer Laz* without the need to kickstart things.

I've even schooled myself to hear *Spencer and Princess Lyra* without grinding my teeth down to enamel nubs.

So why did I end things with him? It's the question, the one *no one* has thought to ask.

I get asked if I'm alright. If I'm brokenhearted.

And if I'm willing to fight Princess Lyra for Spencer.

And if I am, could it be in a public place?

Fenella and Stella pulled me into the Sailor's Salon for drinks the night before I left to start my Suitorette stint. There were many drinks and many surprises: I had no idea that my relationship status was more public in Battle Harbour than if I had changed it on Facebook; I also never realized there was so much support and good will towards me amongst the townsfolk; and that some men really enjoy watching women fight each other.

I guess that's why women's wrestling is popular.

Maybe it's not the name that causes the stutter, but the question.

The question that no one has asked. Do I still like Spencer?

It's certainly a question that a lot of people are going to be asking after tonight.

I can only imagine what the announcer of The Suitorette will say at the beginning of every episode.

After her boyfriend leaves her for Princess Lyra, has Abigail Locke gotten over the man the world considers the

fifth Laandian prince? Will her heart recover in time for her to find love again?

Is imagining the same as dreading?

The announcer will no doubt say something about how I've been tasked to fill the too-high heels of Princess Lyra, taking over for her as the Suitorette in the second half of the season. I'm sure the announcer will echo the viewers' thoughts and express concern if any of the men who came on the show to find love with a princess will stick around for me.

Hopefully, they will make it sound kinder than that.

I'm going to have to get used to people asking that, so it can't really be the question.

Maybe it's the fact that it's *Tema* asking the question that causes my heart to trip over itself.

Tema, the daughter of Prince Bo and my best friend, Hettie Crow, is *nine-years-old*. She should be asking if I like pink ponies rather than if I still like Spencer.

It would have been easier if Tema didn't know anything about me and Spencer, but she's a smart kid. While we dated, Spencer and I had weekly pizza nights with Tema, took her whale watching, and helped her walk the rescue dogs at Stella's shelter. We did a lot of things together with Bo and Hettie and Tema.

Did. Past tense.

Now, Princess Lyra will do those things with Spencer and Tema, and I will be left out of the loop like Cady before the mean Plastics got a hold of her.

I also introduced Tema to Mean Girls. We made Spencer watch it with us.

I'm not touching the FOMO. Those kinds of thoughts are doing nasty things to my heart.

It would have been so much better if I had just kept things as *friends* with Spencer.

I managed for years—all through high school, we had been part of the fab four with Bo and Hettie. Bo and Hettie were *Bo-and-Hettie* and me and Spencer were just Spencer. And Abigail.

There *had* been a few instances where lines had been blurred, but at the end of high school, there had been only one couple in the foursome and that's how I wanted it. And then Hettie and Bo were no longer a couple, and Hettie and I left for Vancouver, and I didn't see or even talk to Spencer for years.

And then we came back.

Hettie and Bo got their happily ever after. We were always together, so I thought it might be a good idea to give things a try with Spencer.

Because it was so *convenient.*

It might have actually worked if it hadn't been for Spencer's *do-I-or-don't-I* dilemma about Princess Lyra—Bo's little sister—that had been going on forever.

Literally, his entire life.

I used to tease him about it in high school, but I'm not laughing now.

The question/dilemma/debate about the two of them that feels as old as time got shoved to the forefront when Lyra decided to become the Suitorette.

She ended up with Spencer.

At least that answered the question: Spencer declared his love for Lyra on the reality show, and Lyra said she loved him right back.

They haven't said *I do* yet, but it's only a matter of time. Royal weddings take some planning, and there's already one scheduled for next year.

The interesting, and another possibly ironic, twist is after *Spencer-and-Abigail* became *Spencer-and-Lyra*, I was offered the opportunity to take over as the Suitorette because Lyra bailed on the show midway through.

And now little Tema—who I have helped Hettie raise since the day she came into the world—asks if I'm over Spencer.

She doesn't ask in so many words, but *she's nine*. She doesn't know those words.

At least she shouldn't.

And if Tema is asking, I can be sure that everyone else is going to want to know that too.

That's what *I* want to know.

I smile at the screen, at Tema's earnest little face. It is sweet that she's worried about me. Not necessary, but sweet.

She's nine; she should be worried about herself.

But no. The newest Laandian princess is more concerned with my broken heart.

Is it broken? Is it really?

Was Spencer *the one*? My Mr. Right? My Prince Charming?

I've been doing a lot of unpacking, and even more self-reflection in the few weeks since we ended it.

It only adds to what I've been thinking about since Hettie and I came home to Battle Harbour.

The main thing—more than adjusting to the fact my best friend is now a *princess*—is that I'm supposed to get used to living without Hettie being attached to my hip and holding Tema between us.

I've had to learn to share her with Bo—*her* being both Hettie and Tema.

I now go days without seeing Tema. A week ago, two days went by without me talking to Hettie, and I drove to the castle in a panic, thinking something was wrong.

She had been busy. With Bo.

A few weeks before that, the two of them went away together for the weekend.

It was the first time Hettie had left Laandia without me.

Getting used to Spencer as just a friend is distracting me from the new normal of my friendship with Hettie, and I'm going to have to adjust.

I know the Fab Four has finished their breakup tour. I've come to terms Spencer will never offer me anything but friendship.

And I can honestly say that my heart is not broken over Spencer.

Just a little bruised.

"I like Spencer as a friend," I assure Tema, not for the first time. Or even for the fourteenth time. "Like you liked that Owen kid on your soccer team last summer."

"I did not like Owen," Teme announces. "He picked his nose when he passed the ball to me. Who *does* that?"

"Maybe I like Spencer differently than that," I concede. "As far as I know, *he* doesn't pick his nose."

"If he does, Princess Aunt Lyra will tell him to stop it."

Tema is slowly becoming more comfortable with Bo's siblings but still unsure of what to call them. It changes day to day.

I'm not comfortable with how Lyra seems to have stepped into everything that was mine. She gets my boyfriend—ex—as well as gets to be *aunt* to Tema, which is a lot more official than my title.

I'm called *mother's best friend*. There's no mention of how I cut Tema's umbilical cord. That the first time she slept through the night was in my arms, how for the first six months of her life, I was the only one who could comfort her when she cried.

I soothed, I sang. I dealt with poop explosions and baby food in my hair moments before I had to be at work. I watched Bluey and Paw Patrol and took her to see Santa every single year by myself because Hettie couldn't deal with Bo missing out on that.

I taught Tema fractions and how to deal with bad friends, and they call me *mother's best friend*.

I'm so much more than *that*.

That is taking a little longer to come to terms with than my bruised heart.

"Your aunt Lyra definitely will," I say, managing to keep all of these complicated emotions from my tone. I would rather set myself on fire than let Tema think she's coming between me and her new favourite, Princess Aunt Lyra.

"As long as you're sure you don't like Spencer anymore." Tema stares at me intently from the screen. Her pigtails are crooked, which means she's been playing with the dogs or Bo did her hair again. "Because you can't have more than one boyfriend at a time."

I press my lips together. I thought I had explained to Tema that I'm about to be the Suitorette, how I will be "dating" several men at once as part of the process of finding true love.

All this will be filmed so viewers can watch. Not Tema, though. I never once told her she'll be able to watch all this play out.

The more than one boyfriend at a time might be difficult to explain to a nine-year-old.

I'll let her mother do that.

Better yet—I'll let her father.

"You don't have to worry about me liking Spencer anymore," I tell Tema instead of getting into the logistics about how I'm about to meet twelve men who all want to be my boyfriend.

Maybe they will even want to be my husband.

Or am I getting ahead of myself?

My hope is that I'll find the men interesting and attractive and worthy of my time. That they'll be smart and funny, and kind and considerate.

I can only hope that I'll have a connection with at least one of them so I don't look like an indecisive dud who can't pick a man when they're laid out for me to sample like a buffet.

If I want to really get down to the bare bones of things, I hope the men like me more than they liked Princess Lyra.

Petty, but at least I'm being honest. To myself, because I'm not telling anyone else that.

"I'm happy that Spencer is happy with your aunt Lyra," I say to Tema.

That is the truth. All I've ever wanted was for Spencer to be happy.

For a while I wanted him to be happy with me, but that's over. I have moved on. Set him firmly in the past and am getting on with my life.

By dating twelve men at once.

"Tema!" I hear Hettie calling from off-screen. "Where is my phone?"

"Are you using Mom's phone?" I ask Tema. "Does she not know you're calling me?"

Tema doesn't pout often, but when she does, it's very cute. "I needed to talk to you, and no one will get me my own phone," she grumbles.

King Magnus, aka King Grandpa, would buy her a phone for each day of the week if she asked him nicely.

Thankfully, she doesn't realize that. Yet. It's only a matter of time.

"Don't try to work your dark magic on me," I warn her. "I'm with Mom and Prince Dad on this. You don't need a phone."

"Daddy came close to getting me one," Tema whispers. "But Mom said no."

Daddy. Bo must love that. Hettie kept Tema a secret from him for the first eight years, and he missed out on so much.

I feel bad for Bo, but if he had been around, Hettie wouldn't have needed me so much, and then *I* would have missed out.

"Tema, give me my—Abigail?" Hettie's concerned face appears upside down on the screen. "Is everything okay? I thought we were talking after you met the men."

"I called her, Mommy," Tema chirps. "To make sure she was in a good headspace."

I press my lips together again to hide another smile.

"And is she?" Hettie frowns.

Yes, I want to say.

Of course, I should follow up with.

I'm excited, would convince her.

Instead, I say nothing.

"Tema, Mom needs private time with Abigail." Hettie takes the phone from her daughter. "Can you go find Daddy and go down for dinner? I'll be right behind you."

"Bye, Absolutely Abigail," Tema sings. "Good luck finding a new boyfriend. I love you."

"Love you, too, Tenacious Tema," I counter. I take credit for her extensive vocabulary since we've played Word of the Day since she was four. She's also already a great Scrabble player.

I wave as the love of my life disappears, then I turn my attention to my best friend. "You can't be late for dinner," I protest. "Especially not for me." Family dinner at the castle is a big thing.

I stop myself from asking if Lyra will be there with Spencer.

Thinking about that only rubs salt into the bruised heart, or whatever makes bruises stick around longer than they should.

"Why not for you? Plus, I can do anything I want." She leaves forward until her nose is almost touching the screen. "I'm a princess," she whispers.

That still makes me smile. "Still can't get used to it, can you?"

"I met with the mayor today," she tells me, disbelief still evident in her voice. "Me. By myself. Who does that?"

"A princess of Laandia?"

"Me." Hettie lets the giggle that has no doubt been building up all day escape, before wiping the excited expression off her face. "No more about me. What's up?"

"Nothing. I'm fine. Great. I'm excited."

Hettie scoffs. "Try again."

I rub my face with my hand. It doesn't matter if Hettie is married to Bo, and Lyra gets to be an aunt, and Spencer will never love me like I deserve—Hettie will always be my person, the one who knows me the best.

The one person I never have to pretend with.

"It's just... why am I doing this again?"

Hettie smiles ruefully. "I'd tell you if I knew, Abs, but I honestly have no clue. I know you love the show, but I never thought you'd actually want to go on it."

"I don't love the show," I cry, surprising both of us. "I watched it because you liked it and got sucked in."

"I don't even like it that much," Hettie confesses with a laugh.

"Why am I here then?"

"Why *are* you there?" she asks in her quiet way that always makes me say more than I've meant to, like pouring rice from the jumbo box into the little measuring cup. It always spills over.

"I want to fall in love," I confess.

Until I say the words, I never actually knew that's what I wanted. Sure, everyone says they want love in their life, but I suddenly realize the need.

The want.

I want the butterflies. I want flowers blooming and rainbows and all the sappy stuff.

I want a partner who will respect me; someone who will make me a better person and love the person I already am without trying to change me.

I want what Hettie has with Bo. It's as simple as that.

For so long, it was the two of us against the world. The two of us responsible for our own happiness as well as for Tema. And then we came back and everything changed.

Hettie and Bo went back to being *Hettie-and-Bo*, and I was left on the sidelines. Spencer was there for a while, but he left me. Eventually.

I'm alone, and it's not a fun place to be.

It kind of sucks, actually.

"You don't need a reality show to find love," Hettie points out.

"But I want it *now*, and this will speed things up. Plus, they asked."

"Abigail..."

"It's not about Spencer," I assure her. "I know everyone thinks it is. And I'm not trying to compete with Lyra, because what would be the point of that?"

"I don't know what to think. You never said anything to me until you told me you were going to take over as the next Suitorette. Because she and Spencer..."

Fell in love, I finish silently.

Or maybe they were always in love, and I got between them. Not that I was much of a block to their happily ever after.

I think they got in the way of each other.

Still... I don't like the optics.

As soon as I set him free, Spencer was on the next flight to Saint Pierre to join the show.

Lyra didn't even finish the show before she and Spencer ran off into the sunset.

Then the producers, prompted by Lyra of all people, asked me to step in to be the Suitorette. To meet twelve men. To date them simultaneously.

To fall in love with one of them.

That's what I signed up for.

And now, when I'm about to start—

Saying I have cold feet is an understatement.

"I didn't have time to talk to you," I admit. "It happened so fast. They were in the coffee shop, and then I was here."

"You've always told me things like this," Hettie says in a soft voice. "Now, I feel like—"

A laugh bursts through my nerves. "Are you upset I didn't tell you before I signed up?"

"I know I shouldn't be, but I'm used to talking about everything with you."

"And now you have a husband for that," I point out gently.

"But I still need you."

I smile at the screen, at the woman who has been my best friend forever. At the woman who is married to a prince of Laandia and mother to the third-in-line to the Laandian throne. "I miss you too," I admit sadly. "It's so hard to get used to not doing everything with you."

"I thought it was just me," Hettie wails and I laugh.

"I've got it worse than you. At least you have Bo to fill the time. I'm stuck going on a reality show."

"You're not stuck," she argues. "You can get out of it if that's what you want."

"I think Grayson Grant would beg to differ."

"I can't believe you met Grayson Grant." Hettie sounds like she's suppressing a fangirl squeal.

"You totally love the show," I accuse.

"I totally love the show," she admits. "And you're going to be the Suitorette."

"I am," I say.

But right now, I don't feel all that good about it.

2

Ashton

I'D RATHER GO OUT in a flaming crash at the first corner of the track than admit I'm excited about being on the show.

Kind of.

Sort of excited.

Excitement is a new emotion for me. Blasé is more me. Nonchalant. I am the epitome of coolness, and cool guys never shows excitement. Has anyone ever seen Keanu jumping around? Or Lennie?

No, because cool guys don't do that.

If my twin sister, Fenella, was privy to my inner monologue, she would also point out that cool guys such as Keanu and Lennie Kravitz would never be a contestant on The Suitorette.

Thankfully, Fenella is not listening to my inner thoughts. There's a twin connection, but that would be truly frightening because I *do not* want to know what goes on in the mind of my sister.

I shouldn't be excited about being stuffed into a hotel, especially one that only has draft beer at the bar. And the rooms—I refuse to sit on the bed because that spread has clearly seen pre-2010.

Don't get me started on the shower curtain.

Three stars, max.

Each contestant has been confined to a room so we can't meet or mingle or potentially threaten/blackmail/extort the other contestants.

Twelve guys, all waiting to meet the woman who might be Ms. Right.

Or Ms. Right now.

One by one—or three by three—we will head to the Oceanview Hotel on the other side of Saint Pierre to meet Abigail Locke.

The Suitorette.

The Suitorette 2.0.

Abigail has stepped in for Lyra because the princess bailed halfway through this season. The promos for this are going to be wild—two women who had been/are in love with the same man.

Spencer had those two women under his spell? C'mon. *Him*?

I'm not under either of their spells and don't plan to be, but still... excitement.

Sort of.

It's not like before a race; more like trying out a new set of tires during a practice lap. Which can be fun.

Being on the show with Lyra was fun—or as much fun as you can have being on camera twenty-four/seven.

Lyra told me straight away that she wasn't picking me, but I didn't believe her until Spencer got here and everyone saw them dancing. After that, it was game over for all of us.

Even though Lyra wasn't a perfect match for me, I never really expected *not* to get the girl.

It's never happened before.

Ashton Carrington, heir to the Carrington toy company and darling of the NASCAR circuit. Tom Ford begs me to be in his fashion shows, Seth Rogan gives me cameos in his movies, and even though I'm far from the most likable in my group, I've never had trouble getting the girl. Even without trying.

After another lap of the room, I brush off the chair and perch on the edge, staring out the window.

Downtown Saint Pierre could be called quaint and cozy. Both are other words for boring, but I'm not saying that.

I'm the one who decided to stick around for part two, so it wouldn't do any good to badmouth the place.

Waiting is getting old. Patience has never been one of my virtues.

My FaceTime chimes just when I'm about to start wandering the halls.

They left us our phones while we wait for the cars, but we're supposed to hand them over before we leave.

I've got a second one hidden in my bags because I don't go anywhere if I'm not connected.

I accept the call because it's my sister, and if I don't, she'll never let me forget it.

"Why are you still there?" Fenella demands.

Since she moved to Battle Harbour, she knows too much about the comings and goings of that country. Lyra and Spencer were supposed to keep a low profile after they left, but that would have been akin to telling a peacock not to do the thing with its feathers.

"You're not supposed to know that," I say with the last of my patience.

I didn't even tell her that I was going on the show. Fenella had been too wrapped up in all things royal Laandian, not to mention her new guy, Silas, to give me the attention I deserved. There had been no time for her brother unless it involved a headline that mentioned her.

"I know everything," my twin announces, and I believe her. "I know you went on the show to fall in love with Princess Lyra?"

She phrases it as a question because it *is* hard to believe. Ashton Carrington does not believe in love.

Even if I did, why would I voluntarily sign up for a reality show to win the heart of a woman?

Not only the heart, but maybe even marry her.

At least that's what they want to happen.

This show gives all the power to the Suitorette—first Princess Lyra of Laandia, and now Abigail Locke, also of Laandia, but only a commoner, albeit one who has the ear of Prince Bo.

She can pick me or kick me to the curb.

It's the ultimate gamble.

A race to the finish line. What men will make it that far? Who will crash and burn?

I stayed in the race until Lyra took herself out, but I plan to make it to the end with Abigail.

Because I am a competitor, and none of these guys have the stamina and strategies that I do.

"I did." If there's one thing I learned from my parents, it's how to lie like a press secretary.

I'm not about to tell my sister the whole truth, because since she's met Silas, Fenella has changed in ways that make her considerate of others. Concerned. Respectful.

Nice.

I blame her falling in love with a barista who is all of those things.

And because of these unfortunate changes, I suspect sister dear will frown upon the real reason I'm here, so it's best I don't tell her. I may not care what the world thinks of me, but I do care about Fenella.

"Why are you still here?" she demands. "Abigail is great, but do you really think she's your type?"

"I think what you really want to ask is if she's our father's type."

The only reason I wasn't disinherited after my father found out I signed up to for a reality romance show is because Princess Lyra was the Suitorette.

For me to stay for Abigail will make him freak out.

I do love a good freak-out from my father.

"That too," Fenella concedes, more than a little guilt in her tone.

Fen had to deal with our parents when she told them about Silas. She's always been the favourite of our father, but our mother did not approve of her marrying a barista, even if he does own the place, as well as being an advisor to the king on his new observatory.

I like the guy because he makes good coffee, but that's not enough for the senior members of the Carrington clan.

"Lyra is gone, so why are you still there?" my sister demands in a voice that is a surefire way for her to get answers.

I know the voice well, because it's the same one my father uses.

I shrug even though she can't see the move on screen. "It's a fun place."

"It's an island in the middle of the Atlantic."

"It's actually in the middle of the Gulf of St. Lawrence. Know your geography, sis."

"It's not even big enough for you to drive around. Like you want to drive."

Fenella knows me too well. I can say I'm having fun, and maybe I am, but she knows what I need.

To quote the oft-quoted film extraordinaire, Top Gun—I have a need for speed.

Or something like that.

I've made a tidy living outside the allowance from my father racing cars, and I'm very good at it.

Some days I need to do it.

But not after that race a few months ago.

I didn't like how I felt after it was over. And since then, I've been trying to keep my distance from the racetrack.

I haven't told Fenella about it, and I won't. All I need to tell her is that I'm looking at trying new things, and my sister—the queen of trying new things—will believe me.

I'll just have to convince myself.

"If I tell you I'm looking for love, will you go away?"

"No, because you don't believe in love. At least, that's what you've always said."

"Maybe I was wrong."

"No, because you believe you're always right even more than you don't believe in love."

I bite my lip to stop the smile. "You have a point there."

"So? Spill it." She narrows her violet eyes at me. We look alike, but not too alike. And I've always been glad I never got the purple eyes. Mine are dark blue, and that's better. "You're not there for fun. And I don't believe you were there for Lyra, because I know Lyra, and the two of you together would be..." She shakes her head, at a loss for words. "It would be bad."

"It wouldn't be that bad. I'm a catch."

"You wouldn't be in Laandia."

"I beg to differ. I think the littlest Laz sister has a thing for me."

"I will make sure to tell Sophie *that* would be a *very* bad idea. When's the last time you spoke to Milo?" she asks suddenly.

There's no way... "What does that matter? Milo has no part in this conversation."

"Are you sure about that? The only way you would go on a reality show—that didn't involve some sort of racing or extreme sport— is if you were forced to do so. And they won't force a person to go on the show because it would make them look bad. So you would need to be compensated more than what a reality show could do for you. So, back to Milo—how much was the bet?"

I stare at my sister in disbelief.

She's good. Very good.

"How do you know it was Milo?" I ask, biding time.

"Rupert doesn't have the cash available, Coral actually *likes* the show, and Lavinia doesn't care enough. What did Milo bet you?"

Shaking my head, I capitulate, because she's my sister and I've never lied to her. "Ten thou if I make it to the last three," I admit.

"And?"

"And a shot at the new Indy car he's sponsoring."

"Ashton," she chides.

She doesn't need to chide me. Even more than admitting I'm excited, I hate that I don't feel great about taking the bet.

I'm a billionaire, always out looking for the latest thrill. The next adventure that will scratch the itch, and irritate my father.

Being a contestant has done both.

Despite myself, I like the other guys. I really liked Lyra, even though I knew things would never go further than friendship, I could have convinced her to keep me around as one of the last three men.

I'm not sure about Abigail.

The thought of trying with Abigail interests me, and these days, so few things are interesting.

Or exciting.

I'll stick around as long as I've got a shot—at driving Milo's Indy car.

3

Abigail

I STILL NEED TO pick out a dress.

These cold feet need to warm up because I've got less than an hour to get myself camera ready. And then get over to the hotel for the make-up artist to work her magic. I'd never regret talking to Tema, but her call did take up some of my picking-out-a-dress time.

I should have shown her the dresses and let her pick.

Instead of going through the three racks of clothes trying to find a dress that 'speaks' to me, I curl up on the bed and let my mind go where it has been trying to go in the four days since I agreed to be The Suitorette.

To say it happened fast is an understatement.

And to say that I'm not here because Princess Lyra took my boyfriend would be a lie.

She didn't take him in so much that I handed him over. I offered Spencer to Princess Lyra like a charcuterie board of all my favourite cheeses.

Can you make him happier than I can? If so, he's yours.

What was I thinking?

I was thinking that I deserve more than to settle for convenient. Which is what I was to Spencer. Not the love of his life. Not the girl from his past that he couldn't get out of his mind.

Those were both Princess Lyra, and the whole world knew it. Except for me, who preferred to play ostrich and keep my head stuck in the sand.

I wonder if the giant birds actually do that, or if it's just an old saying.

Tema likes knowing fun facts like that. My heart gives a tug at the thought of the little girl. The newest Princess of Laandia; Tema, who is not my daughter, but more than a niece.

The pain of missing her eclipses the regret and—let's face it—embarrassment over Spencer, but spurs on thoughts of slipping out the back door of the prefect's house and hotfooting it to make the last ferry back to the mainland to see her.

I don't leave because I stick to my commitments.

Unlike Princess Lyra.

And unlike Spencer, who disregarded everything he ever told me when he went running after Princess Lyra.

I'm not bitter at all.

I've always been proud not to have settled for convenient with Spencer back in high school, and I really wish I'd remembered the 'convenient' conversation before I slipped into being his girlfriend when I came home.

Because it *was* a slip. It was a slide. It was the tiniest of bunny hops from being a friend to a girlfriend.

I deserve more than a bunny hop.

And it's the reason I'm standing here, before three closets full of clothes courtesy of The Suitorette romance reality show, of which I will be stepping in as the new star.

Because Princess Lyra took my boyfriend.

There's a knock at the door.

I swipe at my cheeks to make sure the welling in my eyes hasn't overflowed as I pull myself off the bed.

I hate crying over men. And I'm not—I'm not crying that I lost Spencer to Lyra.

I'm crying because I feel like I've lost a part of myself, and I don't know how to get it back.

But now is not the time to figure out that dilemma. I need to be at the hotel in—oh, wow, only thirty minutes—for them to get me ready to meet the men tonight.

I haven't even decided on the dress to wear.

A dress that will wow them. Wow twelve men.

Twelve, not the twenty-something Lyra started with.

Twelve. Shortened season. Because I'm the replacement. Because Lyra didn't want to finish.

And that's my problem. How can I feel like the Suitorette when I've always been second place to Princess Lyra?

I open the door to Camille and the shy/concerned smile she's taken to wearing around me.

Camille is Princess Camille, but not really since she's married to Prince Odin, who recently abdicated his place in the line of succession to allow Camille to become Prefect of Saint Pierre.

Odin didn't do that because it was convenient. He did it because he loves Camille—a whole lot of love.

I still think of Camille as a princess, but I'm not sure I'm supposed to.

"How is the dress selection going?" Camille asks, hovering in the doorway like a hummingbird waiting for its turn for the sap.

I wave toward the rack of evening gowns. There's another rack of dressy date options, and one for more casual outings.

I'm pretty sure I got more clothes than Lyra, so at least there's that. Not surprisingly, seeing as she's a princess with a princess wardrobe, and I'm not.

She has a whole castle of clothes.

This would be a lot easier if I could just hate Princess Lyra. Or at least seriously dislike her. But I don't. And I can't.

"I'm about to close my eyes and pick. Want to spin me around and make it ever more fun?" I ask Camille. "Come in, by the way."

"That good?" Camille steps into the room, followed by her ankle shadow, Betty White. I feel special because the little dog no longer bares her teeth when she sees me.

Progress.

We survey the colours and fabrics and choices. "I think maybe there's too much selection."

This is only the dresses. I still have to pick shoes and jewelry.

It's not the biggest problem I have, though. That's going to be picking between twelve men.

Twelve.

How do you even go about doing that?

"Are you nervous?" Camille blushes and drops her gaze. "Sorry. I shouldn't have asked."

I know Camille, because, thanks to my connection to Hettie—now Princess Hettie and married to Prince Bo—I'm familiar with the significant others of the royal family.

I'm also staying at Camille's house during the filming.

But neither makes us actual friends, although I'm not opposed to becoming someone Camille can call a friend.

"Ask away." I sigh so deeply that the satin slip dress on the rack shimmers from my breath. "I think I'm on the cusp of freaking out about all the choices in here."

"In here, or in a couple hours when the men start climbing out of the cars?" I stare in wonder as Camille begins to push the hangers aside to look at the dresses. "What's your favourite colour?"

"Go back a second, to when you read my mind." That isn't a slip or a slide into friendship—I jump right in.

That's what I'm used to doing—none of this waking up beside Spencer one morning and realizing that we're in a relationship without any discussion or decisions.

Camille smiles, and this time it's a genuine smile without any shyness or concern for my wellbeing. "It's not that hard. You're going to be faced with a difficult decision, plus following in Lyra's footsteps."

Look at that. Camille just jumped in there with me.

That's what you call instant friends.

"I hated even walking down the aisle after her, and it was my wedding," Camille admits with a laugh that is half serious.

"Yeah, I can imagine. I really can. Lyra has a certain something..."

"I was completely terrified of her when I first met her. Maybe still a little?"

"I think that's common, because I know Hettie and Stella still are," I confess. "Hettie said it was easier meeting the king than Lyra."

"That's because the king—Magnus," Camille corrects. "Is the most amazing person in the world."

"You're not crushing on your father-in-law at all, are you?" I tease.

"He just appointed Odin his Secretary of State, and is letting us keep the titles, so yes, I think I am," Camille says with a proud tilt to her chin.

"I hadn't heard that, Princess Camille. It suits you, by the way."

Camille's cheeks turn pink. "It won't be announced until after the show."

"I'm not sure why, since my being on it has nothing to do with the royal family."

She turns back to the dresses. "Favourite colour?"

"I like them all, but if I had to pick... purple?"

"You really need to work on your decision-making skills before you meet the men," Camille teases in return.

I love new friendships.

"Do you think I'm making a mistake?" I wonder aloud. "I'm putting myself out there to be compared to Princess Lyra, not only by the men, but by the public and the press. They're going to think I'm jumping into a relationship with the first man I find because Spencer broke my heart when he left me for Lyra. Not that he really left me. I gave him permission. To leave me."

Is it the worst move I'd ever made? No.

Is the world about to make me change that opinion? Definitely.

"Is that why you're doing the show?" Camille asks, with her usual serious expression.

"No."

"Then what do you care about what they think?" She pauses for a long moment. "Lyra doesn't."

That's true. Lyra doesn't care what anyone thinks. "That's a good idea in theory…"

"But the reality?" Camille finishes. "Different story. I get it. Look, Abigail, I don't know you very well… yet." She tacks on the word with that shy smile. "But I can tell you're as strong and vibrant as Lyra. She made the show her own. You can too. That's true that they're going to compare you, but who says they will find you lacking?" She shrugs and fingers through the hangers until she finds what she's looking for. "Here. Pink, not purple, but it'll look great on you."

"Do you really think…?" My words trail off as an idea hits me. "Camille. What if…?"

The idea is fully formed and so simple that I wonder how no one had thought of it.

It's a perfect way for me to make the show *my own*. I won't have to worry about the show being a clone of Lyra's, about me being constantly compared to her.

I'll still worry about that, but it won't be that bad. Not if I can pull this off.

Camille stares at me, clearly worried about what's going on in my mind. Because I've never been one to hide my feelings.

And now I'm feeling optimistic. Hopeful.

Excited.

"Should I be worried about what you're thinking?" she asks slowly.

"Maybe?" And then I laugh and share my idea about how I'm going to shake things up with my new friend Camille.

4

Grayson

"I THOUGHT SHE'D BE the punctual one," I mutter to myself as I check my watch for the sixth time. "At least better than Lyra."

Abigail is late.

Granted, we can't start without her, and the crew knows to expect a late night, but I'm ready to finish this season of The Suitorette, and we haven't even begun.

The Suitorette 2.0. Or maybe part two. I still haven't decided what we're going to call it, and I need to make that decision by the end of the day tomorrow.

Because I am an executive producer and I have to make all the tough decisions.

Like stopping halfway through a season to change leads.

We have The Suitorette—Lyra's season. And then because the Princess of Laandia did the unthinkable and actually fell in love with one of the contestants—fell in love after only two weeks—refusing to play nice and finish the season, we now have part two.

Grayson, the former Suitor and romantic at heart, understands.

Grayson, the executive producer and host of the show, is tearing out his hair.

And I have a good head of hair, so that doesn't work for me.

"She's coming," Rue calls as she hurries toward me, She, along with Ria, are both my second-in-command on the show for the season. "We were going over a few things, but Hazel is powdering her now."

"What were you going over?"

"She has ideas for the dates." Rue is being vague, and I notice because Rue is rarely vague.

"She should have come to me earlier," I say with my producer's voice—authoritative but still reasonable. I've learned a lot from being both Suitor and host, especially about what not to do.

"She didn't have the idea then," Rue assures me. "Don't worry, I did some checking when she was in the makeup chair, and everything is doable."

I've also learned that whenever someone tells me not to worry, I do. A lot. "Then why am I worrying? What exactly is doable? And what do you mean by *everything*?"

"Here she comes," Rue says instead of telling her boss everything that is going on. "We'll talk later."

"I think we better," I mutter as I turn to see Abigail in a bright pink dress hurrying toward us. Her gait is slightly off-kilter from the high heels.

"Coming," Abigail calls. "Sorry. There was so much to do, and I couldn't pick a dress, and I had no idea proper makeup takes that long. I didn't give myself enough time."

"That's fine," I tell her, even though it really isn't. I never factored in the stress of being in charge before I took over as executive producer.

"It'll be fun being in charge," my wife Bexley told me.

"You like being in charge," she kept saying.

I really don't think I do.

This would be so much more fun if I were still just the host, saying whatever they wanted me to say, even though I felt like an idiot half the time.

"You're so much more than just a pretty host face," Bexley assured me.

She thought it was a good idea for me to take the job. I took the job. There was no other option.

There never is where Bexley is concerned. I will do anything for my wife.

And because we met when I was The Suitor, I feel an obligation to help others find a similar love.

I give Abigail a last check, a comforting smile breaking through the stress when I notice how nervous she is. "You look amazing," I assure her.

She really does. Abigail is pretty, but Hazel worked her makeup magic, and she's practically glowing. She's done something with her dark eyes that makes them huge, and the slash of pink on her lips is a shade darker than her dress, and makes her mouth look—well, like she's ready to be kissed.

That is a producer Grayson opinion not one from married-to-love-of-my-life Grayson.

"The dress is okay?" Abigail does a little sway and shimmy. "I got Camille to pick for me because I just couldn't make up my mind."

"Hopefully, you'll have better luck deciding among the men."

She meets my grin. "That's what Camille said too."

Abigail's dark curls look like she's tumbled out of bed and onto a boat, only better. They're not polar opposites when it comes to body types, but there are enough differences between her and Lyra so that no one—like some of the elderly viewers—will confuse the two.

And as far as I know, their personalities are very different.

At least I hope they are. Lyra is outgoing and vibrant, but completely unpredictable. Abigail seems like she's a little more level-headed when it comes to getting what she wants.

Again—I hope.

The first car will be here any minute, and Johnny raises his camera to start filming as Abigail fidgets at my side. "All good?" I ask.

I also didn't expect stage fright from Abigail.

"Great," she says brightly.

"Rue said you had some issues with the dates." Headlights flash as the first car makes the turn to the hotel.

"Ideas, not issues." She glances at me, and I can see what I thought of as nerves is really excitement. "Rue said we can work something out."

"Do you have a problem with what we've set up?" I ask with confusion.

"But you haven't really set any up," Abigail points out. "Yet. Rue said that all this has been such a rush that there hasn't been time."

"Plans are in motion," I assure her, the beginning of a headache developing at the thought of going back to organize group dates. It's a collaborative effort, but I have to sign off on all the ideas.

Abigail smiles widely. "Maybe plans can change."

The unease is back and has brought friends. "What kind of plans? What do you mean?"

Abigail laughs. "Don't worry, Grayson. I came up with a way that will help me find my happily ever after, and you don't have to do a thing."

I really dislike when people tell me not to worry.

5

Abigail

THE FIRST CAR PULLS up, and I almost bounce out of these shoes.

I don't mind the shoes, even though I can't walk in them very well. I might be one of the few females in Battle Harbour who don't crush on their shoe collection.

But I'm not in Battle Harbour.

I'm standing in front of the Oceanview Hotel in Saint Pierre waiting impatiently for my Mr. Right to get out of the car.

Only I don't know who my Mr. Right is. Or if he's even here.

I have to think positively. This process has worked in the past. A great example is Grayson beside me. He met his wife Bexley when he was The Suitor.

Then he became the host, and now he's in charge of the whole show.

He likes to think he is. I think Rue is really running things, but I like Grayson, so I'm not saying a word.

"What are you thinking?" Grayson asks.

For a minute, I think he's asking about who I think is really running things, but no. He wants my thoughts for the show. He wants me to tell everyone who is going to watch this my thoughts about how I feel about the possibility of meeting the man of my dreams in the next few moments.

This opening up in front of the camera so the world will fall in love with me—Grayson's words, not mine—is going to take some getting used to.

But I rise to the occasion. "I'm excited," I say, my gaze on the car idling in the drive. I can't see inside the tinted windows, and the anticipation makes me fidgety, like a puppy who needs to pee. "And nervous. But mainly excited."

And I am. Talking to Camille earlier helped get me into the right headspace, and talking to Rue made it even better.

I can do this. I can be The Suitorette.

And I think I can do it better than Princess Lyra.

"How do you feel about following in Princess Lyra's footsteps?" Grayson asks, like I knew he would.

"I'm grateful." That was one of the lessons Mrs. Theissen gave to Hettie when she moved into the castle with Bo—when in doubt, go for gratitude. "I think it will be easier for the men who stayed. They'll know what to expect, and hopefully not take as long to get comfortable with me and the process."

"Are you expecting any of the men not to be comfortable with you?"

I shake my head, slightly alarmed when my hair barely shifts because of liberal amounts of hair spray. "I'm like your favourite stuffed animal. Or an Owen Wilson movie. Or left over macaroni and cheese." I listen to myself and wince. "Maybe that's not a good thing."

The cameras are filming every moment of this.

Grayson laughs. "Well, we're about to find out how comfortable you can make the men. Here comes the first one."

The limo door opens, and legs appear. Shoes so shiny they practically glitter in the lights of the cameras. A torso, and then—

"Rand." I smile as I recognize his red hair. "I know you," I say as he gets closer. "Or at least it feels like I know you."

Rand was one of the original men on Lyra's part of the season. Even though her episodes haven't been televised yet, there has been promotional material out for a few weeks, long enough for me scour the internet for everything I can find for names and faces of the men.

No one has told me how many of them left when Lyra did, or how many were interested in staying for me. There are a few that I hope will stay, and a couple that I'd be fine if they left.

I had no idea how uptight I am about not knowing who stayed and who left until Rand stands before me, smiling.

He has a great smile—warm and friendly with just the right amount of teeth.

Very white teeth.

Rand reaches for my hand. "I'm Abigail."

"Rand. But I guess you know that."

There's an awkward moment when he moves to kiss my cheek and I go in for the hug.

We settle for the hug. He holds me just tight enough, with hands kept in safe spots. And he smells great—like fresh laundry hung to dry in the middle of a forest.

While I'm not opposed to physical contact, I've never been a very huggy person. My parents were affectionate, but gave most of their attention to my younger brothers. And moving with Hettie to British Columbia meant that we were our own support system, and she's not one to go in for the hug unless someone is crying.

Luckily, Tema is all about physical contact, but a sticky-fingered hug from a little girl is a lot different from being held by an attractive man.

And Rand is attractive. He's the boy-next-door, with a bit of a geek side, and a golden retriever energy.

The Golden Retriever book boyfriend archetype, not that I'm comparing him to the breed of dog.

He's got the red hair of Sam Heughan but the gentle, intelligent good looks of Sam Claflin, with a sweet smile.

I like the combination.

I already know I like him.

We chat for a few minutes, but I have no recollection of what we spoke about. I do know that I can't stop smiling.

I'm going to look like a grinning idiot when they show this on TV.

Next up is Boone, the bad boy from Lyra's season. It goes about the same as Rand; he hugs me, I think he's attractive. I remember asking about his tattoos but not much else. And that he also smelled really nice.

I don't remember much about the third man, only that his name is Duke and he sang me song as he walks up.

The fourth man out of the car, on the other hand: "Jakey?" I cry. "Jakey Crow?"

It's been almost ten years since I've seen Jake Crow, and longer since I've spoken to him, and the years—

I won't go as far as to say the years haven't been kind, but there have been enough changes in his physique and... hairline... that sixteen-year-old me wonders what I saw in him once upon a time.

But he still has the twinkle in his eye that suggests he's trouble, and that I might have a lot of fun getting into it with him.

"I'm here as the boy next door," he calls out, arms outstretched. "Or should we call me the one who got away?"

"We might have different opinions about that." Many years have gone by and much water under the bridge, so I accept his hug. "I'd even go as far to suggest as lovers to enemies."

"Ah, Abs, don't be like that. You know I didn't mean anything."

He didn't mean to break my heart? I doubt that. Hettie's cousin—who she gave me explicit orders *not* to date—broke my sixteen-year-old heart not once, but twice.

It might have been over ten years ago, but as Jake heads into the hotel, I can't help but recall the uncomfortable fact that I don't have a great track record in making romantic decisions.

"When's the last time you saw Jake?" Grayson wants to know.

"Not long enough ago," I mutter. "It's been years," I say for the camera.

"Are you excited about reconnecting with him?"

I give Grayson a look. "All I can say, is that Jakey better had smartened up from the seventeen-year-old idiot he used to be, because I don't want Hettie to tell me I told you so twice."

Grayson smiles. "He came to us about the show," he tells me under his breath.

"He always liked the attention." Along with breaking my heart, Jakey also did everything he could to maneuver himself into a friendship with Prince Bo.

It didn't work; *Bo* listened to Hettie even if I didn't.

I take a deep breath as the second car arrives.

Firefighter Dylan is the first one out, and my heart gives a patter at the sight of his handsome face. That's three men who stayed. "I was hoping you'd show up in a fire truck," I say as he approaches.

His smile is butter-melting-in-the-sun good. At least that's how it makes me feel. "Maybe we can arrange that for our one-on-one date."

Lyra never gave Dylan a one-on-one date. I'll have to do better, which won't be a hardship because Dylan is one of the best-looking men in Lyra's season.

Which is my season too.

Next up is a new arrival—Tesh, with dark, drooping curls and a soulful smile. And then Charlie—the dentist.

That's seven. I'm more than halfway there.

And four of those are men who made it through Lyra picking Spencer and stayed. Whether they stayed for me, or wanted their fifteen-minutes of fame remains to be seen, but I have to think that it's for me.

I have to.

And I like to think I'll know if they're only here to get famous.

I've given it a lot of thought, and I'm not sure if I'd prefer a brand-new set of contestants. Knowing four of the men—at least knowing them from the promotional materials—gives me a sense of comfort, like having a friend in a class.

But comfort hasn't done very well for me in the past.

There's no time to mull it over because I hear the next arrivals before I see the car. Engines—at least two—can be heard approaching at a speed that would give them a ticket anywhere else. Saint Pierre is a quiet sort of place, so drivers might have their cars impounded for driving that fast.

There's no one around here who would drive that fast.

I glance at Grayson, my eyes wide as two cars race up to the hotel, one skidding a few feet as they come to a stop.

"He insisted on staying," he says in a quiet voice.

Two men step out of twin Ferraris—one yellow, one orange—wearing tailored suits that might cost more than what Grayson makes on the show.

I catch my breath, because this is unexpected. Not only has Ashton Carrington—billionaire race car driver—stuck around, but he's brought a friend.

"Abigail." Ashton is pretty enough not to need his billions, but wealth gives him a confident air that borders on arrogant.

I know him—or at least I know *of* him, since his sister Fenella is a new resident of Battle Harbour and the girlfriend of my former boss at the coffee shop, and new-to-me friend. I never imagined Ashton wanting to stick around because it's so unbelievable that he was on the show in the first place.

"Ashton." I can't fight the urge to introduce myself because how could someone like Ashton know *me*. But I also can't come up with anything else to say but, "I'm Abigail."

His eyes—the dark blue of the ocean at midnight—scans me from top to toe. Then he gives me a smile of such lazy insouciance that I should be offended. "Oh, I know who you are."

And then he hugs me.

Ashton Carrington, who could buy Saint Pierre if he wanted to, swoops down— because he's very tall—and hugs me.

Arm around my shoulders, one around my waist, and I am being hugged.

Warmth. Strong arms. Musky scent, fabric against my cheek—I take the moment.

And then it's over, and his smile is still lazy, but there's a hint of something I really think is interest in those eyes.

Instant interest?

Sure, why not? This is a reality show.

My words seem to have returned. "You're still here?"

Maybe not the best words.

"I had nowhere better to be." Those blue eyes pack a punch when they focus on you. And I am the focus.

He's here for me.

"Plus, I had to make sure you didn't fall for my friend," he adds.

His friend. I peer around Ashton—he's still standing before me—to check out his friend.

And—oh, my god. Not one billionaire, but two. His friend might not be as well known as Ashton, but I've admired the pictures enough to recognize the face.

If Chris Hemsworth and Chris Evans could have a baby, with Harry Styles' hair and James Marsden's smile—that would be who is standing before me.

"May I present Rupert Lorde?" Ashton drawls. "He's not a real lord, but he likes to pretend."

Rupert elbows Ashton aside and takes my hand in his, which is smooth and soft and, I suspect, manicured.

He *bows* over my hand. "Enchanted to meet you." He straightens with a smile full of straight, white teeth that would make Dentist Charlie proud. "As Taylor Swift would say."

It's impossible not to return the smile. "Already quoting song lyrics. Should I be impressed, or worried that you're into plagiarism?"

At least I can still speak with Rupert.

"Not me. I'm a good boy. Unlike my friend here." Rupert motions to Ashton.

One dark, one light. Is this me being tempted by good and evil?

I really can't stop smiling.

Billionaires. For me.

Rupert tilts his head toward the hotel, his hand still holding mine. "You going to join us?"

"We have to give her a chance to meet the others," Ashton reminds him.

"Why? She's got everything she could want right here."

It's possible at this moment I honestly do. "I have to be fair and at least give the others a chance to meet me," I tell Rupert, caught up in his green-eyed gaze.

"I don't think you do," Rupert argues with a teasing frown. "But I do play fair." He releases my hand and steps back. "I look forward to having all your attention to myself very soon."

"See you inside," I manage, because what do you say when a man like Rupert Lorde looks at you like that?

They head into the hotel, and I turn to Grayson, eyes wide with amazement. "He's— both—really?"

Grayson grins. "Too much?"

"I don't think so." The laugh bubbles out of me. The cameras have been forgotten along with my nerves. "This is going to be so much fun."

6

Tanner

I SHOULDN'T BE THIS nervous.

I've done this before, and I think I did a good job. There had been a connection between me and Lyra. The only problem was that Spencer got there first.

I can't really explain why I stuck around for Abigail.

I wasn't surprised when Grayson came to us to tell us that Lyra had chosen Spencer and was leaving the show well before it was supposed to finish. No one was.

We all saw how Spencer was—he was completely in love with Lyra. At first, I thought it was that they had known each other so long, but there was an energy that surrounded the two of them. I don't know much about love but there is no doubt something connected the two. Lyra is amazing, but I could tell her heart wasn't in it after Spencer got here. And I don't blame her for leaving.

When you find the one, you just want to be with them.

And then they left the show together, finding their own happily ever, leaving the rest of us in the lurch.

It's not a surprise how their love story turned out, but having a new Suitorette dropped in on us definitely is.

If I had anything to return home to, I might have left. Jon did, leaving a hole in the house.

But I don't have anything waiting for me at home. It's the main reason I applied to the show. Yes, I want to fall in love, find a wife and all that good stuff, but I also have been in a weird sort of limbo for a while.

I don't like it.

My family doesn't know what to do with me, and neither do my friends. They stick with me, offering options for jobs, dating, and advice on things I don't need advice for. I know what the problem is: I had a life planned out for me, then I pivoted to play hockey full time. Then hockey fell through, and I've got to pivot again, only I don't have a direction. I have no fallback plan.

My friends and family are great, but I have to be the one to figure things out.

It's taking longer than I expected.

When my buddy's girlfriend heard about the casting call for the Suitorette, she suggested it because I'm the only single guy in our group.

While I wasn't exactly pressured to do it, there were definitely some strong-arm tactics used. I knew my friends meant well, but it wasn't until I got to know Lyra that I got comfortable with the process. But I never really thought I had a chance with a princess.

Lyra is beautiful and outgoing, and slightly intimidating. I would never want to get on her bad side. I also got the sense that she was in the same boat as I am—the S.S Limbo. Without a clue what to do with her life.

Maybe we could have figured it out together. Or maybe we would have kept floundering.

I'll never know.

I stuck around for the chance that *something* could switch things up for me—but also because Grayson had broached the idea of me becoming the next Suitor.

"We usually pick the next Suitor from the men of the Suitorette season," Grayson had explained the evening after Lyra left. "And consensus is, you'd be a popular choice."

I was the hockey player archetype—that's going to be in bold letters after my name. Nothing else.

I'm not even a hockey player anymore. So why would anyone think I'd be a popular choice to be the Suitor?

"Would it be something you'd be interested in?" Grayson asked. "You know the drill—you'd start out with twenty-five women, sequestered somewhere in Canada. We're scouting Ottawa, for a start date in October."

"Sure," I said automatically, without giving it much thought.

I'm thinking about it now, and I shouldn't be, because I'm moments away from officially meeting Abigail and starting the process to discover whether we'd be a good fit.

I shouldn't be thinking about twenty-five other women, but I can't help it. Not the women per se, but what being The Suitor might do for my life.

It might give me options I never considered. A focus.

I could find a partner to work through things with. I would have my shot with twenty-five women—which would almost guarantee I could find the one for me.

I don't know what being on this season of The Suitorette might bring me because it won't air for another month. I don't know Abigail. I have no idea whether there will be a connection between us.

There is nothing guaranteed about my being here, but here I am anyway. Taking my shot, like I do for everything else.

And I find myself back in a car, with the scent of nerves and expensive cologne filling the back seat.

With Basher, of all people.

We were roommates the first time around, and he's still here, in the car with me, waiting for our chance to meet Abigail.

Along with Basher, the third of our trio isn't someone you'd expect.

"You're really a prince?" Basher demands.

Prince or no prince, the guy sits back and adjusts his cufflinks. Real gold, with a twinkle of a diamond. Not like my hockey sticks that my niece Ella got me last Christmas.

"Jonas Erickson," he says in a cool voice.

"Are you—you're related to Lyra?" I ask, wondering about the family tree.

"I *am* a member of the royal family," he confirms, which tells me nothing because now that Lyra is gone, I have no interest in learning about the Laandian family tree. "My father is the younger brother of King Magnus. I'm Lyra's cousin." Maybe he's saving the charm for Abigail because I'm not seeing any of it. "You're obviously not from Laandia," he adds.

"Halifax."

A perceptible sniff gives a suggestion of what Prince Jonas may think of my Nova Scotia roots.

"My side of the family keeps out of the spotlight more than my cousins," Jonas continues.

"Is that by choice or because no one cares?" Basher asks.

Basher has my back better than any of my former teammates did.

Jonas turns his cold gaze toward Basher, who grins in return. "You both failed to win the heart of my fair cousin. What makes you think it's a good idea to stick around for another try?"

Wow. Hope he makes a quick exit.

Basher offers me his hand for a fist bump. "Guys are cool. Most of them," he adds with a flickering gaze toward Jonas. "Plus, next tour doesn't start until the fall, so I've got some time."

"What about you?" Jonas asks me. "Shouldn't you be playing somewhere?"

He knows I'm a hockey player. And either he doesn't know an injury took me out last year. Or he does, and he's being a dick about it.

I vote for the latter.

Part of me wishes I could tell him I'm biding my time before I sign on to be The Suitor, but that would make *me* sound like a dick. Besides, I'm still not sure I want to do it.

And I don't want to tell this guy anything about myself.

So I look out the window instead of answering. The inside of the car is quiet, save Basher's fingers playing "Wipeout" on his knee.

We pull up at the hotel.

Abigail stands with Grayson at the front doors, pretty in pink. Her dark hair, thick and curly, barely hits her bare shoulders. She's curvy, tall.

Even from this distance, I can tell she's the type of pretty that draws you in, rather than intimidates.

She's not Lyra, but maybe Abigail can be something better. Something more.

Someone for me.

Hope blooms inside my chest at the thought, and I can't wait to find out more.

I think this is the point of reality romance shows. They remind you that there's always hope. That you have to take your chance, and keep trying. You can't give up, because there's someone out there for everyone.

There's someone out there for me. "She's pretty," I say under my breath.

Another sniff from Jonas. "Did you have any doubt she wouldn't be?"

Basher shifts to see around me, and I'm reminded that while I might hope that Abigail is the one for me, there are eleven other men thinking the same thing.

My little spark of hope dims.

I sit back to give Basher room to see out the window because watching Abigail will only make me more nervous than I already am.

Basher whistles. "She cleans up good."

"I'm sure the show has certain standards for attractiveness." Jonas's gaze flicks to Basher. "For the women."

This guy. "How do you know I play hockey?" I ask him rather than rising to his petty implied insults.

Jonas shrugs. He hasn't made move to check out Abigail. "I made sure I had approval of the contestants before I agreed to come on the show."

"Why?"

His eyes are such a light blue that it's almost disconcerting. "Adequate competition," he drawls. "I *am* royalty."

Basher turns to me. "He *is* royalty."

The only royal I've met other than Lyra was her brother, Prince Kalle, and he had a much better personality than this guy.

"And I'm not," Basher adds, leaning over to open the door. "But I'm still jumping at the chance to meet this hottie. Later, dudes."

He jumps out and gives a whoop of a greeting, leaving me and Jonas alone in the car. I watch out the window as he practically runs to greet Abigail; at the way she laughs as Basher swoops her up and spins her around.

Is that the kind of man she wants?

Jonas still hasn't looked out. He brushes a piece of non-existent lint off his pants. "Unfortunately, his second time won't be the charm," he says matter-of-factly.

"Don't be so sure," I finally snap. "Basher might not wear a crown, but he's a good guy. Better than most."

"I'm sure your fellow hockey players offer a low bar of comparison."

I let the jab fly over my head and copy Basher's tapping on my knee. Anticipation curls in my stomach. I'll meet her in a few minutes. Five minutes, tops.

Will I be able to tell right away if I have a chance? And if there's no chance, should I just take myself out of the running and wait for my next turn?

I wish Grayson hadn't said anything about me and the Suitor. It's more pressure than I need.

"He's done," Jonas says shortly, finally looking out the window. "You're up."

I glance at Jonas, then out the window at Basher backing away from Abigail. His hands are always in motion, and they are both laughing. "No, it's you."

Jonas shakes his head. Is this a joke? I can't tell anything from his face.

"The order was Basher, you, then me," I insist.

"And I'm telling you that I'm last. Go. You don't want to make her wait."

"But you're next, so it's you who's making her wait."

He crosses a leg over his knee.

"Seriously? You're not going? It's your turn."

Jonas gestures to the door. "After you."

I can't believe this guy. It's a petty thing—who cares who goes next—but it's the principle of the thing. Plus, I can't stand smugness.

"She's waiting," he points out, still not moving.

I'm not ready. I needed another minute to get my head in the game, to push the possibilities back and focus on Abigail.

But she's waiting, and Jonas is... he's a real treat.

With a curse, I open the door. If this were a game and someone treated me with such lack of respect, I'd tuck my shoulder in and knock them into the boards.

But this isn't a game, and I don't play hockey anymore. And I can't let Prince Dick get to me. So I hold my head up high and try to wipe the frown from my face before Abigail sees it.

7

Abigail

BASHER IS ADORABLE.

And he's a rock star, of a band I actually know.

He's like an exuberant puppy who can do tons of tricks and wears a red bow tie.

I love the bow tie. It goes with the sneakers and the black pants that I think might be jeans, but Basher plays in a rock band, so why would he wear a suit?

I like the Basher vibe.

He hugs me, then goes back to kiss me on each cheek. He asks what my favourite band is, then frowns when I stammer out Maroon Five because it's the only one I can think of.

"You're supposed to say Water Rhinos," he says in mock dis-approval.

"They're my second favourite," I assure him.

"We'll have to work on that. I'm much cuter than Adam." He leans forward. "Plus, I'm taller."

I like that he makes me laugh.

I *like* Basher.

I'm still smiling as he backs away from me, almost tripping over Grayson standing off to the side. I keep watching him until he disappears into the hotel, and then finally I turn to see who is next to come out of the car.

It's Tanner.

My smile doesn't fade when I see him. In fact, I think it gets wider.

Tanner McGainey, who made history his rookie year when he played with the Canadian Junior hockey team, scoring a hat trick in his first game, and then taken out by a nasty cross-check against the boards. He was with Team Canada for three years, before getting drafted by the Pittsburgh Penguins.

But after a disappointing first year, with injuries and concussions, Tanner hopped around from team to team, never really finding his footing in the NHL.

I don't think he's still playing.

My family is a hockey family, so I know these things.

And Tema told me about meeting him with Lyra, stories about swimming and slip and slides, and Tanner giving her shoulder rides.

Any man who does that has to be a good one.

It's always nice when he's attractive as well.

Tanner's hair is shaggy and unkempt, but it works with the slightly crooked nose that looks like it's been broken more than once. As he walks toward me, I'm surprised by his height. Tall—so tall that he would be super intimidating on skates—with broad shoulders that practically block the waiting car.

It's fine, because right now, I don't care who is in the car.

He wears a charcoal gray suit that's snug around his shoulders and biceps, and I admit, I have more than a few non-PG-13 thoughts about what may be under that suit.

And then I notice the frown.

He looks angry. Frustrated. He looks stiff and uncomfortable. Maybe it's nerves, but why would a man meeting me for the first time look so upset?

Unless... it's me.

He's disappointed in me.

Tanner is still a few steps away, and storm clouds still collect on his brow, and I'm worried. I'm not Lyra. He's comparing me to her, and he's finding me lacking.

Is this what all the men are thinking, and the others are just better at hiding it?

Tanner should be happy to see me, and that doesn't seem to be the case.

There's no smile. I'm not what he expected. He's regretting coming back.

There was more between him and Lyra that he let on.

I don't like how fast the self-doubt spreads. I hate feeling second best. But what am I supposed to think when Tanner—

He gives a shake of those shoulders and his expression clears. Not entirely happy, but no longer angry.

"Hi," he says, his smile slow in coming. His gaze skates over my face, his own expression relaxing as mine grows more wary.

Tema loved him, and I thought... "Hi."

He looks surprised at the coolness of my tone. "You look amazing," he blurts out.

"You look upset," I point out. "Disappointed?"

Oh, I really don't like how I sound.

This is bad. I glance at Grayson, hyperaware of the camera recording every second of me doubting myself. Can they delete that?

"No," he declares with a confused shake of his head. His eyes are a warm brown that verge on hazel. "Disappointed with you? Not at all."

"When you were walking up, you looked like you didn't want to be here."

"What?" Tanner literally gives himself a shake, like he's a puppy who's gotten sprayed with a hose. "No. I mean, yes, of course, I want to be here. Absolutely. It's just—nothing. It's nothing." He gives me a pleading smile. "This isn't—Can we start again?"

"Is that necessary?"

He looks like he's struggling not to say something, even glancing over his shoulder at the car waiting with the next contestant.

Another shake of his head. "Yes. I would like to start again because I am very happy to be here. And to meet you."

I shouldn't hold a frown against him. He might have tripped getting out of the car, or banged his knee. He doesn't need to be all smiles and rainbows when he saw me.

But I am. And deep down, there was my hope that Tanner would be there. Add on how his little frown made me doubt myself—

Stop it, Abigail.

He holds out his hand. "Tanner McGainey. A real pleasure to meet you."

"Abigail Locke. It's nice to meet you."

It should be nice. It should be more than nice. This is the one I was waiting to meet, and now...

Tanner chuckles, finally managing to look relaxed. "You sure?"

He's still holding my hand, long fingers dwarfing mine. "Maybe we *should* start over."

"I don't really want to go back to the car," he confesses. "How about I have a drink waiting for you inside, where I'll be all smiles and looking incredibly excited to see you. Which I really am."

He smiles. It's not a perfect smile—slightly crooked, mouth a little too wide, but I like it. I like how honest he seems.

I already can read his expressions, so I think this is the real Tanner.

My shoulders drop with relief, and the corners of my lips curve up in response. How can a smile have that much impact?

"Incredibly excited? I think I know what that's like," I admit shyly.

Tanner perks up even more. "You don't say."

"Tema speaks very highly of you. She's getting the king to design a slip and slide for her."

He laughs with delight, and that right there, does more than anything to wipe away the last few moments. "That little miss stole my heart. Ruined me for anyone else."

"She does that."

"She's an amazing little girl. Laandia is lucky to have her."

Tema belongs to Laandia, not me. My smile fades a bit. "They are."

Grayson clears his throat, the sign to wrap it up. "I'll see you soon for that drink," I tell him.

"I'll be waiting. Incredibly patiently. But until then... May I?"

Tanner is asking to hug me. None of the other men did that. They assumed I would welcome the chance to have my body pressed up against theirs.

I've never been much of a hugger, but I step into Tanner's embrace as eagerly as I agreed on the dress Camille had suggested.

Tanner is a wall of muscle, but it's a warm wall, and his arms wrap around me like I'm a precious package he wants to protect.

Citrus and mint and salt air surrounds and for the first time all night, I feel myself relax. "Thank you for staying," I tell his suit jacket.

I feel the rumble of Tanner's chest. "I bet you say that to all the guys."

"Actually, no." I was grateful for those who stayed, but I was interested in the new arrivals. The ones who hadn't done this before, who didn't have a reason to compare me to Princess Lyra.

Whatever good Camille's talk had done for me, I'm still very aware of following Lyra's footsteps, and my shoes will never measure up to hers.

Tanner slowly backs away, keeping his hands on my arms like he doesn't want to let me go.

I've never felt like that from a hug.

I should really hug more.

"I'll see you inside." Tanner walks backward, keeping his gaze on me until he bumps into a planter. And then, with an embarrassed wave, he turns and disappears inside.

Grayson steps beside me. "I don't think that went as well as Tanner hoped."

"No, I... It wasn't what I expected," I admit. "He seemed upset."

"Something must have happened in the car because that's not Tanner. He's a good one."

I glance at the cameraman still filming. "Are you supposed to say that? I thought you're supposed to be objective?"

Grayson smiles, and that is a smile that belongs on television. "I may have my favourites. Are you ready for the last man you're going to meet tonight?"

"Last man? Are you sure no one is going to pop in like Spence—?" I cut myself off before I finish.

I want to take it all back, or at least ask them to edit it out.

But I know they won't.

Spencer will not be popping in to throw his hat in the ring like he did with Lyra. He had his chance with me.

He picked Lyra.

He went on a reality romance show to tell the world he picked Lyra.

Talk about a grand gesture.

I smile tightly. "Let's do this."

"I don't know if anyone will be popping in," Grayson admits.

Great, now he's pitying me. The entire world will be pitying me. Poor Abigail, who lost her boyfriend to a princess and now gets to pick through her rejects. Will they even want her?

"Abigail?"

Guess Tanner isn't the only one whose emotions can be read as easily as a book with large print.

And like Tanner, I give myself a shake. "I'm ready."

"If you're sure." Grayson nods to someone off camera, and moments later, the back door of the car opens.

Legs appear—navy pants with shoes so shiny they reflect the overhead lights. The rest of him—open suit jacket and red tie. And —

I know him.

Not exactly know him, but he looks an awful lot like—

Blond hair, swept back from a brow that needs to be described as noble. Jaw so square that I can see the right angles. Blue eyes...

It's Prince Charming come to life.

"Is that—?" I ask in a hushed voice. "Is that Prince Jonas?"

8

Jonas

I'VE NEVER BEEN AS recognizable as my royal cousins.

The Battle Harbour royals, as they're called. Kalle, Odin, Bo, Gunnar, and of course, Lyra. My cousins.

I'm part of the Peace River royals—brother Mathias, sister Renee, and me. Father Euan, mother Emelia.

King Magnus gave Father a title other than Prince, but no one uses it.

My picture isn't spread as liberally around the world as my cousins, but I'm still well known in certain circles. I don't have People Magazine Sexiest Man of the Year as part of my credentials, but Abigail recognizes me.

I see it in her eyes—the flash. The way her mouth drops open.

I pause for a moment, resting my hand on the car door. I may not have bidding wars for my pictures, but I do know how to pose.

Abigail needs a moment to clarify with Grayson Grant that, yes, I am Jonas Erickson, sixth in line to the Laandian throne.

Seven, now that Bo had a long-lost daughter show up.

Moment over, I stride over to Abigail, buttoning my jacket on the way. "Hello," I call when I'm close enough.

"Prince Jonas." She sounds flustered. "This is a surprise. Should I bow? Or curtsey?"

"Not at all." I take her hand—soft and slightly damp, like she's nervous, and covered in silver rings—and bring it to my lips. "It's lovely to meet you."

I'm constantly asked about my accent, but I'm not about to admit it's from studied attempts to rid the Laandian tone from my voice. A few weeks staying with Harry Windsor at his place in California has helped as well.

"You as well," Abigail says with a nervous laugh.

She's prettier than her pictures, because I have seen her pictures. With Spencer Laz, with cousin Bo and his new wife. So many with the new little princess that I thought Abigail was the child's nanny.

The dark tumble of curls have been styled, tasteful makeup applied. I like a woman to make an effort, but not look overly made up, and Abigail does it well.

I squeeze her hand before I release it. "I expect we're running late, so I'll let you finish out here and meet you inside. I'd love to have a few minutes with you."

"That would be nice," she manages.

I like her smile—warm and friendly and slightly lopsided. She's not perfect.

Perfect women look good on your arm, but there's not much to them, and I find them rather boring.

With a last smile, I head inside. I don't need much time because the seeds of interest were planted as soon as I stepped out of the car.

Last. I made sure I would be the last man for Abigail to meet so I would be first on her mind when she joins us inside.

The main work is to be done inside.

A group of men stands around the hotel lobby, drinks in hand and watching the door. The lobby is suitable—fireplace, bar off to the side, couches grouped for conversations. It's decorated in shades of white and blue, giving it a nautical air. The open wall of windows at the back of the lobby let in the sounds and scents of the sea.

I don't have a love of the ocean, probably because my family's home is on the other side of Laandia. We have a river and lakes, and the border to the Canadian province of Quebec, but no Atlantic Ocean.

My cousins living in Battle Harbour enjoy that.

As I stroll toward the group, there are more than a few confused expressions—as if they recognize my face but aren't exactly sure who I am.

And then there are several who clearly know who I am and aren't glad to see me.

I'm pleased to see the competition is... lacking. "Gentlemen." I nod to the group. "Let the games begin."

The redhead in the tacky blue suit frowns. "This isn't a game."

And then the bald and tattooed behemoth practically growls. "I don't play games."

"Shame. But this is most definitely a game," I correct. "Only one winner, after all."

A scoff, and I turn to find who it came from.

Ah.

Ashton Carrington is here, along with Rupert Lorde. Two of the Billionaire Brats, friends of cousin Gunnar.

Wonderful.

I wasn't exactly truthful in the car—I did manage to see a list of the other contestants, but none had been confirmed at the time. And as much as I pressed the issue, I wasn't allowed a say in who the final twelve were.

I school my expression into one of disinterest to hide my displeasure. "Carrington. And Rupert," I say in a cool voice. "Whose yacht dropped you off?"

"Milo's, actually." Ashton smirks. "You remember Milo, don't you?"

I keep my expression blank. I do remember how Milo Stapleton-Shak won several thousand dollars off me during a private poker game in Monte Carlo last year.

My father was not pleased with the loss.

"Vaguely," I say. "I don't think I liked him."

Ashton looks me up and down with the confidence of a son whose father can buy most small countries. "I know I don't like you."

"How is your sister? Is she still such a ... naughty girl?"

Anger flares in Ashton's eyes at the mention of Fenella. His sister broke up my sister's engagement a few years ago, and Renee had been trolling her ever since. I follow Fenella's various social media platforms because at one time I considered her to be a suitable match for me.

"My sister is a lot of things," Ashton says with a tight-lipped smile. "She can be anything she wants to be. And if you open your mouth about her again, you will not appreciate the consequences."

Silence among the men. I don't bother to hide my smirk.

"We need Jon for this," the red-headed man decides. "He was good at keeping the peace."

"No need to worry about that," I tell him. "I'm just catching up with old friends. And I'm here to make new ones." Without waiting for a response, I head to the bar.

Abigail will be here shortly, and I'll be ready for her.

9

Abigail

TWELVE MEN STAND IN the lobby of the hotel, watching me walk in.

Waiting for me.

They are all attractive. They are nice enough; I don't know any of them well enough to describe them as anything different.

Twelve strangers. Here for me, or so they say.

I can't help but imagine what they're thinking of me. Comparing me to Lyra—shorter, curvier, less charismatic.

Average attractiveness. Not as pretty as Lyra.

My dress is too bright, not glamourous enough. I don't have her poise, her sophistication, or the confidence of being born a princess.

There are so many ways to compare me to Lyra, and I will come up lacking in all of them.

And yet—I'm the one who is here. These men are here to meet *me*.

I give myself another shake because now is not the time to second-guess myself.

Now is the time to get to know these twelve men.

But first—

Now is the time for a drink.

I give a quick wave to the men, holding up a finger in a *I'll be right there* gesture, and head straight toward the bar.

Before I make it there, Prince Jonas steps forward with a glass of sparkling wine. "My lady." He gives a slight bow, golden hair shining in the light. "You've accomplished the first step of meeting us all. You should be pleased and proud of yourself."

I draw a shaky breath. "It's a lot," I admit.

"It's just the beginning." He holds out the glass. "You look like you could use this." Not only does Jonas look like Prince Charming, he's got the chivalry down pat.

"You read my mind." Taking the glass, I take a ladylike sip, even though I'm tempted to down the glass in one gulp.

"Can I steal you away?" he asks.

They all want to meet me. Talk to me. I glance at the group waiting and find expressions of interest, of anticipation.

Of excitement.

Meeting them was only the first step. Now it's time to get to know them.

Game on for the boys.

"You may, but give me just a moment." This time I take a healthy swig of the wine and step away from Jonas. "Hi, guys!" I call out.

A wall of sound hits me—cheers and laughter and everyone saying my name. I laugh with delight. "Hi!" My smile is easy and natural and not fake at all. "I'm really looking forward to getting to know you tonight, as well as in the following weeks, so let's get this party started."

They cheer. For me. And it's... heady. Overwhelming.

Kind of amazing.

These twelve men are here to get to know me, and it starts now.

I turn to Jonas, but see Tanner out of the corner of my eye. He's carrying a beer glass, as well as a tumbler of something pink.

Dismay flashes across my face.

"I'll save it for you," Tanner assures me. "Come find me when you're ready."

"Thank you," I mouth.

Then Prince Jonas puts his hand on the small of my back and leads me away.

He's a prince.

Yes, I have connections with the royal family of Laandia, but Bo never seemed like a *prince* to me, at least not the ones from the fairy tales.

Jonas actually looks like the Prince Charming doll I had growing up, with the blond hair and the blue eyes and the suit tailored to his lean frame. He and my Ken doll used to fight over my Barbies.

Hopefully, these men are better behaved.

Jonas leads me out of the lobby to a patio overlooking the water. There's a fire table, and he escorts me to the small couch before it.

Here we go. Game on for me.

"So. Prince Jonas," I begin, trying to keep the *oh, my God, is this really happening* out of my voice.

"Just Jonas," he says, taking the seat beside me on the low couch. "I don't normally use the prince title."

"Can I say I'm surprised to see you here?"

He shrugs, the simple lift of the shoulder seeming so graceful. Attractive. He's so sophisticated, and it's hard to believe he's from Laandia, part of the royal family of Bo and his brothers.

I shouldn't compare him to Bo.

Bo is quiet and introverted and would never even consider coming on a show like this, even if he'd never met Hettie.

Jonas is here, sitting beside me, looking completely comfortable.

"I heard about Lyra and Spencer," Jonas begins.

My glass pauses on the way to my mouth. Here it comes. Will it be pity? Platitudes about how Spencer made the wrong decision?

"I wanted to see what her replacement is like. For the show." Jonas smiles. "I thought you might like a little support from the family."

That's it?

"Thank you." I take a too-big sip of wine, and the bubbles tickle my nose. "I appreciate any support, not that I really need it. But there might have been an easier way to show that support than coming all the way here," I suggest, my laugh hopefully taking away any possible sting from my reaction.

"But I wanted to meet you."

The way he says it—like why *wouldn't* he want to meet me—adds to the butterflies in my stomach.

I have butterflies. *Instant* butterflies.

Is that going to happen with every man? And if so, how will I ever choose between them?

But now is not the time to worry about that. Now is the time to enjoy myself with a *prince*, and see where things lead.

Twelve-year-old me gives a shiver of delight at the thought of Prince Charming being here with me.

"You live in Toronto most of the time, don't you?" I ask because I really need to say something.

Jonas looks pleased. "Ah. You keep tabs on me, do you?"

"You're a public figure. And a prince."

"Not much of a prince." There's a wry twist of his lips, but I have a feeling there's more than self-deprecating humour underneath his comment.

I'm going to have to find out what's underneath all the comments, for all the men. And as quickly as I can. That's how I'm going to make the decisions.

"So that's why you're here?" I press. "Curiosity?"

"Among other things."

One thing Jonas seems to have in common with his cousin Bo is that they are both closed books. I'm not used to walls. "Why don't you tell me about those things?" I suggest.

"Why don't I tell you how beautiful you look in the firelight instead?"

I laugh. I can't help it. "Oh, you're good."

"I try to be." He turns to face me, crossing his legs in an elegant gesture that shouldn't be masculine, but it is. "Why are *you* here?"

"They asked me," I say immediately.

"Why don't you tell me about the other reason?"

"Who says there is one?"

He chuckles. "I've known Spencer for years. Everyone says he's the fifth prince, but he's more like an advisor. He's the lawyer for the royal family, knows where all the bodies are buried. Nothing more, not really princely. If that's what you were hoping for."

"I wasn't hoping for anything." My cheeks flame. Is that what people think? That I wanted a prince, and Spencer was the closest I could get?

Is that why Jonas is here?

This is a mistake. I want to walk away from this conversation. From everything thinking—

"I don't mean to insult you," Jonas says quickly. "And I apologize for speaking so frankly. I meet a lot of women who are looking for a royal connection."

"*I'm* not."

"You already have one," he corrects. "From what I hear, you and Hettie are thick as thieves. And you practically raised Princess Tema. I like that."

His admission is unexpected and throws me.

"You know the drill, so to speak," he continues. "I've always thought Spencer was an idiot for sticking so close to the family, and now he's confirmed it. To pick Lyra over you—"

"He didn't pick her over me."

"It would have never been an option for me," Jonas announces.

"It wouldn't have been a choice for you, since Lyra is your cousin and we're not back in medieval times where that is accepted," I point out with an awkward smile.

I expected someone to bring up Spencer, to say things like this, and I know I should stop Jonas. We should talk about other things, but I want to hear what he says.

I think I need to hear what he says.

"My cousin Lyra is a complicated woman who has the guilt of the queen's death leading her every decision," Jonas says, staring at the water as I study his profile. "Queen Selene loved Duncan and his son, so it's no wonder Lyra wanted him."

That's something I've never considered. "I don't think that's the only reason."

"Maybe not." He turns back to me. "I'm sure you don't want to talk about Lyra."

"I don't," I say in a flat voice.

"My apologies." He leans forward and sets a warm hand on my knee. "How ever can I make it up to you?"

No one can deny this is a moment. The way he smiles into my eyes. The firelight, the headiness from the glass of wine drank too fast. The fact that I'm here with a prince; that he's one of the men vying for my heart.

Jonas is here for me.

And knowing that helps calm the emotional upheaval I've already gone through tonight.

But there's more to come.

I'm going to have to send at least one of the men home tonight, and I have no idea how I'll that decision.

Jonas smiles at me. He's so attractive, with the cut jawline and those lips. Full. Smiling.

At me.

"There might be one way," I say in a low voice, and lean into him.

10

Basher

I WAIT THROUGH PRINCE Jonas whisking Abigail away, and then Ashton and Rupert tag-teaming an interruption, Jonas again getting back in there, before Abigail puts a stop to it. Then Boone steps in and clears the way for the rest of us.

After all that, I still get blocked by new guys Duke and Tesh before I manage to get in there after Dylan.

I sit on stage for a living, putting my skills on display every night, so there's never been a lack of confidence. Even so, getting blocked and jammed and rerouted trying to get to Abigail is a tough pill. Logistically, it's exhausting. You want to be fair about it—which obviously *Prince* Jonas doesn't get—but you need to stake your claim.

Not that Abigail is something to be claimed.

She's fun. I get that already.

I don't meet a lot of fun girls in my line of work.

They think they're fun, but I see a hardness in a lot of the women who follow the band. A sort of desperation.

Most of the women I meet are those who follow the band, which means the number of relationships I've had that has lasted more than the length of a tour can be counted on one hand.

An ex-girlfriend once told me I wasn't boyfriend material. Not a nice thing to hear.

So I'm here to switch things up.

I finally get Abigail all to myself, and right off the bat, it's great. We talk, we laugh, we—

"You're very twitchy." She points to my always-in-motion hands. I don't even realize my fingers are drumming against my leg.

"Always." I grew up hearing my mom calling me high-energy and spirited, which these days I think are code words for ADHD.

I've never been tested but holding my attention can sometimes be a challenge.

Abigail—who plans on being a teacher and who might know more than me about attention disorders—takes it in another direction. "Song in your head?"

"You know it." My grin falters. "I mean, do you know it?"

She shakes her head. "No musical ability whatsoever. I knew a guy in a band when we lived in Vancouver, though. I'd go listen to them in clubs."

"Ooo, a boyfriend?" I tease.

"Nope, just the friend kind. I didn't do a lot of dating back then."

"Was that in your small child era?"

I like her laugh. It's big and hearty and comes from her belly. "You mean Tema?"

"The wee princess. She was a treat to meet."

"She was. How did you know...?"

"Please. I do my research. Plus, Spencer might have said a few things about you during his time here. But we're not here to talk about Spencer," I add quickly, watching Abigail's happy expression shut like a slammed door.

"No. I'd rather not."

"No. So... no musical ability. I can totally live with that. No competition."

"Do you compete with the guys in the band?" she asks curiously.

"Nah. I'm very supportive. I think I'd make a very good boyfriend," I announce.

Abigail leans toward me, which I take as a good sign. "That is very good to hear."

I rest my hand on her knee and fight the urge to tap. "So what was little Abigail like back in the day if she wasn't a closeted musician?"

"Were you a closeted musician?"

"No, I was way out in the open. It's the only thing I ever wanted to be. Other than a baseball player."

"It was soccer for me," she says. "My brothers played hockey, and I tried that for a few years, but I couldn't compete."

I may be twitchy, but I also pick up on things. Even I can recognize there's something in her tone when she talks about her brothers. "Did you try to compete?" I wonder.

"Very much." She smiles ruefully. "But then I decided my parents had enough on their plate with two future Gretzkys on their hands, and I picked something a little easier. Something for myself."

"You didn't think there was enough room on the plate for you?"

Abigail's smile tightens. "There was a lot of hockey at my house. Still is."

And she's not talking about it. "You must have heard of my man Tanner then? Sounds like he was a pretty big deal back in the day."

She takes a sip of her wine. "I have heard of him," she says, a flash of pink on her cheeks. "And he was a big deal. I guess he's not playing anymore."

"That's what he says. T's a good guy."

"Yeah?"

"You don't agree? Have you had time with him tonight?"

"Just at the beginning. He... he seemed a bit off and I thought—"

I squeeze her knee. "Don't think," I tell her. "I mean, yes, definitely think, always think, but *I* think you were about to suggest something about you turned him off."

"Am I that easy to read?"

I pat my chest. "I am extremely intuitive and insightful. Practically a mind-reader. I mean, I always know what song Slater's going to start with when we jam."

"Again, good to know," she says with a smile.

I like the look of that smile. The way the corners of her mouth curve pushes her cheeks up and makes those dark eyes squint. Abigail smiles with her entire face.

I want to keep her smiling.

Plus, seeing her lips curve up makes me wonder what it would be like to kiss her.

"Don't go thinking the worst of us," I say, hand back on her knee. "Every guy here wants to be here, and if they didn't, they would have gone home. Lyra's time is over." I push away with my hand, like I'm shoving something away. "It's Abigail time now, and I, for one, am right here with you. I assume the best about the other guys, but I know Tanner is in it for you."

The way Abigail takes a deep breath suggests this was really an issue for her. It's got to be hard, following in a princess's footsteps.

Or maybe she's used to is, seeing as how her best friend is now a princess.

I tuck that into the back of my mind. She may have told us she wants to get to know us, but I need to find out what makes her tick as well. I'm a lot to take on, and not every woman can handle all things Basher.

"Besides," I add, feeling the need to clean my buddy's name. "Apparently, there was a little pissing contest in the car after I got out, so that's most likely why my boy was out of sorts."

Her whole face smiles, but also scrunches when she frowns. I don't want to see her unhappy, but I bet she's really cute when she's annoyed. "In the car? So, Jonas?"

I hold up my hands. "Apparently, but I'm not telling tales. And really, I don't want to waste my time talking about what other guys get up to. I'm selfish enough to want your attention on me."

"That's not selfish, that's smart." She leans closer, and that must be a good sign. I'm taking it as one.

Still smiling—lips curved up. That pink lipstick really makes her look kissable.

Might be worth a shot.

I am here to take that shot.

I push a curl behind her ear, and trail a finger along her jaw. "I wonder... if maybe..."

"Mind if I interrupt?" a voice asks, just as I was getting to the good stuff.

Jake is here to stake his claim. The hometown guy.

Grr.

11

Abigail

I TAKE THE SHOES off halfway through the night.

I drink more than I should—not because I'm afraid of getting drunk, but because I have to keep running to the washroom, which makes the night longer than it needs to be.

I've watched the Suitor and Suitorette countless times. The cocktail party is when the viewer make up their mind who they want to see at the end and who needs to go home right off the bat.

Being the person in charge of those decisions is so different.

Every man I talk to, I ask myself: Can I see myself holding hands with him crossing a street? Does he look like a person I'd want to kiss first thing in the morning? What would he look like first thing in the morning?

And the all-important question I ask myself—will his laugh annoy me?

I dated a man once—if you call three dates *dating*—and declined any subsequent dates because he had a laugh like a Canada goose. He *honked*. It was loud, and it made me laugh, which was bad because he didn't think there was anything wrong with honking like a goose when telling a funny story.

His funny stories weren't all that funny either.

So a man's laugh is very important to me.

At the end of the evening, I am tired. The cocktail party goes on much longer than you think it does when you watch it on TV. On screen, they show two or three minutes with each couple, when in reality, I spend at least fifteen minutes with each man.

Sometimes longer, if we're hitting it off.

And sometimes, the cameraman wants a better shot at something, so I have to go back to the same position and pretend we're still talking about what it was that we were talking about, so Johnny the cameraman can film me smiling from a different angle, or take a close-up at a man's hand on my knee.

We actually film Rand kissing me three times.

Which isn't too bad, because—Rand.

At the end of the night, Rand wins my best laugh award, even though I'm the only one who knows I'm handing it out. He's sweet and funny and smart, as well as modest. Did I say sweet? Also cute. And the laugh is one that would not annoy me if I heard it all the time.

Dylan gets the award for best foot rub. I took off my shoes when we were talking, and he immediately pulled my tired toes onto his lap and—wow. My toes are already in love with him.

If anyone saw my face without realizing what he was doing...

One of the producers had to ask me to stop moaning, and I asked her if she wanted to switch spots with me and find out why I was making such a fuss. I think she was game, and it looks like Dylan might have been too, but Grayson put a stop to things.

Dylan is very good looking, and that producer—I think her name is Ria—definitely knows it.

I might say that Dylan is even better looking than Ashton.

Ashton didn't kiss me, but I would have been happy if he had. I didn't kiss him because I wasn't sure if I wanted to kiss him because he's a billionaire, or because he's so good looking.

I guess it's both, because he *is* both of those things.

I have more of a connection with Ashton than with his friend Rupert.

Two billionaires! And a prince.

I don't talk to Tanner until the very end of the night, and by then, I'm so exhausted that my leg is fidgety like it gets when I'm over-tired, and I have trouble keeping names straight. But Tanner is so patient, even when we have to keep redoing clips because I can't stop yawning. We don't have much of a conversation about anything serious, because it's all so fractured—we start talking, I yawn, we laugh, we start again. But he does make it clear that he is excited to be here, even though he doesn't kiss me.

He finally brings me that drink—ice water with extra lemon slices.

Tanner also wins the *who would look best in the morning* question, because his hair is naturally mused, almost messy, so I think it would look the same in the morning.

I think—even though I can't know for sure yet—that he might be the one I'd like to kiss in the morning.

He looks like he would be a good kisser.

Maybe it's because I'm so tired, but I spend an inordinate amount of time focusing on Tanner's mouth while we talk.

I'm still thinking what it would be like to kiss him when we finish up.

All that is left for me is to make my closing statements, as Grayson calls them. Like I'm doing a presentation. Or making a speech.

Both of those things would be less exhausting than being filmed for over five hours. Grayson already told me we have a free day tomorrow, and I plan to sleep for a large part of the day.

But first—I have to get through one last thing.

"I know I'm keeping you all from your beauty sleep," I begin, standing in front of the men gathered at the back of the lobby. The night air is cool and blows against my bare legs.

"And you all need *so* much of it." I punctuate that with an eye roll, and the men laugh like I'm a next generation Tina Fey. "But I still have to say how much I've enjoyed meeting all of you tonight. I don't have to—I want to. Because I have. It's been so much fun, more than ever expected."

"Maybe don't mention not expecting to have fun," Ria points out, and I have to start again.

I keep the beauty sleep bit, and the second time around when I say how much I've enjoyed meeting them, Jakey pipes up about how much fun I've had reconnecting with a certain someone.

I'm proud to say that I don't roll my eyes on camera, because we'd have to start again.

"This is already a different sort of season than usual," I continue. "I'm the second Suitorette, following in the high heels of Princess Lyra." A pause in case anyone wants to give her a shout-out.

None do. Nice.

"And I'm going to tell you that I'm about to change things up a little more."

Cheers for that. Again—nice.

"In the past, Grayson and his awesome team have organized the dates. I'm a huge fan, and I can tell you, they do an amazing job, keeping the dates fresh and real and fun. But I have a little issue with that. With them doing all the heavy lifting, it gives me no idea what *you*—" I point at the men. "—would really do on a date. We're in a reality world here, a little bubble cutting us off from the rest of the world. It's fun, and the viewers want to see all the pretty places we'd go to. Saint Pierre is beautiful, and even though it's a lot smaller than what you're all used to, there is still lots to do."

From the expression on Grayson's face, I can tell he has no idea what I'm about to say.

I feel a twinge of worry about that.

"Our first date—all of us together—will be a fun day at the beach," I explain. "The capelin are rolling, and we're here to experience it."

Blank faces, except for Tanner, who smiles.

"If you know what that is, yay Maritimers. If not, Google it, and I'll quiz you tomorrow. The good part is, I plan on having a lot of fun with all of you. The bad part is, that may be the only date for some of you." I pause for dramatic emphasis, just like they told me to do. The men look suitably chagrined, and I wonder if they were prompted to do so.

"But those of you who make it past the first group date—that really might be your only one. I'm switching it up because I want *more* one-on-one dates. My timeline is short, and I'm taking this seriously. I hope you are too."

I scan the faces of the men. I've never had an entire group pay such close attention to me, and I've taught classes in fractions where kids really need to pay attention.

When I look at them, I can't help but wonder if one of them is the man for me.

Is the love of my life in this group? Someone who will end up being the partner I want—not because it's convenient, but because they'll love me enough to put me first.

I want that. I want it so badly that I stumble over the next words and have to redo it again.

"If you're here to make an impression, to let me really get to know you, I'm giving you that chance. I want you to plan a date." Murmurs from the group, and instead of worrying that no one looks really happy about the idea, I plow ahead. "I want you to plan a date for me. A one-on-one date with me. I want it to be what *you* want, not what you think will impress me, but what you would do with your girlfriend. Which, I guess, is me."

I have twelve boyfriends. Tema will not be impressed.

12

Grayson

I THOUGHT TONIGHT WOULD never end.

I like Abigail, I really do, but she's just made my job so much more difficult. What was with her little announcement? Little *huge* announcement.

Men planning the dates? What was she thinking?

"What was that all about?" I bark at Rue, loud enough for Camille's dog Bea Arthur to think I'm yelling at her, and slink out of the room.

I like dogs. And I like dogs named after Golden Girls, so Bea Arthur's departure makes me even more upset. I glower at Rue across the table from me.

Ria just arrived after making sure the men got settled in their rooms. With only twelve, no one needs to double up—a plus with this group.

I expect more drama this time around, with Jonas and Rupert in the mix. I don't think Rupert will be the problem, but he gives Ashton a sidekick and an audience, both of which the billionaire doesn't need.

I rub my temple, wishing I took Camille up on her offer of a drink.

Why did I think it would be a good idea to replace Lyra mid-season? I could have forced her to stay.

My internal monologue laughs at the thought of forcing Princess Lyra to do anything.

Maybe I could have sued her.

That idea gets a shiver of fear. Lyra is a *princess*, and even though Laandia is a small country, it doesn't mean its treasury is tiny.

I'm not looking forward to talking to Abigail about her *idea*. What was she thinking, telling the men to plan their own dates?

I thought she'd be easy-going. Low maintenance. I knew what I was getting into with Princess Lyra, but at least *she* never hijacked my show.

Having the men organize their own dates? And everyone gets a one-on-one from the start? What about the drama of the group dates? The competition? What will this do to the show?

My blood pressure spikes just thinking about it.

Being the executive producer would be fun, they said. Having control over the show meant I could make it better, not having it taken over by—

"I think it's a good idea," Rue says in a gentle voice, like she's trying to soothe my spiking blood pressure.

"How do you figure that?" Abigail insisted on changing before we could do the recap and make the decisions on who gets the roses tomorrow, leaving us waiting in the kitchen for her.

My head is spinning with the decisions that need to be finalized before tomorrow.

I could have shut it down, but the guys were so excited. And there is a deadline to get the footage edited, so I let it go.

Not smart, Grayson.

"The guys love the idea," Rue points out. "It gives them more time with Abigail. Plus, it will really bring out their personalities when they plan their dates. We can film all of that. Spend more time in the hotel, watch for drama, the guys competing with each other. See who cracks under the pressure."

I stare at my second in command. "That doesn't sound fun for them."

There's a gleam in her eyes as she rubs her hands together. "Yes, but it will be for the viewers."

I almost expect her to cackle.

"Seriously, Grayson, it's a good thing," Ria chimes in, thankfully without Rue's gleam. "I don't know why we never thought of it ourselves."

"Too much choice isn't always a good thing."

"But look where we are." Rue lowers her voice so Camille won't overhear. It's never a good idea to have your host hear you griping about their country. "There's not much of anything to do. The guys will really have to work on this. It'll be great."

"That's what I'm afraid of. The nothing around here thing. We're going to have beach walks and beer tastings, and that's going to get boring."

"Maybe not," Ria argues. "We can give them gentle suggestions for those who go first. Some of the guys have been here for almost a month. They know what to expect."

I shake my head as Abigail arrives, ready for bed in flannel pants and a Halifax Heroes T-shirt. "You've made my life a lot more difficult," I grumble.

"Challenge is a good thing," she says with a grin, sinking down on the chair across from me. "Change is too."

"Uh huh." I give her a mock glare and then move on to the business at hand. "Other than your little announcement, it went well tonight. Any thoughts?"

"Prince Jonas?"

I can't tell if Abigail is excited or not.

I can't tell if *I'm* excited or not. I'm not in charge of casting, but I have veto power if there's something sketchy about them. Which makes it ultimately my decision on who is on the show. Prince Jonas refused to deal with Paula in casting and insisted on coming straight to me.

Negotiated with me. None of the contestants ever negotiate. They take their contracts with a smile and do their thing. I can't always tell who signs up to try to win the love of a good woman or get their face ready for fame, but ninety percent of them are here for the right reasons.

I have no idea why Prince Jonas agreed.

"We thought it might be a good idea to have someone in the royal family continue on," I explain. That was my main reason for agreeing.

The other being the thought it might create some drama with Ashton and Rupert. Looks like I was right about that.

Abigail rolls her eyes. "Because I am not?"

"We toted it as the Royal Reality version," Rue points out. "Prince Jonas fills in nicely."

"Does he really expect us to call him Your Highness?" Ria asks in a low voice.

"Have you ever met him before?" I ask, ignoring Ria's comment.

Abigail shakes her head. "The two families aren't really close these days. And I wasn't friends with Bo back when they were."

"You could bring them together," Rue suggests with another gleam in her eye.

"If you want to keep him around," Ria adds.

"I'll keep him." We share glances at the excitement in her voice. "At least for now."

Everyone saw them kiss.

Jonas got the first kiss. Not surprising—he *is* a prince. And a good-looking one at that.

I hold my breath, waiting for Abigail to comment on the kiss. Some of the Suitorettes need a confidant on all the kissy details. One of them kept trying to talk to me about open mouth versus closed mouth until I pushed her off to Ria.

But Abigail doesn't get into who and how and everything else.

"There might be some issues with him and Tanner," Abigail says instead.

"What kind of issues?" This might be an issue for *me*, since I have plans for Tanner and need to keep him looking sweet for the viewers.

Abigail frowns. "I don't know. Basher said something about the car."

"Tanner did take the prince's turn," Rue says in a low voice.

"Or maybe Prince Jonas wanted to go last," Ria points out.

From what I know about the two men, I will go with the latter. "Does it seem like it could develop into a big deal?" I ask the table.

Abigail shakes her head. "Seems a bit petty if that's the issue."

"Drama is usually caused by something petty. And the viewers eat it up." Producer Grayson makes a mental note to find a reason for Tanner and Jonas to interact during the group date, while host Grayson will ask the men if there are problems that need to be addressed. "Thoughts on anyone else?"

"They seem great," Abigail says. "Ashton's friend—" She shakes her head in disbelief. "Two billionaires. How...?"

"Don't forget the prince," Rue adds.

I grin at Abigail. "Only the best for you. Unfortunately, we're going to need two names to send home tomorrow."

This is the worst part of the process—telling men they're out of the running. It's bad enough to have to tell women, but no man with a healthy ego wants to be told the girl doesn't like him.

I know, because it's happened to me. My first go-around with The Suitorette show, Chrissa sent me home. I got over it, and it was for the best and all that—obviously—but at the moment, it wasn't fun.

I've learned to be gentle and considerate of their emotions. If that doesn't work, I send in Ria to interview them.

I expect to have a discussion about who will be leaving. Names thrown out, reasons to keep them. Pros and cons, and usually the conversation veers off to who might look better in a swimsuit.

These are the discussions among the women about the men.

But once again, Abigail surprises me. "Duke," she says firmly. "And Charlie."

Never before has the Suitorette been so decisive. And so quick.

"Any reason why those two?" Ria asks, marker at the ready. The list of names is already printed out on the whiteboard, ready to be crossed off.

Abigail huffs with disgust. "Duke's here to get a music deal. He told me he was a musician as soon as he got out of the car, and within five minutes of talking to him, he pulled out his guitar. And he was all over Basher." She scrunches her nose. "I get that not everyone is here for me, but don't make it so obvious. Plus, Charlie told me."

"Fair enough." Ria crosses out his name. "Charlie too? After he told you about Duke?"

"He *tattled* on Duke," Abigail corrects, crossing her arms. "I've never liked tattle-tales. I could have easily figured out on my own that Duke wasn't here for me. I don't like men who try and force my hand to control me. Plus, there's lots of guys wanting to talk to me—if you get some time, shoot your shot. Don't go bad-mouthing the rest of them."

I try and hide my smile at her vehemence. "Some may say he was only looking out for you."

A shake of her head. "I make my own choices, and by telling me that, he was taking it away." She takes the colourful elastic on her wrist and ties her hair back. I take the move to show that she means business.

"Never looked at it like that." I nod to Ria, and she crosses out Charlie's name.

I don't have a problem with either one of those choices. This is moving along quicker than I expected. I still won't have time to call my wife tonight, but I might get a full six hours of sleep.

"They will get the yellow roses in the morning." Rue makes a note on her tablet. "And first date rose goes to..."

I have no clue about what Abigail wants for this.

The producers used to make suggestions about the coveted first date, but none of the dates were a success and they would invariably go home. Under my rule, the Suitor and Suitorette get full control of who goes home.

Although that didn't really work well with Lyra.

"All of them," Abigail announces. "I want a group date tomorrow. I'll decide after that."

That's not how we do things here. Maybe this will be a long night after all.

13

Abigail

A HOCKEY PLAYER, A rock star, and a prince meet two billionaires in a bar...

Meeting the men sounds like the beginning of a joke.

The fact that I'm here, in Saint Pierre, getting ready to start my turn as The Suitorette, seems just as unbelievable.

But here I am, ready to find love.

Yesterday was a 'free' day. The men stayed at the hotel, getting to know each other and hopefully planning their dates with me. It wasn't free for me—I did get to sleep in, but from late morning to early evening, I was with Rue and Grayson, doing promotional shots and confessionals where I talk about my first impressions of the men.

I had to keep changing my clothes to make it seem like it all didn't happen on the same day.

It was interesting, getting a firsthand view of the making of the show, but it was a long day.

The original Suitor show aired only weeks after Hettie and I left Battle Harbour. The timing always makes me feel like I have a connection with the show, both of us starting fresh at the same time.

I followed my best friend from Laandia to Vancouver, Canada, almost ten years ago. I was young, without a plan about what I wanted to do with my life. I thought it would be an adventure, that I was brave and loyal leaving with Hettie. I was supposed to take care of her, but couldn't do anything about her broken heart.

There was nothing I could have done about that. It all happened so quickly. The secret wedding to Prince Bo. The accident that killed his mother, Queen Selene. Bo, blaming himself for her death and sinking into a grief so severe that he pushed everyone away, including his brand-new wife.

I was supposed to protect my friend, but I couldn't do anything about her heartbreak at losing Bo, so I pledged my fealty and left Battle Harbour with her.

She had no idea that she was pregnant with Tema when we left. And she never told Bo that she had his child, so scared that he would take Tema away from her.

Of course, Bo, or the royal family, would have never done that. And I should have known that, but I had a child I considered my own. If Hettie had told Bo—if I had pushed her to do so—I would have lost Tema.

There's still so much regret and guilt that I didn't do anything to heal the rift between them, mixed with the slow realization that I put my life on hold for my friend... There's a lot I need to unpack about the last ten years.

I never gave much thought to what I was giving up by going with her. By staying and helping Hettie raise Tema, basically keeping her from her father.

Yeah. A lot to unpack.

But as we settled in Vancouver, with me trying to ease Hettie's grief in any way I could, we stumbled onto The Suitor.

It was the Canadian version of The Bachelor—one man, tasked with finding love among twenty-five women. Reality romance at its best. The Suitor had slight differences, but it was pretty much the same formula as the American version.

We were hooked after the first episode, although Hettie made many comments about how everyone was idiots for believing in true love.

The comments stopped after a while, but we never stopped watching. Both The Suitor and The Suitorette.

And now, here I am. Full circle. I'm The Suitorette.

Hettie didn't say much when I told her, because I didn't give her a chance. It was my decision, and I made it quickly—maybe too quickly.

It was the first decision in years that I had made where I never considered Hettie.

She's with Bo now, happily married and living in the castle. *They* are raising Tema. My role... I'm not sure what my role is any more.

I'm not sure what I'm supposed to do anymore.

I was a mother to Tema for eight years. Maybe she wasn't my biological child, but I loved her as if she were my own flesh and blood. And it wasn't like I was a supporting role; I was an equal parenting partner with Hettie.

In some ways, I think I might have been more.

Hettie was caught up in her pain and heartbreak, dealing with her family issues. I stepped up with Tema, and kept stepping up.

Until Hettie decided to tell Bo he had a daughter. And then everything changed.

I try not to think about those changes. I constantly wonder about my role in Tema's life—how to keep my role because I love that little girl desperately—but I don't push. Hettie and Bo have a lot to deal with. Tema has a lot to deal with.

I'm there when they need me, but I have something of my own.

Spencer wouldn't have been mine. He's so connected to Bo, to the other princes and the castle, that I would have been forced to share him.

He would have allowed me to keep my place with Tema though, and I think, deep down, that was the real draw. Of course, I love Spencer. I've always loved him.

But I was never *in love* with him.

There's a difference between the two, a slight shading of the line between a man and a woman. There needs to be friendship between a couple, and a level of comfort. That's love.

But to be *in love* with a person... I've never had that.

I think it should be more than simple love. I want it to be. I want to wake up thinking about him, and go to sleep with his head on the pillow beside me. I want to do things with him, and when I don't get to, I want to tell him everything.

I want to share what's important to me with him, tell him silly stories about my day, and have conversations about the latest movies and whether Game of Thrones was really ruined by the last season.

It's simple—I want to fall in love.

And being here, being on the cusp of maybe getting everything I want—it's terrifying. And exciting.

And I'm ready to go.

After meeting the men and giving them instructions to plan dates with me, I switched it up and insisted on a group date.

I know Grayson doesn't love the idea of everyone getting a solo date. I can tell Grayson is very frustrated with me, but the other producers, Rue and Ria, are behind me all the way.

I hope.

And I hope my plan helps me find love.

This process won't be easy. Narrowing down twelve men to one means cutting those I don't see a future with. Those I don't feel a connection with.

I'm not looking forward to the tough decisions about who needs to go home.

But it was surprisingly easy to pick the first to go home.

During the cocktail party, Duke attached himself to Basher. So much that when offered the opportunity to talk to me early in the evening, he stayed with Basher, talking music.

Basher is the drummer for Water Rhinos, and Duke seemed to be more than just a fan.

I'm a fan. There was a bit of fangirl shrieking when I found out Basher was part of the group that stayed.

Even if Charlie hadn't told me Duke was here to give his music career a boost, I could have figured that out myself. I've seen every season of the show, so I think I would know when a man is here for his fifteen minutes of fame.

At least I hope I'll be able to tell.

They gave Duke the archetype of 'golden retriever', but I didn't see it. They should have changed it to 'wannabe rock star' when they filmed him leaving. Charlie was 'dentist', which is at least true, but I didn't feel any connection with him, even before he turned into a tattletale.

They both received the yellow rose of friendship yesterday morning, and today, should already be back home, wherever home is.

I didn't even get far enough with them to find out details like that.

After today's date, I have to send two more men home. There are ten left, and I feel some measure of interest in all of them.

There's also attraction for quite a few.

I think that's a good thing.

But after talking with them, I feel quite *a lot* of attraction to a few of them. That's what makes it difficult. What if I can't pick between the men? What if I like more than one? What if I actually fall in love with more than one of them?

I honestly never really considered that possibility—until I met them. Tanner and Dylan, and Rand... Prince Jonas. Ashton and Rupert... bad-boy Boone. Basher.

There is more than one possibility here, and I'm big game pumped up, raring to go.

It's a heady feeling to know this is all *my* decision. It comes down to what *I* want. It's all my responsibility to send home who I want, and keep who I like.

Who I like, not who I think it might be convenient to have a relationship with.

I'm going to pick one man from this group, and that's a scary sort of power.

But I think I like it.

One of the first things I did when we came back to Battle Harbour was to visit the beach. Hettie and I took Tema onto the pebble-strewn sand to look for pretty stones, just like our mothers had taken both of us when we were small.

And then Hettie's mother left, and my mom started taking both of us.

I've always wondered how she could have left her family. Her children. Her friends—my mother. They had been as close as sisters for a time, and then she left. Without warning. Without even a note.

Now, after Tema, I completely don't understand how she could have made that irrevocable step of leaving her kids. I may not be Tema's mother, but I miss her every minute I'm away from her.

I told Hettie to make sure she and Bo took Tema to see the capelin roll. And now I'm here on a different beach watching it with the men.

The capelin roll is a Maritime staple I missed when I lived on the west coast of Canada.

The capelin roll is just that: the waves roll in with thousands of small, silver fish catching a ride so they can crash onto the shore to spawn. It's a crazy, hypnotizing scene because there are literally fish everywhere, a noisy carpet of splashing along the water, flopping and wriggling as they rush to the sand to lay their eggs.

This is the backdrop for the first group date.

I want the men to experience it with me.

The waves are silver with the tiny fish, and there are so many that the water seems to boil. Half of the island seems to be here, families as well as tourists with their buckets and nets to collect fish.

I watch as a little boy wades in with red boots, catching two fish by the tails and holding them up for his parents.

It's the third day of the roll, and the fires are lit along the beach, with men manning each one, to clean and cook the fish.

"Hey, guys!"

I wave as a horde of testosterone swarms toward me like the defensive line of a football team. Only no one is about to tackle me.

Instead, they hug me. One after another—Fireman Dylan is first one to reach me, and then Tanner. I'm passed from arm to arm, some kissing my cheek, a few whispering how glad they are to see me.

Most say how good I look.

"Perform for the cameras," Lyra had told me, and I rise to the challenge.

"Are you all ready to get wet?" I ask them when the hugs have finished.

"What is this?" Rand demands, googling at the fish, the families, and the birds dive-bombing it all.

"This is part of Maritime culture," I tell them.

"The noisy part of it," Jakey chimes in. "I haven't been to one of these in years. It's never this extreme in Laandia."

"I've never seen anything like it," Jonas says, shaken out of his cool.

"I can see why," Ashton mutters.

"Look—whales!" Tanner cries and, in unison, everyone looks out in the distance where a humpback breaches.

My heart feels like it's swelling with Maritime pride.

"This is a capelin roll," I explain.

"Why are they rolling?" Basher asks cautiously. "And what *is* a capelin?"

"They're fish. Little fish who come to shore to spawn and they taste good, so we're going to help catch some for the fish fry."

At least the men cheer at this, because there's a lot of skepticism on faces.

I don't really care if they're not as into it as I am. This is my date, the one I planned and a capelin roll has always been a favourite memory.

Dylan helps me hand out buckets as I give the men a few facts about the experience. Like how many fish are here to spawn, and how the sea life, like the birds and seals and even the whales further out, are taking advantage of the easy pickings. I tell them about the time in Laandia where the fish came in with a storm and completely overran the beach, and how people ran around in the rain throwing the fish that got stuck on shore back into the water.

I've been told I talk too much when I'm nervous, and now it's on camera, so everyone will agree.

Each man gets a bucket, and I tell them to get to work.

"You've got to be kidding me?" Ashton mutters, staring as Jakey and Tanner lead the charge into the tide of fish.

Ashton is runway ready in a periwinkle polo shirt that brings out the blue in his eyes, and a pair of light gray shorts that would be more suitable on the golf course than in the water.

"I am not kidding you," I tell him with a grin. Ashton may look good, but I want to see if he's able to get messy. "I can guarantee your sister will be doing this today or tomorrow."

"I am not my sister," he points out, still staring at the waves of fish.

"Not looking at settling down in Battle Harbour?"

This is Ashton Carrington. Just because his twin found love in my hometown, why would I ever think the same will happen to him?

With me.

But even as, deep down, I might not really believe I'm about to end up with a billionaire race car driver, I still want to find out what all the men are thinking. Their ideas, options. Hopes and dreams. What is a hard no for them.

It's a lot, and I'm starting with Ashton?

But if living in Battle Harbour is a hard no for him...

"I'll follow you anywhere you want," Ashton says in his slow drawl. The tone that already makes my stomach tighten, and when added to the smirk-smile and the hooded glance of his dark blue eyes, makes Ashton Carrington so very attractive.

It also makes me think that anything is possible.

I guess that's the point of this show.

I point to the others. "Into the water."

Ashton shrugs good-naturedly. "You got it, princess."

I stiffen. Ashton was here for Lyra, not me. "I'm not the princess," I say coolly.

But Ashton only smiles and takes my chin in long fingers. "Every woman is a princess to me, sweetheart," he says, so cool and so casual.

But then something shifts in his expression. A flash of something I can't understand, and Ashton almost looks... vulnerable? Like he—

He kisses me.

It doesn't start off as much of a kiss—it's only a quick brush of his lips against mine, like I'm a favourite aunt or a fashionable friend, but then he pauses.

It's a long pause, where our lips are still pressed together and he tastes of mint. It's like he's asking a question and I'm answering.

And then Ashton's cool fingers slide onto my neck, and his lips shift. Everything shifts because we're kissing. Really kissing. Soft and sweet, mouths moving together like we do this all the time.

It's a real kiss, right here for half the town, as well as the other men, to see. Also, all the viewers because the cameraman is filming it all.

Ashton Carrington kisses *me*, just like that, just as if I'm the one he wants to be kissing.

He finally pulls away because I'm unable to do so, and he's smiling.

His *smile* butterflies fluttering just as much as that kiss. "Well, then."

I'm unable to form a word. I can only stare at the mouth that just kissed me like I'm a fairy-tale princess and he's the man sent to break the spell.

"I'm off to catch you a fish," he promises, his gaze still holding mine.

I nod. And then he takes his bucket and wades into the water.

14

Tanner

EVERYONE SEES ASHTON KISS Abigail.

It's not something I want to see, but I find I can't look away, like the worst kind of accident on the side of the road.

It's makes me... sad. Regret that it's not me standing there laughing with her. Kissing her. And the look on Abigail's face when they pull away from each other...

That's a tough one to stomach.

It's day one, and I already feel like this?

But it's not a new thing. I dealt with this when it was Lyra we were competing for. I saw her kiss other men just like Abigail kissed Ashton, and it was tough as well.

I liked Lyra, and for a few days, I thought I might have a shot with her, as unbelievable as the thought of me with a princess would be to anyone who knows me. But Abigail is different.

When it was Lyra, I thought I had time to get to know her. To slowly open up, to let her peel back the layers.

With Abigail, it needs to happen *right away*. It's game on, because if Ashton is kissing her, then that's going to open the floodgates and everyone is going to want to kiss her like that, and I don't want to miss my chance.

I want a chance with Abigail. Even though the idea of being the next Suitor is there, like a safety net below, I still want my shot with her.

Game on.

The beach is packed with both locals and tourists. Saint Pierre isn't an easy trip—flights to Newfoundland, ferry only comes twice a day—but there are many who have made the trip.

And there are more here who are curious about the cameras.

Johnny is filming everything: Abigail giving us our marching orders. The kiss. He's right there when I show Rand and Tesh how to catch a fish with their bare hands. He gets the shots of Dylan helping others more than filling his own bucket.

My favourite is how he managed to get the shot of Ashton and Rupert laughing at the others and not watching the waves—until one comes in quick and soaks the full length of their backs.

There are so many shots of Abigail as she flutters around, giving everyone her time, trying to be as fair as possible. I watch her with the others, trying to gauge who I need to worry about. Who will be my competition?

And then I wonder why I bother.

Why did I stay?

Is it only because they want me to be the next Suitor, and that wouldn't work if I don't stick around? The producers don't want me to fall in love with Abigail, but for the fans to fall in love with me.

I could fall for Abigail, but not end up with her. Apparently, heartbroken Suitors make good TV.

I still haven't decided if that's what I want to do.

Deep in thought, I don't notice when Abigail appears at my side. "Having fun?" she asks brightly, tossing a fish into my bucket.

I glance at the bucket and then down at her. "Does this mean I'm getting special treatment?"

I like her smile. It lights up her entire face like a little kid at Christmas. I like the way she smiles at *me*.

I *don't* like the way she smiles at the other men. But I got myself into this, so I'm going to have to get used to it.

"You were so deep in thought, and I didn't want you to lose ground if you were having a moment," she says with a teasing gleam in her eye.

"Moment over," I tell her. "At least that moment."

"Ah."

"Yes. Ah." Is this a moment? Am I already having moments with Abigail? "I love the ocean," I manage, wrenching my gaze away from her face.

Heart-shaped. Big, dark eyes. Cute nose.

I've already got it memorized.

I wave toward the water, the happy chaos on the beach. "I haven't seen this in years."

"Halifax, isn't it? That's where you're from?"

"Stalking, or doing your homework?" It's my turn to tease now.

"I prefer to call it homework." Her attempt to sound regal fails as the salt-and-fish scented breeze suddenly attacks her curls. "Calling it stalking sounds like I don't have a life."

"I can tell you have a life because you're on the show." I watch Boone pick up a child knocked down by a wave. Rand and Basher laugh as they wade deeper into the water.

There are fish everywhere.

I love it.

It reminds me of home.

"It's actually East River," I say. "Where I'm from. It's about halfway between Halifax and Lunenberg."

"I've always wanted to go to Lunenberg," she says wistfully. "My parents took us to Halifax for a tournament once, but we didn't have time to do much looking around. We were a hockey family," she explains.

"You sure you weren't stalking?" I tease.

"I do know you played for the Mooseheads," she says, nose scrunched up like she's embarrassed. "And I *might* have caught one of your games."

"Really?" Even though I prefer not to have my former career brought up, the thought of Abigail seeing me play makes me happier that I thought it would. "So you've been stalking me for a while now?"

She brushes my side with her elbow. "Definitely."

I almost reach out and tuck her hair behind her ear, but she beats me to it. "Did you play?" I ask.

"No, but thank you for thinking that I could."

"I am very supportive of women's hockey."

"And I'm very glad to hear that. I tried it for a few years, but no go."

"Don't tell me you couldn't stand the cold."

"Ha. No." She pauses for a moment, gathering her thoughts, and I watch her.

I like watching her. It's almost too easy to read her emotions.

"My brothers played." I get the sense that there's more to that.

"As brothers often do. Are they any good?"

"I'm not sure," she admits. "It's been a while since I've seen them. I used to love to watch them play. Little brothers and everything." This time there's a much longer pause, and I wait. I see Jonas in the distance making his way over to us, and I know he's coming to interrupt, to take his turn with Abigail.

The only problem is that Jonas feels like he's entitled to more turns and time with her than the rest of us.

I plant my feet in the sand because I'm not giving up this moment that easily.

"You know," Abigail finally manages to sort her thoughts. "When you grew up listening to something over and over again and you just don't want to listen to it anymore? Or watch? That's how it is with my brothers." And then her eyes snap wide, and she turns to look to see where Johnny is positioned. "Oh, god I just said that out loud and they're filming and it's going to be on TV, and my brothers—"

"It's OK," I soothe. "You're being honest. That's never a bad thing."

"It kind of is. My father grew up playing and he really wanted to make it to the NHL, but injuries and meeting my mom..." She shrugs. "He wanted the best for my brothers. Still does. It was a lot because—"

She presses her lips together. It's times like this I wish there were no cameras, that it was just me and Abigail getting to know each other.

But if it were just me and Abigail, then there would be no show. And if there was no show, we wouldn't have met in the first place.

I wonder if there was a time in our lives where we could have met. I saw Lyra once; maybe there had been a time when I crossed paths with Abigail.

I like that thought.

"I'll have to look them up," I say. "Check them out."

"They would love that."

We stand together in silence for a few moments, watching the others in the water. Jonas has almost reached us, but I want to keep talking to Abigail. I want to be in the middle of a great conversation when he shows up, so Abigail will want to keep talking to me. I want her not to let him interrupt.

"Ashton, huh?"

No idea why I bring him up. I mean, I've always thought I had game, but not too sure now because why would I bring up the guy who kissed her in front of everyone?

Abigail looks just as surprised as I am, and maybe a little more embarrassed. "Did you see that?" she asks, nose scrunching again.

It's cute, like a little girl caught with a crush on a rockstar.

That would be Basher. I suspect he would be easy to have a crush on.

"Sweetheart, the whole beach saw that." I grin, letting the word roll around my tongue. Sweetheart. I'm not the type of guy—or at least I didn't think I was—that would call a woman sweetheart. Sweetie. Honey. I've never used terms of endearment before, because I've always thought they sounded condescending.

Maybe it's how you use it. And who you use it on.

I think I like it.

Well... Yeah," she admits.

Her cheeks are red, whether from the kiss or from the thought of so many people watching her kiss. I don't want to point out that it's not just the people on the beach. There are going to be a lot of people interested in her season of the Suitorette, after news of Lyra and Spencer gets out.

And if I become the next Suitor.

I don't want to think about that when I'm talking to Abigail. No decisions have been made. There are still options.

Lots of options.

"I'm not sure what I'm supposed to say about it," Abigail says a touch defensively.

"You don't have to say anything. It's none of my business who you kiss," I assure her. "I shouldn't have brought it up."

"It kind of is," she hedges. "Since I'm... and you... And you can bring up anything." The way she studies my face makes me think for a moment that yes, I can tell her anything. She'd listen and understand. She'd get me.

"Ashton took a shot," I say matter-of-factly, like the thought of Ashton and Abigail didn't just tie me up in knots. "Ashton saw the moment, and he took a shot. There's no need to say anything about that."

"Yes, but the rest of you..."

"Will have to wait for our moments." I'm sure there will be another moment for one or more of the men today, and I'm going to have to watch that too.

I've never been a jealous man, but I don't like the thought of that.

It's not a nice feeling, knowing I'll be a witness to a private moment—especially that it will be *Abigail* having a private moment with someone else.

When I want to be the one having a private moment with her.

So why don't I take this moment?

"And... are you waiting for a specific moment?" Abigail asks like she can read my mind.

The tone of her voice... it makes me think that I could kiss her here and now and she'll be happy about it.

But something holds me back. "I am waiting for a specific moment," I say, my voice low. "I want the right moment. You only get one chance at a first kiss, and I'm going to make the most of mine, seeing as how I didn't do too great with the first impression." With a rueful smile, I tuck her hair back, letting my fingers linger on her cheek.

Her skin is soft, with a spatter of freckles across her nose that weren't there when I first met her.

"I think you did fine," she protests.

"Fine doesn't cut it for me. So I'll make sure the kiss—our first kiss—will be special. Maybe you won't be expecting it. Or maybe we'll be looking at the stars, or laughing at something you said. I don't know when, but I'm willing to wait for the perfect time for us to have our first kiss." My thumb brushes her bottom lip, free of any lipstick or gloss.

Maybe this *is* the moment.

And then someone calls her name. I don't know who it is, and Abigail doesn't turn away from me, only lifting her hand in *just a minute* response.

"At least that's what I want," I finish.

The corner of her mouth creases up, like she wants to smile but isn't letting herself. Like she appreciates me wanting to make it special. Or that she wants that too.

Abigail leans against my hand now cupping her cheek. "That sounds nice," she whispers.

"Yeah." I stroke her jawline, like I'm trying to memorize the contours of her face.

"Do you think we'll have to wait long?"

"No."

I lean down, thinking that with all my talk, the only thing I want to be doing is kissing her right now. I want to know how she feels in my arms, how she tastes, if she'll run her hands through my hair or stroke my back or—

Another voice calls her name and there's a burst of raucous laughter.

This can't be the perfect moment. I stop myself, pressing my lips against her forehead. "Maybe this isn't it," I admit.

"There are a lot of people around," she concedes, and I know I'm not imagining the hint of disappointment in her tone.

"Too many. But they'll be other moments." I pull back and smile at her, reminding myself to breathe normally so my stomach can stop jumping. "Ones where I don't start off talking about other men kissing you."

Abigail laughs, and the sound is music to my ears. And then her face softens, her dark eyes fixing on mine like there's a secret between us. "I'll be waiting for that moment," she promises.

I've never had a woman look at me like that, a look that makes my knees feel as weak as if I've skated an entire game without a break. I can't seem to catch my breath.

Is this what it's supposed to feel like? "Me too."

"If you caught the most fish…" She glances down at my bucket.

"I'll need to catch up for that," I say ruefully. "I better get back to work."

"I'll be watching," she says with a flirtatious note in her voice.

I can feel her eyes on me as I head back to the water.

I'll be smiling for the rest of the night.

15

Abigail

Tanner...

I watch him wade back into the water, and yes, I am admiring the view. Those gym shorts can hide a multitude of sins, but I'm not seeing any at the moment. Tanner saunters rather than struts, straight into the water without giving a thought to the fish thrashing at his fish.

A waves gets him, splashing around his knees and I laugh.

He turns like he can hear me, and sees me watching.

I can't stop smiling.

First Ashton and then Tanner—this group date was a great idea. Maybe I should rethink the idea of more one-on-one dates.

But solo dates would give me more private time with the men. More moments like the one I envision happening between me and Tanner.

I *really* wanted him to kiss me. I don't know if it's possible, but the *almost* kiss from Tanner affected me more than the real kiss from Ashton.

That kiss from Ashton was unexpected and ... unexpected. As much as I wanted a second kiss this afternoon, I think Tanner's right—it would be weird if he kissed me right after Ashton.

This is going to be confusing

A little confusing; it's not that I can't keep the men straight and separate, but it's my thoughts and feelings toward them that will need to be compartmentalized. Ashton has a box, Tanner has a box. The boxes need to stay separate, and that's the only way I'm going to be able to handle this.

Rue told me to keep a journal, and while I've never been a writing-things down type of person, that might be a great idea in this case.

After Tanner heads back into the surf, the target resurfaces on my back. Tesh immediately joins me, and I find out he's a CEO from Toronto. When I met him the first night, I thought his lack of smile was because of nerves, but now I can see he's the grumpy archetype.

His reserved manner reminds me of Spencer, so I'm not disappointed when Jonas interrupts. We talk about the royal family, and Camille's attempts to bring the tourists to Saint Pierre.

For Camille, I'm glad to see the tourists. For the show, it's got to be difficult to film the men when there are so many people milling about. Most of who would love to have their face in a shot.

But Johnny manages.

Boone interrupts Jonas and I'm happy to see the emergence of a soft side under his bad boy exterior. When he smiles, it's like the sun comes out. I only wish he did it more often.

Rupert sidles up when Boone is telling me about his motorcycle trips—every Friday the thirteenth, regardless of the month, a mass of motorcyclists descends on the small town of Port Dover in Ontario. I've never been on the back of a bike, but after listening to Boone, I want to.

Rupert chimes in with his experiences, and the two discuss motorcycles for a few minutes, leaving me the outsider.

Fireman Dylan comes to my rescue.

It's like that for the rest of the afternoon—it's like the men are bees, targeting Flower Abigail to take their turn, one after another. They interrupt each other, claiming my time for themselves. Some are more polite than others. Some join a conversation already in process and seem happy to share me.

It's clear most of them like each other, especially those who have been here from the beginning.

Everyone makes an effort, and it's unbelievable how special that makes me feel.

Yes, it's exhausting—I have to be on at all times, my smile at the ready, changing topics at the drop of a hat. The boxes pile up in my mind as more information is collected and curated.

I mess up once or twice, but no one gets upset.

It's a fun day. It's an amazing day. The sun, the salt air, the scent of the fish adds to the experience, and I'm happy that the men are enjoying themselves. Everyone is so nice and hospitable and interested in the filming.

Ten men, all here for me. I make time for all of them, giving them my attention, and asking questions to find out as much as I can in the short time I have with them.

But they don't know me yet. They can only see the outside, know a bit of my history and make assumptions about why I'm here.

I'm sure they all can assume why I'm here.

But they don't know anything about me. Not really. No one knows what I like, and don't like. I keep things light and surface level because I'm not ready to dig deep.

Not yet.

There will be time on the individual dates to let them get to know me. I just have to figure how to best do that.

I'm a strong, healthy, attractive woman, but with very little experience with men.

I've dated, but I've never really made time for anyone. I've never carved out a place for a partner. For years, it was me and Hettie, together against the world. We had Tema, and she was the centre of our universe. We had each other.

There was always an underlying of guilt when I met a man. When I went out with someone, and Hettie would stay home with Tema.

I felt like I was betraying her, prioritizing someone other than our little makeshift family.

Hettie continually told me to get out and meet someone. She even set me up a few times, and I did go on dates. But I never let anyone in.

I'm sure I'm a lot like Princess Lyra in that way.

I'm supposed to let these men see the real me. All my hopes and dreams, all the big stuff and a lot of the little stuff too. And I only have four weeks to do it.

Four weeks to discover if any of these twelve men—ten now that Charlie and Duke have left—would be a good match for me.

My Mr. Right.

My soulmate.

That seems a lot to ask.

But this could work. This process will force me to be vulnerable, to ask the questions I need to ask to make sure I'm not a convenience for anyone.

That they want me. Really me.

I better get started.

I don't expect to start with Jakey.

He's the first to fill his bucket.

Tanner and Rand are with me when Jakey trots up to me with a bucket overflowing with fish, with a big smile and even bigger expectations of getting his reward.

Not only that, but his loud whooping cheers make it clear that he won. The rest of the men follow him out of the water like he's the Pied Piper, with a few grumbles and good-natured trash talk. Jakey's chest puffs with every step toward me.

"Abs! I got you! I got your fish, and now I get my reward." When he sets the bucket on the sand before me, water slops out and onto my feet, along with a capelin.

Tanner reaches down to tuck it back into his bucket.

"He stole my fish," Jakey cries. "He's cheating."

"Just getting it off Abigail's foot," Tanner corrects. "It's not cheating if the game is over. Like you said, you won."

"Thank you," I say to Tanner. He smiles, and I want to keep looking at him. I could spend all day looking at him.

"What happens to the fish?" Rand asks and I'm pulled back to the reality of ten men surrounding. All looking at *me*.

I point down the beach where a group of men are cleaning and frying the fish over an open fire. "Fish fry for everyone. You have all just contributed. We can go and sample now."

"Wait just a minute," Jakey explains. "I need my reward before we do anything else. You promised a kiss."

I glance over at Rue, close but keeping her distance. She's the one who promised the winner would get a kiss, not me. It's awkward kissing on command, but this is my show and the cameras are focused on me. "Of course," I relent.

I take a step toward Jakey, about to give him a chaste, perfectly platonic peck, but he has other ideas. Grabbing me around the waist, he hauls me against him, mashing his lips against mine.

There's nothing chaste about it, and nothing enjoyable, as he all but forces his tongue into my mouth.

"Dude," one of the men mutters.

There are none of the tingles I got when Ashton kissed me. None of the butterflies from the almost kiss with Tanner.

None of the weak-in-the-knees sensations I used to get when Jakey would kiss teenage me. There's... nothing.

I break from his embrace as quickly as I can, to find unhappy expressions from the men, and one huge smile from Jakey.

"Let's go get something to eat," I say brightly, resisting the urge to wipe my mouth.

Seems like I can learn a lot from kissing the men.

I now know Jakey doesn't have a chance with me.

16

Rand

J AKE. HUH.

Don't like seeing that.

There wasn't much debate among the men when Grayson gave us the option to stay on after Lyra left. There were some grumbling, most of which came from the men who I didn't consider having much of a connection with Lyra, and therefore, not much of a chance to win her heart.

Charlie, for instance, made quite the fuss, and it might be petty that I'm pleased that Abigail sent him home.

Jon made the decision to leave, and I'm not surprised. I don't think his heart was ever really into it. I am surprised at how I miss having him around. I didn't expect to make friends—real friends—here, and I know I'll stay in touch with Jon.

The rest of us were quick to decide to "stick around," as Ashton put it. I came here to find love and deep down, never really expected it to work out with Lyra. A princess and me?

Longshot, but not unheard of.

With Abigail? She's just as beautiful, just as smart, funny, ticks all the boxes—and she's not a princess.

I think that's a plus.

But while I stayed, along with Tanner, Basher, Ashton and Dylan, new men arrived, and I can't say I like the sight of them already making their move to kiss Abigail.

If you can call that face mash a kiss.

Ashton kissing her is one thing because I feel he put in the time. Jake, on the other hand—

He doesn't deserve it. And Abigail definitely deserves a better kiss than whatever that was.

If I were to kiss her—when I get to kiss her—I'll start slow. I think I made a mistake with Lyra, moving in for the kiss on the first night. I've already decided to wait with Abigail, wait for her to be ready. For her to want it as much as I do.

There's no point kissing a woman if she doesn't want you to.

What I just saw was a bad kiss, and that's on Jake's head.

"Who is this guy?" Tesh asks under his breath as Jake escorts Abigail to the firepit, leaving the rest of us wet and smelling of fish.

The scent of fish doesn't bother me, but I caught Rupert surreptitiously sniffing himself.

Away from the shore, the noise of those on the beach drowns out the flapping of the fish. The entire town must be out here, along with countless tourists. You can tell them apart—the tourists all seem to be having more fun than the townsfolk, with their resigned expressions at the antics of the newcomers.

Sort of the way I must look right now.

"Hometown boy next door," I tell Tesh.

"I thought there was another one of those?"

"He left. He was sent home," I correct. "Most of us who were still here decided to stay."

Except for Jon, which I'm glad. Not only was Jon a really good guy, I think he would have been a good match for Abigail. With him gone, it's easier for the rest of us.

I've never been the competitive type, so that thought surprises me.

"What do you think of her?" Tesh asks as we carry our buckets to where the crowd gathers.

Tesh is tall and athletic, with dark curling hair and soulful eyes. He's some sort of CEO or CFO or something with initials. From Quebec, so the French accent adds to the package.

I'm sure Abigail admires the package.

He needs to go home.

"I think she's great," I say. "What's your thoughts on her?" I might want to weed out the competition, but I can still be friends with them.

"I haven't had much time to talk to her," he admits. "The Prince interrupted me both times last night."

Jonas Erickson. He's walking ahead of us, and with his golf shorts and polo shirt, and looks like he belongs on a golf course or a yacht club. But there's a hunger in his eyes, like he'd be very willing to throw any of us under the bus to get what he wants.

He also kind of looks like Harvey Spector from Suits.

Does Abigail like that type? She liked Spencer, and he had the same effortless poise and polish. But Spencer was decent and lacked the undercurrent of ruthlessness that I see in Jonas.

I don't think Jonas would be a good match for Abigail, but I have a feeling he's got the charm and tenacity to convince her that he is. He's part of the Laandian royal family after all, and they have charm to spare.

"You can just call him Jonas," I say, more to lessen the intimidation of Jonas for me than Tesh.

"I've never met royalty before," Tesh says, his eyes following Jonas as he catches up to Abigail. The way she smiles up at him—

I think I'd rather see Jake face mash with Abigail than watch her smile at Jonas like that.

"You obviously have," Tesh continues. I give myself a shake. Competitive, feelings of jealousy—what's going on with me? "You met Lyra. Princess Lyra."

"I did."

"What was she like?"

"It doesn't matter," I say, my gaze trained on Abigail. "We're here for Abigail now."

17

Abigail

WE STAY ON THE beach until after dark. There are bonfires, all the fish you can eat, and fireworks. There is music for dancing and singing, tons of food. Good conversations with the men.

The producers bring bottles of champagne, as well as a cooler of beer, and we sit by the fire as the sky lights up with colourful rockets.

The men sat by the fire—I'm led away from the fires by the men, one by one, for walks in the sand, wading in the water and to explore the rocks at the far end of the beach.

They have the routine down pat, and tonight they were much more polite than they were the first night.

Basher pulls me up to dance. I talk all things Laandia with Jonas. Rupert steals a bottle of wine, and we perch on the rocks as he explains the difference between champagne and sparkling wine. Tanner tells me about living in Halifax. Rand takes me for a walk along the beach, and Dylan finds me a sweater before he kisses me.

It's a nice kiss.

That's three tonight.

I look at the men differently after they've kissed me. It definitely reaffirms that they are here for me, but it also shows confidence.

Or cockiness when it comes to Jakey.

There are definitely a few of the men I'd still like to kiss, and who haven't even made an effort to make a move.

I wonder if I'm allowed to kiss them.

Which is stupid, because why not? I did with Jonas, but that was mainly because he was a prince and I might not have even gotten that chance again.

I should have asked the producers if that was allowed. If the viewers approve. It's awkward pulling someone aside *now* to ask if I can initiate the kissing.

But still... I'm tempted.

With Tanner.

Also, Rand because he intrigues me with his earnest sweetness.

It's hard to keep some of the men separate in my head. I find myself forgetting who told me about holding their sister's baby for the first time and whose girlfriend took their shared cockapoo when they broke up. A few have distinguished themselves, but I'm not sure if it's simple attraction or I'm actually interested.

It's been so long since I've been interested in anyone other than Spencer.

And we all know how it turned out with him.

Eventually, the night at the beach ends with hugs and promises to see me soon. There's an aura of confidence among the men, like they all expect to get their own date with me.

Some of them will.

The night isn't over for me. Decisions have to be made, and big ones.

Who will be going home?

On the ride back to Camille's, I sort the men into conversations and kisses, compartmentalizing them into boxes of yes, no and maybe.

This is to be my routine: long days and late nights with the men, then back to Camille's kitchen table with a bottle of very nice wine to talk with Grayson, Rue and Ria about everything. Men. Dates. What I want.

The last part is going to take some getting used to.

I never realized just how much I truly cared about other people's feeling until I started arguing with myself about sending Duke home because I was afraid it would hurt his feelings. Grayson may think I was quick and decisive about who to send home the first night, but there was a lot going on in my head that I never told anyone.

Tonight is worse.

Ria tells me to decide what *I* want and that's a new concept. For years, I've put everyone—I've put what Hettie and Tema and my parents—needs and wants as a priority before deciding on my own.

Being here, being on my own, I don't need to ask Hettie what she thinks. There's no need to arrange that someone is staying with Tema before I do something. And I don't have to step back with what I want to make things easier on my parents and my brothers' hectic schedules.

I only have to think about what *I* want, and that's more difficult than I ever thought.

After today, I'm firm on five of the men I'd like to keep around. The ones I feel where there is already a connection growing, or I'm interested enough to try to develop one.

Two more that I'm on the fence about, but not ready to give up on.

That leaves three.

"You need give out two yellow roses again," Rue reminds me. "Those are the men who will be going home."

In my head, I know who it should be.

In my heart, all I can think of is I what if I make a mistake on who to pick? How can I disappoint these men, who have given up so much to be here? Should I give them another chance? That wasn't enough time to make a decision.

What if I'm sending the wrong one home?

"Don't second-guess too much," Grayson advises. "Go with your gut, your first instinct. I know you haven't had much time to spend with them, but you can't have a spark with everyone."

"That will be a very different kind of show if you do," Camille says with a quiet smile. She joined us tonight to see what our thoughts on the capelin festival were. It was the first time the little island had such a celebration, and we told her she needed to make it an annual event.

I'm glad she stayed because I like the moral support.

"Who is it going to be?" Rue demands.

Ria stands ready at the whiteboard, marker in hand. "Tesh," I finally admit. "He's... I'm not much for the grumpy type."

"Plus he reminds you of Spencer," Rue points out.

Yes, that might have gone through my head once or twice, but I certainly didn't tell anyone that. "Did you do that on purpose?"

Grayson shrugs. "We had to make sure you were over him or this wouldn't work."

"I'm over him," I tell them with enough vehemence that my hand on the table almost knocks over my wineglass. "I'd appreciate you not second-guessing *me*."

"Whatever you say." Grayson nods, and I'm reminded that while this is my life we're discussing, it's also the basis of a television show that Grayson's responsible for. I'm here to find love, but he's here to make it a good show, with enough drama and swoony moments for the viewers to love.

What happens if my search for true love gets in the way of his plans for the show?

I guess that's what happened with Lyra and Spencer.

Grayson can't have an easy job.

But this is *my* life. I need to get used to putting *myself* first.

They're waiting for me to decide, and so, with a big inhale, I make my choice. "Boone," I say sadly. The motorcycle was a plus, but not enough. "I just—it's not there."

"It won't be there for all the of them." Grayson nods at Ria, who crosses off Boone's name.

Done. Tesh and Boone will be leaving in the morning.

I tell myself it's the right choice. It's what *I* want.

Or don't want.

"And for the first date, I thought Jake," Grayson continues. "The viewers will be eager to see you reconnect with him."

That might not be what *I* want. I think about the kiss that afternoon. "What if I'm not in a hurry to reconnect with him?" I ask slowly.

"Which is why the First Date rose is a good idea."

I've watched the show—I know all about the first date curse. In the past, whoever gets the First Date rose goes home. It happened for Lyra, it happened for Esme, and it's been that way since the second season of The Suitor.

That's the only reason I agree to give Jake the First Date rose.

It might not be fair, but it is what I want.

Or don't want.

18

Jonas

I AWAKE TO MY hotel room smelling of fish.

It's not a pleasant scent.

But I have no time to dispose of the clothes I wore yesterday, or call for someone to freshen up my suite because we've been told to be in the hallway outside our rooms at ten-thirty.

Not to be early, but to open the door at exactly that time.

Camera ready they said. Make sure you smile, they instructed. Be ready to be seen.

The red-haired guy—Rand? Andy?—had explained to us the first night that was how we would find out who was going home.

It's not until ten twenty-eight, that I come to the realization that I could be sent home at any moment.

It's not a comforting thought.

I knew it wouldn't happen the first night—unless I completely offended Abigail in a way I wasn't aware of, there would be no reason for Abigail to send me home. I knew there would be enough interest, even intrigue, about why I was there. There would be no possible way that I would be sent home before the first date.

And then she kissed me.

The kiss itself had been a little tentative, but Abigail herself had initiated it, so I could understand the hesitation.

But last night on the beach, it seemed like every time I turned around, someone else was kissing her.

I had assumed this would not happen until the individual dates.

I staked my claim with Abigail—and then others moved in and reclaimed.

And now there's a possibility—as slight as it may be—that I might be going home?

I don't like this.

She kissed me. There's an obvious connection between us. Why should I have to go through this camera-ready circus act, since I *will not* be leaving today?

I keep telling myself that. It's better to be angry with this process than feel vulnerability in any way.

At least I assume this is what being vulnerable feels like. Definitely a new sensation.

I don't like it if this is how it feels.

The producers told us that success will only come if I open myself up to Abigail and allow myself to be vulnerable.

I think not.

Abigail knows what I have to offer. The viewers do as well.

I'm royalty.

Intelligent, handsome, wealthy. I'm a prince of Laandia, the most popular monarchy in the world.

I can make this process a fairy tale for Abigail.

Instead, there's a chance I might open the door to find a yellow rose lying on the floor in the hall. That would send me home because yellow is the colour of friendship, and it would indicate Abigail wasn't interested in pursuing a connection with me.

Implausible but... possible?

I *could* be reading the room completely wrong, but I doubt it. Our first kiss may have turned her off, or after last night, she might have a stronger pull towards the other men. There's a chance my lifestyle and everything I could offer her intimidate Abigail.

I can offer her a lot.

I can offer her a title, a life of luxury and expensive things.

Plus, it would be the perfect way for her to get back at Spencer, should she choose to do so.

Which makes it more unbelievable that is even an iota of a chance of me going home in the next—

It's time to open the door.

They told me ten thirty, but I find I can't open it. I'm not ready to find out if it's me with the yellow flower at my door.

What if it's me? What would people say? My cousins—my father.

If Spencer broke up with Abigail and then she sent me home, what would that say about me?

But it won't happen. It can't.

It could.

Best to rip off the bandage.

I yank open the door a minute behind schedule, so the reveal is already in progress.

Ashton's door opens after mine, and he gives a self-satisfied smile at the sight of the pink rose at his feet.

There's a pink rose at my feet as well.

Years of experience keep my face expressionless as I draw in a breath that is a little too shaky for my liking.

I'm safe.

Rupert is across the hall from me. He's got a pink rose too, and after he scoops it up, he smirks at me. "A little nervous there, Prince?"

"Why would I be nervous?" I demand, trying to match his usual insouciance. I know of Rupert more than I know him, but his father's billions will never give him a crown, and he needs to stop thinking he's better than I am.

Because he's not.

The men are saying goodbye to the ones selected to leave. The biker and the businessman are clearly not Abigail's type.

But Jake, the other Laandian seems to be. A red rose still lies on the floor outside Jake's door since he's too busy congratulating himself to bother to pick it up.

I may not understand all the rules yet, but it's clear that getting a red rose means Jake will have a one-on-one date with Abigail tomorrow.

I have no idea why it's him and not me who gets the privilege but at least I'm not going home.

19

Abigail

I TAKE GRAYSON'S SUGGESTION and give Jake the First Date rose.

It's mainly so I can find out just what the heck he's doing here.

Does he actually think he's got a chance with me?

I dated Jakey Crow when I was fifteen years old. I'm sure he's already told the others the dirty details, embellished to make him look like the good guy.

I doubt he mentioned the relationship lasted all of two months, and that he broke my heart—or as much of my heart as he held in his hand.

Looking back, I know we would have never lasted, that it was just a blip in my romantic history, but try telling your fifteen-year-old self that.

It also says a lot about my romantic history that they would bring in Jakey as the one who got away. Or for a second chance.

I have no idea what they have in bold after Jakey's name, but the fact that he's here at all...

Vigorous eye roll.

Jakey was my first date, my first kiss, and also the first—and last time—I didn't listen to Hettie.

She said, don't date my cousin.

I said, Jakey's different.

He wasn't. She was right.

And now Jakey has appeared back in my life. For a second chance? It would be laughable if I didn't have to do anything about him.

But no—I'm going on a *date* with him.

I'm sure Hettie will have a few things to say about that.

Because I pick Jakey for the first date, I don't expect much. He's only been in Saint Pierre for a few days, so he can't have been inspired to plan a romantic, fairytale-like date in that short of notice.

Plus, it's Jake.

I'm not disappointed.

The SUV drops me off at one of the two bars in town. Somehow, I just knew that I wouldn't need more than jeans and a white tank top for our date.

"Jakey." He sweeps me up into a hug. For one tiny, little moment, I let myself appreciate the feel of his arms around me, the heady scent of his cologne, which hasn't changed in all those years. I let myself think *what if*—

And then the moment is over.

"Beer and pool," Jakey says, brandishing a pool cue. "Just like what we'd be doing back in Battle Harbour. By the way, I go by Jake now." He grins. "A little more manly, don't you think?"

I smile in return, only mine has a bite to it. "But you weren't exactly manly when I knew you, so I think you're stuck with Jakey."

Does he actually think he's going to end up with me in Laandia? Jake was what I wanted when I was fifteen, but things change. Things *have* changed.

If they hadn't, there is a pretty good chance that I would have married Jakey right after high school. He would have gotten one of the Crow family fishing boats to captain. I would have worked at the school, or maybe stayed at Sweets and Treats, where I worked during the summers.

I might have thought we were happy.

There would have been no fab foursome with Hettie, Bo, and Spencer because the Jake Crow's father hated King Magnus. I wouldn't have left with Hettie.

I would have never have known Tema.

Then again, there's a chance Hettie and Bo wouldn't have split up.

I definitely wouldn't have been the Suitorette.

There are a million and one paths my life might have taken, and there's no sense *what if-ing* any of them. The fact is that I'm here. I'm The Suitorette.

And Jakey Crow better be ready to prove that he's changed if he doesn't want to be sent home before my first beer is finished.

"But we're not back in Battle Harbour," I remind him, taking a look around as I follow him to a table in the back. This could be any Maritime pub, with fishing accoutrements hung as decorations and weathered faces watching us suspiciously as we walk by. There are two cameramen and another crew member holding a light to brighten the dim interior.

I'm supposed to ignore everyone but Jakey, but it's difficult in the small space. I haven't gotten used to constantly being on camera. Lyra ensured me I would, but Lyra spent her life in the spotlight. I spent most of mine shielding Hettie from it.

Two pints of beer wait at the table, but most of the froth has disappeared. "So." Jakey lifts a glass with a beaming smile. "What do you say? Abigail and Jake back together?"

"Is that what you really want?" I can't hide the skepticism in my tone, and Jakey's smile dims a bit.

"I'm here, aren't I?"

"You are, but I'm still trying to figure out *why*."

Grayson said the viewers would appreciate a reunion between me and Jakey, but I don't feel like giving it to them. Yes, Jakey deserves this date, this chance, but suddenly I don't want to waste time when I'm sure nothing is ever going to happen between us. Ever again.

Taylor said it best: We are never getting back together.

"Maybe I'm looking for another chance with you," he suggests, holding my gaze as he drains half of his glass.

"Maybe you are. Have you changed that much, Jakey?"

"Like I said, I go by Jake now," he points out. "You're the only one who calls me Jakey. Have *you* changed, Abs?"

"No one calls me Abs but Hettie."

"And how is our newest princess? She got her happily ever after. Time for you to get one, isn't it?"

"Hettie is happily married to Prince Bo. And I'm very excited to be here meeting all the men."

"You could have stayed home and met men," he points out.

"And miss out on this?" I smile to take away any sting. "What have you planned for me tonight?"

He lifts his glass. "Beer. Pool. I thought we'd play for a kiss."

"What do I win?" I ask with a straight face.

"Well—I mean, you could kiss me. That's a good prize."

"Been there, done that."

"It wasn't all that bad." Jake grins, dimples on full display. It's the same smile that got him more female attention than he could handle in high school. And he thought he could handle a lot.

"No, it wasn't all that bad," I concede. Before I knew Jakey had enjoyed the company of at least two other girls, I had liked being his girlfriend. He was fun and popular, and I had gotten a lot of attention when I was with him.

But then I found out about the other girls and things ended. I don't need to air my dirty Jakey Crow laundry for the world to see. And with Johnny standing off the side, trying to blend into the background as he films every moment of this strange reunion, I am well aware everything I say will be shown to a lot of people.

People who we both know.

"So what do you say?"

I take a healthy sip of beer and push back my chair. "Sure. You win—you get a kiss. I win—you have to tell me what you're doing here. Full disclosure and no trying to look pretty for the cameras."

"But I do look pretty for the cameras." And he looks directly at Johnny and smiles. "And I'm here for you."

"Uh, huh." I grab the pool cue. "Let's play."

Twelve minutes later we're back at the table.

"So why are you here?" I demand. "You're not the reality show type."

"How would you know?" he shoots back. "I haven't seen you in ten years."

"I could say the same about you."

He raises his eyebrows. "You haven't spoken to me in longer."

"There didn't seem like a need to do so after you broke my heart."

"I didn't break your heart," Jakey accuses. "I was always second choice for you, after Spencer. Every guy was."

I drop my gaze. I didn't expect that. "That's not true."

"No? Why are you here, Abigail? Other than getting back at Spencer for finally picking Princess Lyra over you?"

"He didn't pick her," I say firmly. "At least he didn't pick her over me. I let him go."

"That's really big of you. Is that because you knew you were going to lose him to her? She's part of the royal family, Abs. They're not like the rest of us. Although," he muses. "You were the only one he'd ever been interested in who didn't have a spot at the royal table."

I don't want to talk about Spencer, especially not with someone who knows him. And definitely not with someone who clearly saw behind the curtain I held up around my teenage feelings for him.

It may be true that I had enough respect for myself in high school not to give in to someone who saw me as a friend and a convenient partner.

It didn't mean I didn't want to give in.

Spencer may have been in love with Lyra for most of his life, but can I say anything different about me?

No one in Battle Harbour could have measured up to him. No one I met in Vancouver ever did.

I only hope *desperately* that one of these men here can.

"Maybe they're not like us, but that doesn't mean they get everything they want," I say, gritting my teeth. I need to find a way to get off this topic without looking like I'm trying to get off this topic. "Spencer had been in love with Lyra since before I knew him. You don't come between that."

He raises his eyebrows. "It would have been good to see you try. It would have been good to see you at that table, Abs, and not because you're joined at the hip with the new princess."

"Wow." I lean back in my chair. "This is not where I saw this date going."

"And where did you see it going?" Jakey's smile has changed from the self-satisfied smirk to something genuine. He looks like he... *cares.*

Not about me. He can't about me. But something.

"I don't know. I thought we'd reminisce. Tell stories about high school. You could tell me what you've been up to and who's married to who."

"We could do that," he agrees. "Or I could let you know that all of Battle Harbour is rooting for you."

"What do you mean?" I'm stunned by his words, spoken in such an off-handed tone. Jakey could be simply saying that to prolong his fifteen minutes of fame—which is what I've decided he's here for—but the expression on his face tells a different story.

He looks like he means it.

"The town wants the best for you." Jakey leans forward and takes one of my hands in his. "I know this isn't going anywhere Abs. I know what it feels like when a girl doesn't want to kiss you back."

"I hope you stop kissing me then," I can't help but say.

"You kicked my butt in pool so you wouldn't have to kiss me."

This offends me. "Did you honestly think I'd let you win?"

"Ten years ago, you would have."

"I was a very different person then. I beat you fair and square because I spent my nights playing pool at the King's Hat, while you were underage drinking at Sailor's Salon," I point out with a laugh.

"That's because no one would give me beer at the King's Hat," Jakey protests.

"That's because you were *underage*. We were there to play pool, so they let us."

"Being good friends with the owner's brother might have helped."

"This was before Kalle bought it."

"Even then, the town wanted you to do well."

"Who, exactly, are you talking about?"

"Abs, everyone knows what you did for Hettie," he says gently. "What you've done, and still do. You gave up your home for her, and everyone—me, included—wants to see you start living your own life."

My heart stutters at his words. The town... *saw*. Jakey is Hettie's family, but there are so many more who aren't. I don't see how the entire town knows anything about me.

Jakey squeezes my hand. "I might have come here with the tiniest of chances—" He presses his thumb and finger together to show how that tiny chance was— "—to have another chance with you, but I'm really here to wish you good luck. To tell you that everyone at home wants you to win this thing."

Jakey was always a bad liar. It's how I knew he had taken Jessa Donovan behind the high school when we were together, even before the rumours started swirling.

He's not lying now.

A rush of emotion that I can't begin to understand pours over me, and I have to blink to keep the tears from pooling. Growing up, I felt like my identity was so linked to Hettie's that no one saw me as her big-mouthed protector.

Knowing they want me to win...

"I think it's pretty tough for me not to win this," I say with a shaky laugh. "Seeing as how I'm the Suitorette at the centre of all of this."

"You could decide not to try. You could settle. Take the easy choice."

"Who is the easy choice?"

Jakey shrugs. "No idea. Maybe me? Because I could bring you back to the world where you could have been all this time. But you need more than what Battle Harbour can offer you. You deserve more, anyway."

A tear spills down my cheek. "Jakey..."

"Jake," he corrects with a grin.

This time I give him a hug.

20

Rand

J AKE GOT SENT HOME after his date with Abigail.

I'm not surprised, nor am I disappointed. He came back and told us the news with a rueful grin, a little different from the cocky smirk he sported when he left for his date.

I don't like how familiar he seemed with Abigail. True, he knew her when they were younger, but people change in ten years.

I know I have.

While I'm not surprised to see Jake leave, I am astounded to find a red rose before my door this morning.

I get the second date with Abigail.

There had been a moment's regret when Jake got the first date, quickly followed by relief. Especially when he came back from the date only to grab his suitcase.

The curse of the First Date rose continues.

I have the Second Date rose, so let's hope a new curse doesn't start with me.

I spend the next day planning the date, which isn't difficult since there is not much to do in Saint Pierre. Producer Ria helps with the logistics.

Now all I have to do is get myself ready.

I change my shirt three times. My hair dries funny after my shower, which is a big deal when you're a redhead, so I wet it again, splashing my third choice for a shirt, so I go back to the first choice, a blue polo that looks like the one Ashton wore at the beach.

I hope Abigail doesn't think I'm trying to copy Ashton's look.

I hope she likes my idea for the date. What if she doesn't? What if she hates it?

What if she sends me home?

When they gave me the option of staying for the new Suitorette, I didn't hesitate.

My sister had watched the show since the first episode, and since I spend a lot of time with her, I've become a reluctant fan. But it was Rayna who signed me up, first to be a Suitor, and then to be a contestant. I went along with the idea because it made Rayna happy, and it wasn't as if my dating life was booming.

"Nothing that exciting will ever happen to me, so I have to live vicariously through you," Rayna had said the day before I left for Saint Pierre to meet Princess Lyra. "You have to do this for me."

I've lost count of how many times she's said that to me since the accident.

She lost the use of her legs at seventeen.

I had been in the car as well; my best friend had been driving. We had been coming home from a concert when the drunk driver had hit us. I had been fine; my friend and his girlfriend had escaped with barely a scratch. Rayna's friend had broken her arm, but that was it.

Rayna had taken the worst of it, and never walked again.

She could have been bitter. Turned resentful that she had been the only one who had been hurt. But Rayna forced us to live our best lives, becoming an inspiration to us all.

So if she wanted me to try to win the heart of the princess, I would give it my best try. And if that didn't work out, and I got a second chance to find love with a smart and beautiful woman, there was really no choice. I would stay and give it a try.

I liked Princess Lyra. I admired her and, yes—I was a little intimidated by her. I didn't think there was much chance of my ending up with her, not after Spencer showed up, but I'm proud of the connection we'd forged. I like to think we ended as friends.

Abigail is different. She's much less intimidating, more real, probably because she's not a princess.

I say that's a plus.

The SUV picks me up for our date and takes me into town, where Abigail will meet me. Anticipation buzzes, but the nerves aren't as bad as I thought they would be. I'm looking forward to seeing Abigail, and yes, I'm nervous that she won't enjoy herself, but not as much as if I had planned this for Lyra.

I wouldn't have the first clue of how to plan a date for Lyra. But Abigail—

Is here.

Standing up, I watch her walk in, taking in the stage, the microphones and screens. She's wearing red pants, snug at her hips and leaving her ankles bare, and a flowy cream-coloured that shows off her shoulders and bare arms.

Her dark hair is loose and curly, and she's wearing purple-framed glasses.

Her smile takes up her entire face.

"Karaoke night?" Abigail guesses after we've hugged hello. It's hard to get the perfect closeness ratio right with the hug—too much squeeze, the woman will try to pull away, not enough, and she won't know how much you want to be close to her.

I don't think I squeeze enough, so I overcompensate with a quick kiss on Abigail's cheek just as she pulls back.

She smells nice, like flowers mixed with cherries.

Abigail gazes around with a big smile, like she actually likes the idea of performing karaoke with me in front of a crowd of strangers.

Or else she's good at pretending.

We have a table close to the stage area, but with enough distance from the speakers to prevent hearing loss the next day. The bar begins to fill up, which is both good and bad. I'm not sure if it's because the karaoke is a new thing in Saint Pierre, or word has got out that we're filming tonight. Johnny has brought another cameraman, and they take up their positions on opposite sides of the little pub.

I made sure it's a different bar than she went to with Jake last night.

"It is," I say, watching her face take it all in.

"I had no idea they did karaoke here." A waitress arrives and they talk cocktails, which results in Abigail asking to be "surprised."

I order a beer. "I don't think they usually do," I admit. "Ria helped me set it up."

Her dark eyes widen with delight. "So all of this is for me?"

"You said you wanted us to plan the date." I spread my arms. "Welcome to my date."

Abigail bounces on her seat. "I... This is...*Thank* you," she finally manages. "For setting all this up."

"Well, thank you for giving me a date rose." I feel my cheek flush, a common occurrence for a redhead. "And not the First Date rose."

"Yeah, well, Jakey..." She shrugs.

The DJ steps up to the microphone before I can respond. He welcomes the crowd, gives a shout-out to Abigail and the show, and points me out as her date for the evening. The line to sing has already started, and an older man is the first to take the stage.

N'Sync pours out of the speakers and the crowd cheers. His voice is shaky to start but improves once he gets going.

Abigail leans forward. "This is so much fun," she speaks loudly over the music. "I've never done this before."

"Oh. Is this okay?"

"It's better than okay! I've just never had the opportunity. I like to sing in the car, so I'll be fine once I get a drink for courage."

"I always need one."

"Is this something you do a lot?" Abigail has to shout so I can hear her over the crowd singing along, but it also means she leans closer.

I nod just as the waitress returns with our drinks.

We do the obligatory toast, and Abigail's eyes widen as she takes a sip. "Strong," she says with a cough. "Want to try?"

She passes me the glass like we've done this hundreds of times. She smiles like we've known each other for years.

That's what it feels like.

I take a sip of her drink, and a few different types of alcohol swirl and settle into my belly. But the warmth running through me isn't from the liquor.

I like Abigail. I'm already comfortable with her.

This does not feel like a first date.

I like being with her, even if I'm about to show off my lack of talent as a singer.

"So this is your date." When the next singer stands up and starts to belt out a Cher song, Abigail moves her chair beside mine. "You have to tell me why you picked *this*. That's one of the requirements."

"There were other requirements?"

She leans on the table, close enough that her elbow touches mine as she slowly sips her drink. "I wanted it to be something you enjoy, that you do in your regular life. That if this were your hometown, we'd be doing the same thing." She glances over her shoulder. "Minus the cameras."

Johnny steps around an over-enthusiastic fan of the Cher singer to keep the camera on us. "Have you gotten used to them yet?"

She shakes her head. "Not really, but hopefully soon. But you must be used to them. You made it pretty far with Lyra."

I didn't intend to bring up Lyra, but if Abigail does... "Does that bother you?" I ask carefully.

Abigail's expression is blank. "Should it?"

"Well... yeah. I think so," I decide. "At least it could. You take a group of men competing for a princess of all things, and they start to have feelings for her, and then she leaves with someone else. And then there's *you* coming in after her, and you have to wonder..."

I stop myself, because maybe Abigail isn't thinking about any of that.

Maybe I just opened mouth and inserted foot.

"I do wonder," Abigail admits, and I let out a huff of relief. "It's... not easy. And I think I'm in my head too much, but it's tough, you know? I'm taking over for *Princess Lyra* and she's..."

She pauses like she wants me to continue. "She's a lot," I offer.

That seems to be the right answer because Abigail's shoulders relax, and she smiles. "She's a lot of everything. And I'm just... me."

"Well, I happen to like just you."

She drops her gaze, noticing how close our hands are on the table. "I think of the men, how you were developing feelings for her, and then you got thrown a curveball. And then I'm here. And you have to start all over with me. Did you have feelings for Lyra?"

I'm surprised at the question. Not surprised that Abigail would want to know that information, but the abruptness of her asking. She never even took a breath.

I get the sense there's no beating around the bush with her.

I'm not used to that. I'm too much of a people pleaser to be so direct.

"I liked Lyra," I admit, unsure of how carefully I need to tread. I sort of expected we'd discuss Lyra, but not right away. Maybe it's best to get it over with. "And I liked getting to know her. But I don't know if I really knew her all that well. And for me, I need to really know someone before I can say I have feelings for her."

Abigail leans back in her chair, a relieved expression crossed her face. "Thanks for being honest. I'd rather have the truth than people telling me what they think I want to hear."

"And what do you want to hear?"

"Oh, maybe that Lyra doesn't have anything on me, and you're all so happy to have me show up because no one liked her. Something like that." She grins.

I like the way her eyes shine when she smiles. "*I'm* happy to have you show up. And I'd say the other guys feel the same."

"The ones who didn't come back. Did they have feelings for her?"

The slight hitch of hesitation suggests this is a question that bothers her, maybe something she's been thinking about too much.

I shake my head. "It was only really Jon. And his heart wasn't really in it from the start, so I'm not surprised he didn't stick around. Good guy, though. He was the Alpha."

"I've never really gone for Alphas before," she admits. "So maybe it's for the best. Now that you've heard all my insecurities, I still want to know, why this place? Do you sing?"

"Not very well. But I do a lot of karaoke at home."

"Home is..."

"Oshawa. Ontario. Close to Toronto."

"Do you go with your friends?"

"Sort of." My friends are more than just friends. Rayna was family, and the others—that night had bonded us forever. Rayna was the centre of our group, and we revolved around her, doing whatever we could to make her life a little easier. To make her happy.

"When I was eighteen, I was in an accident," I offer. "Four of us walked away. My sister ended up in a wheelchair."

Abigail looks stricken. "I'm so sorry."

"She's not. I mean, she lost the use of her legs, but she still manages to have a great life. She kind of pushes the rest of us to do the things that she can't."

"Does she sing?"

"Horribly. But she loves it. There's a bar back home that's accessible, and we go there about once a month. For her. So she can make an idiot of herself. She loves it."

"What's her name?"

"Rayna. She's kind of the reason I'm here."

"She made you come?"

"She signed me up, and wouldn't let me back out."

Abigail moves her hand so that her finger brushes mine. "I'm glad she didn't let you back out. Thanks, Rayna." She smiles. "You're close with her."

It's not a question. "She's my best friend," I confess.

"I love that." She pushes back her chair. "Let's sing for her. How do we do this?"

"We pick a song. And we get up on stage."

It's easier to get on stage then picking a song. The two girls with serious plans for a Sabrina Carpenter song let us go since they're still debating dance moves.

And then the lights are on us and we're singing "Don't Stop Believing" at the top of our lungs.

It's as bad as I thought it would be. Abigail throws herself into it, but her voice is as bad as mine, especially when she's practically screaming the lyrics.

Still, it's amazing.

So amazing, that we do it twice more. We spend the rest of the evening cheering the others on.

It's a good date. Even maybe a great one.

And it makes me think that maybe I've got a chance at this.

21

Abigail

I don't send Rand home.

In fact, I'm looking forward to getting to know him better. It was a fun night. We sang three songs together, and the last one got the whole place on its feet.

Neither of us are great singers, but we sound good together.

I saw our reflections in the bar, and we look good together.

There's a sweetness about Rand that I've never found in a man before, and I like it. He may be sweet, but there's also a strength to him. And a thoughtfulness that is refreshing.

Maybe it's because he takes care of his sister, but I get the sense that Rand is a protector. That he would take care of me.

It's a novel concept to me.

I've been on my own since I was eighteen, and while I might be back living at home with my parents in Battle Harbour, it's only a short-term solution. I already know I'm too independent to stay for long.

I like the thought of Rand taking care of me.

Opening the doors when we left the bar. Offering me his sweater because the breeze was chilly. Asking to kiss me and angling my chin to make sure it was the optimal position for me.

It was a good kiss too. Soft, at least at first. Sweet, but with some heat.

I'm starting to like the kissing aspect of being The Suitorette.

I liked kissing Rand. I *like* Rand.

He's considerate. Spencer was too, but I never came first for him. There was always something else on his mind when he was with me. *Someone* else.

I need to stop comparing everyone to Spencer.

I *told* myself not to do that. That was Hettie's main advice, as well as Camille. And what am I doing?

Exactly that. I've got a chart ready in my head for Rand and Spencer, with pros and cons listed for each.

Neither one of them should be on my mind, because I have my date with Rupert today.

Rupert Lorde. Friend of Ashton Carrington and his twin sister Fenella. Full-time member of the Billionaire Brats, which is what the internet calls their group of friends.

He's a *billionaire*.

"Why is he here?" I had asked Grayson the first night when we went through the list of men.

Grayson shrugged. "Ashton suggested him."

"But why? And why is Ashton still here?" The idea boggled my mind. I know more about Fenella than actually know her but Fenella is neck and neck in the intimidation race with Lyra. The thought of her brother, someone so close to her, being *here*, with me...

"You'll have to ask them," Grayson told me.

And I plan to. Because hockey players and rock stars and even princes are one thing, but these are *billionaires*. Young, really attractive men with so many zeroes after their names that I need both hands to count them. They travel the world and race cars and date supermodels. They are in another league. Another galaxy.

Because I am me—Abigail Locke. Soon to be a teacher. And they're *billionaires*. Ashton races cars. I have no idea what Rupert does.

They both should have *opposites attract* after their names.

But even as overwhelming as it is to know that men of their means want to spend time with *me*, I'm still excited about the date.

Rupert meets me at the marina the next afternoon. "My lady." He takes my hand and bows over it.

"Rupert." Note to self: Rupert is not a hugger. "I'm excited to see what you have planned for me this afternoon."

He told me to bring a bathing suit and to dress for a day on the water. I expect that he booked one of the catamarans offered for the tourists, and an afternoon of sailing sounds perfect.

"I could prolong the anticipation, but I won't." Rupert points out to the water where a boat is anchored.

That's no catamaran. It doesn't even have sails.

It's a *yacht*.

Even from the dock, it looks massive, like something moored around a Greek island.

"Hope you're okay with boats," he adds with a smug smile.

I try, but I can't completely wipe away my expression. "We're going out in *that*?"

"See anything you like better?"

I look him straight in the eyes. There's no point in feigning nonchalance here—I'm spending the afternoon on a *yacht*. "I don't think so, no."

"I didn't think you would."

"Either someone is overcompensating, or likes to make a big effort," I mutter under my breath as Rupert takes my hand and leads me to the tender docked at the end of the pier.

"I like to make efforts, if the person is worth it," he says over his shoulder.

Rupert thinks *I'm* worth it?

It's a quick trip to the yacht as Rupert explains that the size of the boat means it can only come in so far. And then we pull up, and Rupert helps me onboard.

Everything is white; too polished, too perfect. It's like I've been transported onto a movie set, some romantic comedy where the heroine is completely out of place and comedy pratfalls ensue. The crew, in uniforms straight from Doctor Odessey, greet us with flutes of champagne and snacks.

The captain even looks like Joshua Jackson. It's so pretty and perfect that it must be unreal.

The moment my foot touches the shiny surface, everything shifts. The boat rocks on a rogue wave, and I grab for the railing.

It's more than that, though. For the first time, I realize *this could be my life*.

Not life-on-a-yacht—life with one of these men.

My life is about to change.

If I pick Rand, my life will be Ontario weather and karaoke with his sister. If I pick Rupert—or Ashton—my life will be big boats and movie premieres and fabulous clothes.

The choices couldn't be more different, and there are *a lot* of choices.

Nine, to be exact.

And my life will change depending on who I pick. If I pick anyone.

"You okay?" Rupert asks as I continue to grip the railing. I've been on boats my entire life, so it's not the wave that has spooked me.

I give my head a shake. "Yes. I'm fine."

"Is it too much?" Rupert is serious. He thinks this whole fish-out-of-water thing has completely stunned me.

I'm not sure if that's sweet or offensive.

"Of course not." I give a theatrical toss of my head. "I'm worth it."

Rupert nods with what I think may be admiration. "That you are."

We drink champagne and eat lobster rolls. We swim, and the drop into the cold Atlantic Ocean makes my heart stop, even in the summer.

Rupert, I quickly find out, prefers swimming in the Caribbean, but tolerates the Mediterranean. He spends the rest of the afternoon in a sweater with a blanket nearby.

I'm not sure what to think about Rupert. He's the perfect host, asking my opinion and what I need, making sure my glass and belly are full.

The crew helps with that as well. Apparently, there is an actual chef on board.

I can't imagine living with this much opulence. And as the hours pass and Rupert and I talk about everything—and nothing—I still have no way of knowing how Rupert feels about it.

Does he take it for granted? Does he feel entitled to his wealth, this way of life? Is he grateful for everything he has?

He's charming, attentive, and funny. I feel seen and heard and even listened to. He asks all the right questions and laughs in all the right places. As far as being good boyfriend material, I've no doubt Rupert could fit the bill.

But I need more.

Rupert may be the perfect host, but even after spending hours with him, I still have no clue what makes him tick. What beliefs he might have. Values. He doesn't even talk about his family.

It makes it very difficult to imagine starting a life with him.

As the sun sinks lower, I lean my arms on the railing to watch. We toured the mouth of the St. Lawrence, and I can just make out the colourful houses of Saint Pierre from this distance.

Our date is almost over, and I think I know him *less* than when I got on this boat.

"Is this your boat?" I ask. Even the boat—I should have known that by now.

Rupert shakes his head. "A buddy of mine."

I wait, but no name is coming. "If we're going to end up together, I'm going to have to know names," I tease.

"Milo Stapleton-Shak. Heard of him?"

"The name may ring a bell." I manage to feign nonchalance but anyone who has seen a tabloid in the grocery store has heard of Milo. And the internet is full of his exploits, along with the rest of the Billionaire Brats.

I am so out of my depth.

Not so much *depth*, since I can't really tell how deep Rupert goes, but this life they

lead—it's not me. Still, I've got some time left, and I want to keep trying.

"You must be close to him."

Rupert cocks his head like I've commented on peace in the Middle East. "Why do you say that?"

"He let you borrow his yacht. Or is that what you and your friends do?"

He clinks his glass against mine. "That's what we do, my lady."

I'd let Hettie borrow my car, so maybe it's the same thing. "And is this what you usually do on a date?" I prompt.

Again, so non-committal. "I thought you'd enjoy a day on the water."

"What would *you* enjoy?" I press. "I wanted these dates to be what *you* wanted to do."

"I like this."

"But is this what you want to do? If you could choose any-thing. Which you probably could." Rupert doesn't reply. "I'm trying to get to know you."

"Why bother?" The perfect host masks slips, and bitterness coats his words. "We both know you're not picking me at the end."

I rear back and stare. "Why would you say that?" As much as I've tried and failed to get to know Rupert this afternoon, I haven't given up.

"Pretty lady, my life would chew you up and spit you out," he drawls, sounding more like Ashton than himself.

Or maybe this is the real Rupert.

"Because I don't have money?" I demand coolly.

Rupert smiles into the setting sun before turning to me. "Because you're too good for me." He tilts up my chin like he's about to kiss me, only there's nothing loving in his expression, only sadness. "You've lived, and you've loved. I hear you talk about that kid—Bo's daughter—and your face lights up, and all I can think of is that I want someone to look like that when they talk about me. And no one will."

"You don't know that."

Rupert drops his hand. "Oh, but I do. Abigail, I live in a bubble—a very small bubble, where I can buy anything I want and I'm surrounded by other people who can do the same thing. People don't say what they want because they're too busy trying to impress me."

"I thought you were supposed to impress me? That was my idea, anyway."

"Is that what you really want? You want the men to fall all over themselves trying to impress you? Trust me, it's not all that fun."

I'm stung by his words, but not enough to second guess myself. "I thought it was a good way to get to know the men. Find out more about them, let them show me the different sides of themselves."

I turned this show on its head with my idea, so I better not doubt myself.

He shrugs and looks back at the water. "I have no idea how to do that."

"I wanted you to be yourself. I'm trying to get to know the real Rupert."

Rupert huffs a sigh, like he's a student and I've given him homework that takes away from his time to play with his friends. "The problem is that I don't know who that is."

There's a truthful tone in his voice. I think we're getting somewhere now.

"I'm one person when I'm with my friends, another when I'm with people I don't really know," he continues. "And I'm another person when I'm with my family."

Issues with family. That is coming through clear as a bell. And there's no point pushing there because I can tell he's not about to dive deep.

"What would your perfect date be then? Anything at all," I urge.

"I had a perfect date once," Rupert surprises me with his admission. "It wasn't really a date, but it was... it was pretty perfect."

"Tell me." There is more to Rupert—I can see it now. And I want to know more.

I just don't know if we'll have time.

"I was with a group biking through France. I like to bike," he says off-handedly.

"We should have gone biking."

"I saw the bikes at the hotel, and this—" He pats his backside. "Is not getting on one of those."

I laugh.

"I was with a group, and I got ahead of them," he continues. The sadness in his voice is back, and I watch his face, mesmerized by the layers unfurling before me. "It was somewhere in France, and I blew a tire. I managed to stop, no injuries, but my tire kit was with the van behind me. I could have waited by the side of the road, but I saw this girl in the field. Lavender. Beautiful. It was warm and sunny and I could hear the bees. She was staring at me because I might have been swearing a bit. And then I stared at her." He smiles, his focus on a place, on a person, that is nowhere in sight.

"We stared for a bit, and then I waved. And then... she took me to her farm. It was all peaceful. She had no idea who I was and could barely speak English. She gave me lemonade and took me walking among the lavender. I saw the van and the other bikes go by, but I stayed with her."

I can see it—a smiling and happy Rupert walking in the fields with a woman. His blond hair would be gleaming in the sun, and he'd have a bunch of lavender in his hand. Of course she would be beautiful, and soft, and delicate. Someone who would want Rupert for himself—and be able to bring it out for the world to see. "What happened?"

"Her father came home," he says with a rueful shrug. "He wasn't pleased to see me taking up his daughter's time, especially when she was sort of engaged to some neighbour's son. The father could speak English. At least he gave me a ride to meet the bike group. But those few hours?" Rupert tips his head to stare at the sky. "It was pretty perfect."

I rest my hand on his holding the railing. "I'm happy you had that."

"Are you?"

"Of course. Everyone needs some happiness, and perfect days are hard to come by."

"Right now would be a good time to say that today was perfect." Rupert grins at me, and it's more of a real smile than his usual sardonic twist of his lips.

There is more to Rupert than meets the eye. But the timing...

"It would be great for the cameras, but what would be the point when we both know your heart is still in France?"

He laughs, then glances over his shoulder. "I didn't think I could get used to the cameras, but you make me comfortable enough for me to forget all about them."

"That's good to hear. I'm getting there, but I'm not quite forgetting they're always around yet."

"Give it time and a perfect date, and you won't even think about them."

I nudge him with my shoulder. "And who do you think I'll have that perfect date with?"

"Ah, but I'm not a betting man. Ashton, on the other hand—" Rupert points to a black dot moving fast toward the boat.

If I squint, I can make out a jet ski.

"There's your ride back, by the way."

22

Ashton

I pick up Abigail from her date with Rupert because she's with Rupert. I wouldn't have done it with anyone else.

And plus I know Rupe isn't into her like some of the others might be.

Like I am.

I haven't stopped thinking about her since I kissed her.

When I kiss a woman, there's usually three reactions: gratitude and awe—He *kissed* me; smugness—He kissed *me*; and entitlement—of *course* he kissed me.

All three get old pretty fast, which is why I haven't been doing much kissing in a while.

It was different with Abigail. It kind of made me remember how much I like kissing.

The last woman I dated was a model I met at the Victoria's Secret Fashion show and we spent two months in Europe, not seeing much more than the inside of hotel rooms, until she found someone with a bigger wallet. The one before that was a small-time influencer, who used our six months together to catapult herself into the million-follower bracket.

The one before that was an Oscar nominee who used Method acting as an excuse to cheat on me with her co-star.

There's a pattern, as my sister has pointed out more than once.

Abigail is different, and honestly, I don't have the self-awareness to figure out why I like her. But despite the fact she's dating ten other guys—nine now that Jake was sent packing—I trust her. She's strong, and smart, and funny. *Fun.*

She's a good kisser.

I feel safe with her, and that is something I never imagined would be important.

As soon as I board Milo's boat, I can tell things aren't really meshing with Abigail and my friend.

It might make me a bad friend to admit I'm glad that I didn't walk in on anything other than the two of them standing at the railing, barely touching.

And neither of them protest when I tell Abigail I'm there to whisk her away for our date.

"We'll see you back at the hotel?" I ask Rupert.

Rupert doesn't answer. Instead he watches Abigail like he's expecting her to say something.

She doesn't. I don't know how it worked when she sent Jake home, but I don't think it was like this. As far as I can tell, Rupert is still in the game.

I'm not sure Rupert realizes that, however.

"I don't think you will." With a deep sigh, he takes Abigail's hand. "I think this is as far as I go."

"Rupert," Abigail says softly.

"You agree?" he asks.

Now I feel like I'm intruding on something.

Abigail's smile is sweet and just a little sad. "It was lovely to meet you. What will you do now?"

"I might go back to France."

That is news to me. But I don't say anything, just try to be unobtrusive as Rupert takes himself out of the game.

"You should definitely do that." Abigail gives him a hug and after a moment, Rupert relaxes enough to hug her back.

She must be truly special if she can get him to hug someone. Rupert avoids displays of affection as much as he can.

Family issues. We've all got them.

"Dude." I step forward to clasp his hand. "You're really out?" Rupert lifts a shoulder in acknowledgement. "See you soon?"

"Not *too* soon." He nods at Abigail. "I expect you'll be sticking around her for a while."

"True. She's not getting rid of me."

"*She* is standing right here," Abigail reminds us with a grin that is truly adorable.

"Let's get out of here then." With a last wave at Rupert, I get Abigail into a life jacket and position her on the jet ski.

"Can I drive?"

"No," I tell her, swinging my leg over the machine. "Hang on tight to me."

"Why?"

"I go fast. You have a problem with that?"

Abigail winds her arms around my waist. She's surprisingly strong. "What do you think?"

I think I like her arms around me.

"Where are we going?" Abigail shouts as I gun the motor.

"It's a surprise."

And then we're off.

I race anything with a motor, and once I hear the squeal of delight from Abigail, I don't hold back.

I do donuts, splashing both of us. Skim the waves, almost jumping a few of them. I go fast, like I promised, and from the sound of the laughter behind me, Abigail seems to enjoy it.

Which makes me show off.

Her hair flies everywhere because I forget to tell her to tie it back, and her hands grip my life jacket, body pressed against mine. I like how she leans even closer when she wants to say something. For a few moments, I wonder if I should let her drive, see how she does, but I like how she feels behind me.

Besides, I'm not the type who likes to relinquish control.

It takes longer to get back to the marina because I'm enjoying myself. And I think Abigail is too.

Her eyes are certainly shining when I hand over the Jet ski, and something tugs in my chest at how happy she is.

"I want you to take me driving," is the first thing she says.

I don't bother masking my smirk. "That can be arranged."

"I wasn't even scared," she announces as we head to the SUV waiting for us.

"You should have been." I laugh. "I won't tell you how fast we were going."

"But I wasn't." Abigail takes my arm, the gesture so natural that I look around to see if she's confused me with someone else. "I wasn't scared at all. Because... of you."

This is a first. Usually, I'm the one scaring people with my driving.

I disentangle her arm and take her hand instead. Her hand is cold and instinct has me taking it in both of mine to warm it. "Most people are scared to drive with me."

"I'm not most people. I knew you wouldn't do anything to hurt me." I look down at her in disbelief. "What?"

"Blind faith," I tell her. "I'm not used to it."

The way Abigail looks up at me... my gaze flicks to her mouth, soft and smiling at me and I think—

Not *now*.

But there's a moment as I open the back door of the SUV for her, and she looks at me—

Giving in to the temptation, I press my lips against hers. They taste like salt, and are cold as ice, which is why I linger for a moment longer. "I'm glad you had fun," I whisper.

Those dark eyes are still shining as I get into the car beside her. "So what are we doing now?" Abigail demands like she expects me to amuse her.

I don't know if I've ever planned a date for a woman. I never go on traditional dates. There have been women I've enjoyed spending time with, but I've never taken them to a movie or stopped for a coffee or anything ordinary like that.

I wonder what that would be like.

I have a variety of acquaintances that I can call on when I need a plus one to some gala or event, or when my father insists I show my face at some business thing.

But I don't plan dates because I don't think I've ever had a woman I've thought of as a girlfriend. I've *dated,* but that's as far as it goes.

I've never told a woman I love her.

They might have referred to me as their boyfriend, but it's never gone both ways.

And because of this, I hate to admit it, but I was at a loss when Abigail announced that planning dates was our responsibility.

So I used the phone I hid in my bag and called my sister for help.

"There's something that no one knows about me," I begin.

"And you're going to tell me," she says practically bouncing with her eagerness.

"If you let me."

"I'm letting you."

"So the one thing that no one knows about me, my deep dark secret is…" I draw it out as long as I can, if only to watch Abigail's eyes widen. "I love to… shop."

The look on her face is priceless. "Shop? Like in *shopping*."

"Shopping. Shop. Retail therapy."

She shakes her head in bewilderment. "I never saw that coming. What do you like to shop for?"

"That's the embarrassing part. See, I really like to shop with my sister." I hunch my shoulders. I'm playing this up, but it's all true. And it's a little embarrassing.

Fenella takes me with her when she meets with designers because she needs dresses for events. We've gone to malls all over the United States, popping into Gaps and Foot Lockers like normal people when we travel. If we're in the same city, we meet for brunch and a few hours in the stores.

Sometimes we're recognized, but Fenella is good with disguises. It's one of the few times the two of us can relax together.

I don't tell Abigail any of this. It's bad enough to admit that top driver Ashton Carrington spends his spare time shopping for shoes with his twin sister.

Abigail clasps her hands together. "That's so sweet."

"It's really not, but what can I do?"

"So we're going shopping?" She looks confused, mainly because we pull up at the hotel.

"Not exactly, because I'm not allowed to take you away from Saint Pierre. And if I want to get a T-shirt with a lobster waving at me, this is the place, but there's not a lot here if you're looking for fashion."

"I'm confused."

"I called in the cavalry. Fenella. She talked to the shops in Battle Harbour—she's impressed by them—and they sent a variety of things for us to try on."

Hands clasp again. "Is this like Pretty Woman?"

Her eyes… I've never seen a woman's eyes glow like that. I don't know if Abigail really likes shopping, or this is something else.

But I like it. I like that I've made her happy.

I really didn't think it would matter so much. "Yes," I say, leaning over to unbuckle her seatbelt. "But without the snobby salesgirl. Just me."

23

Abigail

I DID NOT EXPECT this from Ashton.

I did not expect a lot of things from him.

When we get back to the hotel, he whisks me up to one of the King's Suites on the top floor before any of the men realize we're here.

And for once I'm glad to miss out seeing them, because I don't want to miss one minute of this.

The entire suite is filled with racks of clothes.

The bed is covered with bags and purses, scarves and shoes, including a brown pair of ankle boots that I grab and clutch to my chest.

And the washroom looks like a Sephora sample sale.

"That's Fenella's doing," Ashton calls as I marvel at the variety of skincare products strewn across the vanity. There's even some in the bathtub. "She gets tons of samples, so she sent some over for you."

"That is *some* of them?" I laugh.

"I'm not into makeup stuff, but she loves it. Take whatever you like."

I stand in the doorway and spread my arms. "And the rest of this?"

Ashton pulls out his phone. "Fen told me to write them down so the stores would get credit. Here." He takes a step toward Johnny and stares into the lens. "Thanks to Arnold's Attire, Helen's Hunt, and Sera Sports for providing the collection we have here. You can find all this and more in Battle Harbour, Laandia. And maybe on their websites?"

"I don't think they have websites yet," I admit.

"Maybe they should look into that after this. So?" Ashton grins, looking younger and happier, with a little mischievous thrown in. "We doing this?"

I laugh. "I'm not exactly sure what we're doing."

"We are going to look through these clothes. Boys," he points to one side. "Girls. You're going to pick out three outfits for me to try on, and I'm going to do the same for you. After that, we'll do some serious shopping. But you only have ten minutes to pick for me."

"You did all of this... for me?" I ask in disbelief.

"For me, too. I said I liked shopping."

"But..." This is stepping up. This is what I hoped the men would do, but I never expected it from *Ashton*.

His kiss on the beach made me look at him in a new way, and this makes me see him in a totally different way. Gone are the smirking playboy, or the man with the need for speed.

Ashton looks like he's having *fun*.

And it's a very good look for him.

"Grayson said there wouldn't be enough time with the new format for you to have the wedding dress date," he says. "I didn't want you to miss that, because Lyra—it seems fun. Fen got a few sent over for you to try on."

Another surprise. "You're doing the wedding dress shoot for me?" Things are soft and melty when I look at Ashton. That he went to so much trouble for this, for me—

"You want to hug it out or something?" he asks abruptly.

My mouth drops, because this is another new side. And before I can respond, Ashton pulls me into his arms.

I expect rigid, and I knew from clutching him on the Jet ski, that things are quite firm, bodywise, but Ashton hugs with a sudden softness that is a surprise.

And then— "I'm not used to making people happy," Ashton whispers into my hair, soft and muffled so it won't get picked up. "I'm not used to it."

"You seem to be very good at it," I tell him, squeezing my arms around his waist. "I appreciate it."

He pulls back with a lopsided smile. "You haven't seen what I picked out for you to wear," he threatens.

"Oh, we're on." And we break and head for the racks.

So many colours, so many styles. I have no idea what Ashton would go for, which makes it even more fun.

The pile of clothes I pick for him grows bigger.

I grew up with these stores, but spent my teenage years resentful that my shopping habit—as weak as it was—was limited to what was around the square in Battle Harbour. There was no mall, no big box stores, only stores that had been passed down for generations, with sometimes outdated attire.

All these colours and fabrics and different styles are a revelation, and shows me what I have been missing in the local stores.

Ten minutes flash in a blink, but I'm ready for it. I sort my pile and select three outfits for Ashton to try on. Then he disappears into the other room while I survey his choices for me.

A pair of ultra-high-waist jeans, dark wash and slightly flared, with a one-shouldered bodysuit the exact shade of purple as my glasses. He paired that with a pair of black boots with stacked heels and even added jewelry.

A pair of white, wide legged pants with a matching vest, just short enough to show a glimpse of my belly.

And a dress—purple so dark that at first, I think it's black, with an asymmetrical hem and a lace overlay that drips down to my knees.

Ashton even added a strapless bra. Not sure how he knows my size, but he got it right.

I try everything on—and love it all.

Having Ashton look at me as I model it for him doesn't hurt either.

And I like watching him, because it's clear he's enjoying himself. His face softens, and his smiles are easier—real smiles, not smirks or smugness. He laughs.

The man really likes shopping, even in a hotel room.

I keep on the dress, and he wears the black dress pants I picked out, and the black shirt with the design that looks like silver lightning as we browse the rest of the racks. Ashton has good taste, encouraging me to try on things out of my comfort zone, and everything he picks out looks good on me.

I feel good in the clothes too.

While we look, we talk—about his sister, my family, living in Vancouver, living all over the world. Ashton's voice brightens when he talks about racing, and I even get him to admit how he felt after the crash in his last race.

We talk about his friends, and how close they are.

"I trust Rupert... maybe not with my life, but with my sister." Ashton hands me another pair of shoes to try on. My pile has tipped over on the bed, and I've started to feel guilty about picking too much. But Ashton insists. He keeps looking, and keeps picking for me, and I keep trying them on. He chose four other dresses for me, in a rainbow of colours and different styles, and all flatter my body type.

I don't know how he does it; he looks at a shirt or a skirt and then at me, and he can somehow tell what will look good on me.

"I like Fenella—what I know of her. She's like fresh blood to Battle Harbour."

"She's like a punch in the arm," he grouses.

"I can tell you're close. And I'm jealous—I have younger brothers, and they're still more into hockey than anything I can do for them."

"What can you do for them?"

"Be a good big sister. Give advice, opportunities. Buy them alcohol before they're legal."

Ashton laughs at that. "I knew you were a bad girl."

"I am the least bad of any girl," I say ruefully. "I follow rules. I do what I'm told."

"You moved across the country with Hettie. That sounds like breaking a few rules."

"Maybe."

"I'm not trying to be nice. I'm not nice. But I am observant when I want to be. And I can tell you don't see yourself like others do."

"Does anyone really?"

"I'm rich and good-looking and I like to go fast. That's how the world sees me."

"I don't see you like that."

I had fun on my dates with Rand and Rupert, but this is different. I feel close to Ashton, a different kind of close.

It's as if he's shed some of his crusty outer skin as he tries on different clothes.

"I know," Ashton admits. "And I think that might be a problem. Want to try on the wedding dresses?" he asks before I can respond to his cryptic comment.

I shake my head. "Not all of them. Just one. And you pick."

"You want me to pick the wedding dress you're going to show up on TV in?" Ashton says skeptically.

I point to the pile on the bed. "You picked that. I trust you."

"You trust me." He shakes his head like it's a foreign concept.

"People trust you."

"Not like this." He turns away, focusing on the few white dresses hanging on the rack.

I hadn't thought much of the wedding dress date that is part of every season of the Suitorette. Rue had told me that we wouldn't be doing that for my part of the season, and I had been so overwhelmed with everything else that was going on, I didn't let myself be disappointed.

I hadn't let myself think of the men as potential husbands.

I want to find love. I want to have fun. But when I signed up for this, I hadn't given much thought to what might happen after the show was over.

But now—Ashton hands me a white dress. A wedding dress. A dress to be worn during a wedding. "This one," he decides.

"I..." The satin is slippery in my hands. "Is there something for you?"

He raises an eyebrow. "White dresses aren't really my thing."

"You know what I mean!"

"You want to see how we look together?"

I give a huff of exasperation. I've gotten Ashton to be vulnerable tonight, to be open and honest and tell me real truths. And then he slides back into his grumpy billionaire persona, and it leaves me floundering. "Why do you do that?"

He stills. He shrugs. "It's who I am."

"I don't think it is. I like you, Ashton—you, not all this." I wave at the racks. "You're not just a billionaire with me, if that's a real thing."

He shrugs again, and I see the challenge. Yes, Ashton has opened up tonight, and shown me different sides, but there's so much more that is still closed off.

I need to decide whether I want the challenge of pushing through. If he's worth it.

"There's a couple of suits for me," he says in a gruff voice. "You want to pick?"

I shake my head and start for the other room. "I think we both know you have the better taste."

And the dress he picked for me proved it.

It's exactly the dress I would have picked for myself.

Simple, but not plain. Form-fitting, but not tight, skimming my curves as it puddles around my feet. An inch of thick off-white satin, heavily embroidered along the bodice and the hem, with tiny straps.

When I see myself in the mirror, my eyes fill with tears, and I wish my mother were here. I want Hettie to see me in this, because this is the dress I would wear for my wedding.

Whoever I marry.

I take longer in the bedroom because there is some swishing of skirts. A little jumping around with excitement. And I have to call Ria in—she's been here the whole time, standing quietly with Johnny, witnessing it all—to help me do it up.

Finally I step out to show Ashton.

He's been busy.

The bed is empty of my piles, the clothes now packed neatly into bags. The racks have been pushed back, and the table is pulled out to the middle of the room with a bottle of champagne and a plate of cheese.

All this, and he's even had time to change into a tuxedo—classic black and looking like it was tailored for him.

"You look beautiful," I tell him honestly.

"I'm supposed to say that about you." He takes my hand and spins me around, the skirt swishing around my ankles. "Magnificent."

The expression on his face—intense and admiring, and slightly guarded—makes me suddenly shy. "You must say that to all the girls."

"I don't. I would tell them they were beautiful or lovely. But you—" Still holding my hand, he assesses. "This is you. It's perfect.

Glorious. This is what every man who ever dreamed about getting married wants to see walking down the aisle. You look utterly delicious, Abigail."

Delicious. I draw a shaky breath. "Thank you."

"Thank *you*." Ashton clears his throat. "I had some food brought in because I always get hungry when I shop. But... dance with me first?"

I didn't even realize there was music playing. I saw Ashton, and how he looks in that jacket hugging his shoulders, and what he's done for me, and blocked out everything else. But now—he pulls me into his arms.

I have no idea what song is playing, and I don't need to know as Ashton leads me in small circles, his arm tight around my back, his gaze holding mine like a caress.

There are shivers and butterflies and racing pulses. The shivering butterflies are racing faster than Ashton ever could.

This is what I want. This is what I've been waiting for.

This is why I agreed to do the show.

And this is even before Ashton kisses me.

Which he does, and it's... glorious.

24

Grayson

I CAN'T HELP BUT smile as Abigail sits down at the table across from me. Her eyes are glassy and staring, and she's more stunned than smiling.

"How was your date with the billionaire brats today?" I ask.

Ria, who has been with her for the day, smirks. She texted me the news that Rupert wouldn't be returning, but I've heard nothing about Abigail's date with Ashton.

From the look of her, I'd say it was a success.

"It was—they were... nice," she manages.

I smirk. "Nice is a start. I'd wager you'd like to keep Ashton around?"

"I... oh my god." Abigail breaks then, laughing, almost giggling. She hugs herself.

"So... good?" Rue presses.

"So good." Abigail takes a deep breath, still with the glazed smile. "One minute he's Ashton, the grumpy, snarky guy with too much money, and the next—*most* of the time—he's this incredibly sweet and considerate... Do you know he goes shopping with his *sister*? And he doesn't think anyone trusts him."

Rue rolls her eyes. "Oh, boy."

"His name is staying on the board then?" I ask. Ria isn't hovering with her marker this time—she's busy pouring more wine for herself.

"I had to watch it," she mutters when I meet her gaze.

"What did you watch?"

"Them." She flicks her hand toward Abigail. "It was sweet—almost sickeningly so. They danced... Johnny got some great footage. After this, Ashton's going to end up as a front-runner with the viewers. This will get him tons more fans. The sight of him driving that Jet ski." Ria shivers.

"I know, right?" Abigail leans forward. "His hair whipping around, and those *arms*? I was behind him, but still, I could see enough of him."

"Great footage," Ria repeats. "Lots of fans."

Do the producers act like that around the female contestants? "Well, that's all very good," I say, trying to block the sight of a smitten Ria from my mind. "I'm sure Ashton will be happy with his new fans. Now onto the next round of dates."

"More dates?" Abigail sounds almost disappointed, and I waste no time nipping this in the bud.

"Yes, more dates. Many dates. Dates with everyone. Four more to go," I tell her firmly.

"And then another with Ashton?"

I glance at Ria, who shrugs. "That bad?"

"That good," Rue corrects. "There was some chemistry with Rand, but it's been lacking with the others."

"I don't have chemistry with the others?" Abigail demands. "Don't they like me? I like them."

"It's more than liking each other," Rue tries to explain. "There's something palpable that comes across to the viewers when there's chemistry. We've got good guys here, but there's not been that spark with you. Lyra had the same problem."

"Except with Spencer," I say without thinking. "Sorry, Abigail."

Her smile vanishes. "Don't apologize. I'll do my best to create some chemistry with the men so you can have a better show." She pauses for a beat, glances up at the names still on the board. "Are we done here?"

25

Abigail

I DON'T HAVE CHEMISTRY with the men?

It's the first thing on my mind when I wake up the next morning.

How do you *create* chemistry?

I like the men who are here and am fairly certain the interest goes both ways. I'm also attracted to them.

I've kissed... a few... and they were good kisses. What more do they want?

Maybe I should have asked for an explanation, but hearing you lack chemistry with men you're interested in is a little offensive.

But it is good to know that Lyra had the same problem.

Except with Spencer.

It's always about Spencer.

And I get it. I've seen the two of them together. I'm sure when the episodes with Lyra and Spencer air, the chemistry between them will be electric. I've always known they had that connection—I just tried to forget it.

I'm not sure I've ever had chemistry with anyone.

Being with Ashton yesterday was different. He made such an effort to get all those clothes brought in. Yes, his sister might have done most of the legwork, but he came up with the idea.

At least it sounds like it was his idea. And that was the first time a man had gone to that much effort for me.

First time *anyone* had.

I always took the lead planning things with Hettie because she had so much on her plate with Tema. But even in high school, I came up with plans for us to go to dances, summer fairs, spend the day on someone's boat. Bo called me the social convener because I planned it all.

Even growing up, my parents accepted that I would organize my own parties, since my birthday fell within the inevitable play-offs of my brothers' hockey seasons.

I assumed I took on this role because I was organized and the type of person who liked to make sure things were done right.

Now I wonder if I became that type of person because no one else did.

Maybe that should have been one of those realizations I saved for the confessionals. Ria told me that there will be a lot of self-reflections to be filmed, but I'm not ready for big ones to be televised yet.

But I'll talk about the lack of chemistry with the men and what utter *crap* that is.

My date with Dylan is today, and I'll prove there is a *palpable* connection between us. He's a bit of a mystery to me, and that might be my fault because I have trouble seeing past his good looks.

If Henry Cavill and Ryan Gosling produced a child, he would look like Dylan. He's got old-fashioned gentlemanly charm mixed with Canadian cool, plus the hero aspect of being a firefighter.

I have to have chemistry with someone like that. Who wouldn't want that?

Not only that, I'll pick Dylan up at the hotel so I can see the other men and show off the chemistry there too.

Maybe I'll see Ashton.

I'm still thinking of Ashton and our date when I arrive at the hotel later. Dylan told me to dress comfortably, so I wear a pair of high-waisted leggings and dipped into some of my new clothes to find the purple cropped T-shirt Ashton picked for me.

I want him to see me wearing it.

It's just a shirt, I keep telling myself as I head for the door. He took me shopping. It's not like we saved puppies.

But I still feel the glow of the date, and I tell myself to stop. To settle down, because Grayson was right—there are still many more dates to go.

And I can't fall for all of them.

Being here, being around such good-looking men, makes me realize how quiet my romantic life has been lately. Sure, Spencer took up the last few months, but before that? A California drought has nothing on my dating life.

Fun, but things can quickly get out of control.

Look at Ashton: he's not my type. So very good-looking, but we have nothing in common. Realistically, I know that. But he did something nice for me, and we shared a few kisses.

They were really good kisses.

But still, if I had more of a robust dating history, would I be so drawn to him?

I'm a woman off her diet, heading into Costco when they're handing out samples of Krispy Kreme donuts. It's dangerous.

Fun, but dangerous.

"Abigail."

Rand is the first of the men I see when I walk into the hotel. He's wearing blue shorts covered with hibiscus blooms and a shirt to match. Unbuttoned, so the bare chest is on full display.

It's a surprisingly nice chest.

Rand is the cinnamon roll hero, with the boy-next-door vibe and a sweet geekiness.

I didn't expect such a nice chest.

"Hi, Rand." I pull my gaze off the said chest with difficulty. "How are you?"

I'm not sure how to do this. We're supposed to be open and honest and vulnerable. On the dates, I have to pour myself into conversations, tell my deep dark secrets, be affectionate and some-times, physical.

And then I have to do it all again with someone else, but still retain the connection.

On my date with Rand, we talked in-depth about families. We laughed and joked, and got serious about things.

We shared the stage together, singing our hearts out.

He kissed me at the end of the night, with soft lips and just the right amount of urgency.

And then, the next day, I did the same thing again with Rupert and Ashton.

Maybe not with Rupert.

Now, seeing Rand, I'm not sure how I'm supposed to act with him.

Have I done something wrong because I had such a good time with Ashton? Because I kissed him, and can't stop thinking about him? Did I betray Rand?

It might be easier if I could literally compartmentalize all the men, not just my thoughts about them. If they weren't all *here*.

Physically here, with open shirts and flowers on their shorts.

Smiling like he's so happy to see me, giving me a hug like he hasn't seen me in weeks...

Rand obviously doesn't share my hesitation. He swoops me into a hug, pulling me off my feet and swinging me around. "Hey," he breathes. "It's so good to see you."

It is. I'm very happy to see Rand. Even though I'm here to pick up Dylan, and I hoped to see Ashton...

Am I doing this right? Am I supposed to be feeling all the feels for two different men?

At least two?

I tighten my arms around his neck, breathing in his Rand-scent: sunshine, sea air, and citrus. "It's so good to see you, too."

"Really?" He sets me down, and the expression on his face tugs at my heart because it's so hopeful. He looks like he really wants me to mean it. To like him.

And I do, but how can I tell him that if I feel the same way about Ashton?

What about Tanner? Basher? Jonas?

My head is starting to spin, and it's not because of Rand whirling me around. "Really," I admit. "I came to pick up Dylan but hoped to see... well, see you all."

I'm not confessing that I came with the hope of seeing Ashton because now Rand is here, I'm not thinking of Ashton quite so much.

He hugs me again. "I'm sad because it's your date with Dylan today," he says into my hair.

"Oh..."

"I'm happy for Dylan, because he's looking forward to having time with you, and I'm happy for you, because Dylan is a good guy, but I'm sad for me." Rand pulls away with a rueful grin.

"I honestly don't know what to say to that," I admit.

"There's nothing to say because that's how it is. I know that."

"Is Dylan...?" He can't be late, because he's Dylan.

"In the kitchen, giving Basher a little talking to. There was a dish towel left a little too close to the stove this morning. He's quite thorough in his fire safety." Rand threads his fingers through mine, and I love how easy this is for him. "You look amazing."

"Thanks. I love your shorts and..." My fingers reach out on their own accord and pull at one of the buttons on his shirt. "This."

"I should do it up. We didn't expect to see you."

"Definitely *don't* do it up." I give the fabric a tug, and Rand smiles.

He blushes, and my heart gives a soft *aww*.

"Abigail."

I turn at my name to see Jonas coming in with bags of groceries. "You're a little early for our date."

I drop my hand from Rand's short. Dylan date this afternoon. Jonas tonight.

And Rand... I'd like another date with Rand.

"What a lovely surprise." Jonas sets the bags on the nearby couch and comes to hug me.

It's different from Rand's exuberance. Firmer, somehow. More rigid. Straight-back and stoic, like he's holding back, and doesn't want to put too much of himself into his hug.

I prefer Rand's hug.

"I hope you're ready for our date tonight," he continues.

Rand is still there. How does he feel, standing there while Jonas talks about dates? He knows what goes on during the dates, can guess what might happen with Jonas...

Still, Rand stays, like he's offering me support.

The only support I need is if I'm doing this the right way. That I'm supposed to feel so conflicted.

"I'm looking forward to it," I say. "Do I get to know what we're doing?"

Jonas gives me a tight-lipped smile. "There's no sense keeping you in suspense now that I've seen you. I'm making you dinner. And Camille and cousin Odin will be joining us."

Surprise blooms, and I can't hide it. "Oh, wow. That sounds wonderful. I didn't know you cooked."

I can't picture Jonas in a kitchen.

"I've had lessons at the Cordon Bleu in Paris." It's not a brag, but only a matter of fact. Jonas can come across as arrogant, but I'm sure it's only because he grew up in a royal family.

He is a prince after all.

I take a step to the couch so I can peek into the bags. "Do I get to know what you're making?"

"Bouillabaisse. I'll start it here in the kitchen since it takes few hours."

And takes a few years to learn how to make it right. "Sounds amazing."

"Better get in there to get your lesson in fire safety from Dylan." Rand's earlier happiness seems to have vanished, and he's staring at Jonas with disapproval.

He knows I'm here for Dylan, but he's annoyed with Jonas? Does he sense Jonas is the bigger threat, or is it more personal?

Jonas sniffs as he picks up the bags. "I would have thought Dylan would prioritize his date with Abigail rather than teaching kitchen skills."

"He'll be along in a minute," Rand says coolly.

There's something between them, and I sense Jonas isn't a favourite among the men.

I'm not sure how I feel about that.

"Is Dylan making you wait?" A voice calls, and I turn to see Tanner approach.

Tanner.

I've been so caught up with Rand and Jonas that I never noticed Tanner... and when I take him in, I have no idea how I could have missed him.

It's like one of those slow-motion montages from a rom-com movie, when the hero comes toward her, and time slows as she takes in everything.

Bare shoulders, thick with muscles. Thin tank top gray with perspiration. Running shorts that hug muscular thighs.

A thin layer of sweat coats it all.

Normally I don't go for sweaty, but it... works... on Tanner. Everything works on Tanner. He might have stopped playing hockey, but his body doesn't know that yet.

I blink twice to stop the ogling.

"Hey." He wipes his face with the hem of his shirt and...

I draw a shaky breath at the quick glimpse of his abs.

So. Many. Good-looking men.

And all for me. "Hi, um, good to see you." More blinking because I can't seem to turn my gaze away from Tanner.

In other words, I can't stop staring.

"I didn't expect to see you." His grin starts slow, but quickly makes its way across his face.

"I, uh, thought I'd stop by."

Dylan. I have a date with Dylan.

I completely blanked on his name because I'm caught off guard at my reaction to Tanner's smile... plus there's a rivulet of sweat running down the side of his throat, and I fist my hand so I don't swipe my finger through it.

What is wrong with me?

"Good run?" I manage.

Tanner points to the nearby rise of land. "I did that trail, all along the coast. I think I saw a whale."

"We are at the edge of the Atlantic, so that would be likely," Jonas drawls.

Tanner's smile fades. He looks between Jonas and me, at Rand hovering nearby. "Are you having a group date or something?"

"I came to pick up Dylan. I have a date with him this afternoon," I say, unable to stop my tone from sounding apologetic.

"He's in the kitchen," Rand offers.

"Ah. Another date." Tanner holds my gaze, and at that moment I want to forget all about my date with Dylan.

Forget about all the dates and step into that circle of warmth around Tanner. I shift my weight, leaning away from Jonas, closer to Tanner.

"Want me to hurry him along?"

I blink. Tanner *wants* me to go with Dylan? He's offering to help? "Um, okay, but I'm sure he'll be out in a minute."

"I'll go check."

I take a step back. "Thank you."

Tanner nods and wipes an arm across his face. "I hope you have a nice time with him. Looking forward to tomorrow," he says, almost off-handedly as he moves away from me.

Walks away from me.

"Um. Me too?" I ask quietly.

What just happened there?

26

Tanner

I'M SUCH AN IDIOT.

I've been in my head about my date with Abigail tomorrow, trying to make up for the mess I made with meeting her the first night.

Trying to figure how to create the perfect moment to kiss her.

Because I really want to kiss her.

And then last night, Ashton came in with that smirk, telling us about his date with Abigail. Not really giving details but letting us know that there were details that had happened.

He kissed her.

And Rand kissed her, and Jonas, that.... I grit my teeth at the thought of his smug mouth anywhere near Abigail's.

He's kissed her too.

I want to kiss her.

So I'd been thinking of her, which is why I went for a run in the first place, so I could sort out my thoughts. I almost didn't see the whale far out in the water because my head was all about Abigail.

And then I come back, smelling like a locker room, covered in sweat, and she's standing right here.

All I wanted to do was hug her, but... sweat. Smell.

I get away from her before her smile can turn into a frown of disgust. Before she can look at Rand, dressed like he's on vacation in Mexico, and Jonas, who always looks like he shops at Tom Ford, and compare them with sweaty me.

Awkward. Uncomfortable. So glad to see her.

Completely messed up... again.

"Dylan," I snap as soon as I walk into the kitchen. He's standing, laughing with Basher.

Both of them look up in shock at my tone.

"Dude?" Basher asks.

"Abigail's waiting for you," I tell him. "You don't make her wait."

"I..." Confusion on Dylan's face. He is the best-looking of all of us, so why am I trying to help him? "Thanks. I didn't know she was here."

And why do I sound like I'm one step away from ripping off his head?

"Get it together," I tell him, softening my voice, not missing the looks Basher and Dylan give me as I stalk off.

Every time I see her, I think I have a chance with Abigail, and I want it.

I really want that chance.

And then I do whatever I do to self-sabotage it.

I should have kissed her on the beach, and then, at least, I wouldn't have the pressure riding on me.

I should have done a lot of things differently.

I'll make it up to her tomorrow.

27

Abigail

"I DON'T UNDERSTAND TANNER," I complain as I change for dinner with Jonas. Camille is lounging on my bed, Betty White curled up in her lap. "He doesn't show interest."

"Maybe he's shy."

"He's a hockey player," I say irritably, as I try to tame my curls with no luck. I reach for a clip. "How can he be shy?"

"What does playing hockey have to do with being an introvert?" Camille asks with serious confusion.

"Did Lyra say anything about him?"

It's something I haven't wanted to ask Camille, something I've held off talking about as our friendship grows. She was with Lyra when she met the men. She was here as Lyra realized what she felt for Spencer was real and long-lasting, and finally needed to be said.

I didn't want to discuss anything about Lyra's time here in case it came around to Spencer. But seeing Tanner today, having such a reaction to him, and then him just walking away…

Desperate times call for desperate measures.

"I never discussed the men with Lyra." Camille gives me a sympathetic smile, like she knows what I'm thinking.

How can she know what I'm thinking when *I* don't understand what I'm thinking?

I do know that I'm thinking *a lot* about Tanner, and I haven't even had a date with him.

Seeing Tanner has totally blocked out the warm giddiness from my date with Ashton.

"Besides, I thought your date was with Dylan today?"

Dylan. Sweet, handsome Dylan. "It was." I sigh, turning from my hair to what to wear tonight. "I saw Tanner when I picked him up. And Rand. And Jonas. He's cooking tonight? For all of us?"

"He asked, and I wasn't about to say no. I thought it might be nice for Odin. Sorry if we're hijacking your date," she apologizes.

"No, it's fine. I haven't figured him out yet," I admit. "He's a prince on a reality show. How often does that happen?"

Camille cocks her head.

"Oh, right. My bad." Odin and Camille are so in love that it's hard to remember that it only started because Odin had been one of the men on The Suitorette. Esme, who had starred in his season, had made the right choice in sending him home, but I wonder if she had truly known that at the time.

Have I been completely confident in sending the men home?

I think of Jakey. Yes, I have, at least with him. The others? There had been a lingering uncertainty that I hadn't known them well enough.

Things will change after tomorrow. All the men will have had an equal amount of time with me. What they chose to do with that time is up to them, but at least I won't be able to say I don't know them.

Maybe not well enough, but I do know them.

"Are you trying to figure out all the men?" Camille pulls me out of my thoughts. "Any luck with that?"

A dress tonight, for Jonas. Something pretty and casual... not too casual.

And not one of the dresses Ashton got for me yesterday.

"Some are easy." I hold up a midi-length sundress with a sprinkling of purple and green flowers. Camille shakes her head. "And some... I think I do need a little more understanding. Like with Tanner."

"He's on the list for tomorrow, so hang in there. What did you do with Dylan this afternoon?"

"He took me to a spa."

"That sounds nice."

"It was. Very nice," I admit, still searching through the racks. "Dylan is very nice. And very nice to look at."

"I think I would have a hard time with a man that pretty," Camille decides, stroking Betty White.

"I know, right? He's the best-looking guy here. Plus, he's sweet and considerate, and heroic, of all things. He's got everything going for him."

"I sense a but..."

I hold up a green dress, only to receive another shake of Camille's head. "He's a great kisser. He gave me a foot rub on the way back to the hotel because I mentioned the masseuse didn't spend enough time on my feet after all the high heels I've been wearing, and I practically *swooned*. But..."

"But it's not there," Camille finishes.

"Not there," I agree. "And I'm sad."

Dylan will be getting a yellow rose tomorrow morning. I couldn't bear to send him home during our date.

I told myself I wasn't sure, but it was cowardice, plain and simple.

I don't feel good about that.

Jakey was the only one I told to leave, and both of us knew it was going to happen. Dylan has no idea. He was smiling and happy when I dropped him off at the hotel. Maybe he was feeling the butterflies.

And now I'm about to squash them.

"You shouldn't be," she argues. "You're eliminating them, and that's the point. You don't want to feel the same about all of them. Do you feel... anything... for any of them?"

"Ashton," I confess, with an embarrassed smile. "I never would have expected that. And Rand. And Tanner... I think. That afternoon on the beach, he gave me butterflies. And seeing him today... I don't know what to think. The butterflies might have flown away."

The butterflies were still there, but Tanner walking away definitely put a damper on their flight.

I sigh. "I guess I'll figure Tanner out tomorrow."

"You have your work cut out for you tonight with Jonas."

"If I can find something to wear."

Camille pulls herself off the bed, and Betty White jumps down to follow as she heads for the far rack of clothes. It only takes a moment for her to make a selection—a dark-blue dress cut through with black embroidery and fluttery cap sleeves. There are cut-outs around the waist.

"That looks regal," I decide, unsure of the style.

"And perfect for Jonas. He's a prince," she reminds me. "He'll expect a certain... style."

"I don't need a reminder of his royal status," I say, but the flash of *oh-my-god-I'm-dating-a-prince* hits me with enough power to rival one of Tanner's slapshots.

I wish I could ask Hettie if it was like that for her with Bo.

She married Bo. She's a princess in her own right now.

I wish I could talk to Hettie about all of this.

But no. I know my best friend well enough to hear her words in my head. She'd be so excited about Jonas, just as she was excited about Spencer.

Me ending up with a man who would keep me close to her? That's all she had ever wanted. Ending up with Bo's best friend is no longer an option, but what about his cousin?

Hettie would be rooting for Jonas to be the last man standing.

Am I? Because it needs to be all about me now, not all about Hettie.

I'll find out more tonight.

28

Jonas

I CAN'T BELIEVE ODIN gave up life in Battle Harbour to come here.

He was a prince of Laandia, the second to the throne. And now, living in Saint Pierre, he's no better than a consort to Lady Camille as she runs her little island nation for the French.

I simply cannot understand his logic.

My father was beside himself when Odin announced he was abdicating during his wedding.

I understand why he did it. Or at least I know why, but I don't understand. It was love. Odin fell in love with Lady Camille, and this was the best thing for her. But what about Odin? Is this the best for him? Is living here good for him?

And why should I care?

We are related by blood, but we've never been close, even though we are the closest in age. We've never been friends.

I've always felt regret about that.

There was nothing I could do—there is so much bad blood between my father and his brother the king that Father can't bear to hear anything positive about the Battle Harbour royals.

I wonder what Father would think of Abigail.

He would be intrigued by her connection to the castle. To Bo and Spencer. And I know Father would want me to find someway to use that to my advantage. I don't know for what reason, but there are always schemes and plans in play with Father, always waiting for the opportunity to take more power.

He would take the throne of Laandia in a heartbeat if given the chance and spare no sympathy to those in his way.

He was the one who suggested I contact the show, to offer myself as a contestant.

Father knows nothing about reality shows, nor about what would be in store for me, but he saw an opportunity. A possibility.

I still don't know what the possibilities might be, but I agreed. I've always agreed with his schemes and plans for revenge, to boost our family over the status of our cousins.

Until I got here. And met Abigail.

Now, the straight path I'd always followed seems to have veered off the side a little.

"How are you enjoying your time on the show?" Camille asks.

I do like Lady Camille. She was considerate enough to assign other tasks to her house manager so I could have use of the kitchen to finish the meal. Cooking for me is best done alone. I've never liked it when people hover.

Even though she and Odin are hovering, using the guise of asking for my suggestions on wine pairings for the meal.

"I enjoy it," I say dutifully, adding the mussels and tiny clams to the pot.

"That smells amazing." Odin leans over for a glance. I'm sure he has no idea what he's looking at.

My cousin has grown up with someone to make his meals for him, and I doubt he could feed himself without help.

"It's almost ready. Thank you," I add, giving the pot a stir rather than slamming the lid back on.

I'm here to mend fences with my cousin, I remind myself. It's the one instruction of Father's that I agree with.

I don't know why he would want better relations between us and the Battle Harbour royals, but after Mathias's disastrous attempt a few months ago, it's obvious Father sees me as the last option.

"But how are you really doing on the show?" Odin asks. "I've been there, remember? Not as long as you," he adds ruefully. "I left quickly."

I'm glad Odin admitted that because I have to bite my tongue not to point it out.

But because he did, I have to give him something. "The other men," I say after a pause. "They're not what I expected."

Camille glances at Odin. "We met most of them when Lyra was here. They seemed nice enough."

"They're very nice. I'm just not used to the fraternity lifestyle."

I'm also used to being the most famous face in a crowd, and at the hotel, I'm clearly not.

Basher is a drummer in a band. Tanner is a Canadian hockey hero—or at least that's how the others describe him. And Ashton Carrington...

At least Rupert has gone home. I was glad to see him go.

"I'm sure it takes some getting used to," Camille concedes.

"I thought there would be more competition between them. Us," I confess. "We're competing for the same woman, and I thought—the atmosphere is much friendlier than I expected."

Like Tanner offering to get Dylan for Abigail earlier, so he wouldn't miss out on any more of his time with her.

I'd rather think Tanner had some ulterior motive, but I doubt it.

"I noticed the same thing with Lyra," Odin says. "Of course the reality is one thing; how they edit you might be very different."

"Every season seems to have a villain," Camille adds.

Is she suggesting it might be me?

That doesn't sit well with me. Having Camille see me as the villain, as well as the rest of the viewers? I don't like that.

"I think I've had more than enough of being thought of as the bad guy." I don't glance at Odin, but sense the look passing between him and Camille.

It's a start.

Forks clink against bowls, and a comfortable quiet has fallen over the table as we finish our meal.

The meal I created.

The sauce was perfect, the seafood tender and flavourful. I relished their surprise turning to amazement as they taste the food I made.

Cooking fills me with a sense of pride, of accomplishment that I don't normally feel.

It's even more tonight, not only because I've done this for Abigail, but because it's something I can clearly do better than my cousin.

"This is amazing," Odin announces for the third time. "This is a new side of you, cousin."

I smile tightly and offer him more wine, like I'm the head of the table.

Which I feel like I am.

"That's what I like about the show." Abigail spears a chunk of lobster and pops it into her mouth with a soft, "*Yum.*"

She might have dined with my royal cousins, but she'd need a tutorial before sitting down to dinner with my father.

"I get to learn about all these new sides of everyone," she continues. "Did you know today was the first time Dylan had ever had a massage?"

The casual mention of Dylan yanks me out of my self-satisfied good humour. "That's what he did on your date?" I'm not able to hide my contempt. "Got a massage?"

Abigail shakes her head. She's pulled her wavy hair into a clip, accentuating her eyes and strong jaw. I like the look. "No, Dylan took me to the spa and asked one of the therapists to give him a lesson so he could give a better massage. Halfway through, when I found out he'd never had one himself, I made him switch. My hands weren't strong enough to do much good, so the masseuse did most of the work. He seemed to enjoy it, though."

Camille tries to hide her smile. "You gave Dylan a massage? You didn't tell me that."

Abigail talks to *Camille* about the dates.

Interesting.

"Sorry, I shouldn't bring up the others on my date with you," Abigail apologizes.

I want to give her reasons to talk about me later, not Fireman Dylan. "He seems like a good man," I concede, feeling the expectation to say something nice about him. "The hero type. If that's what you like."

"I think everyone here is a good man," Abigail says loyally. "They did a good job picking the contestants."

"Even me?" I ask, only half-teasing.

"Even you," Abigail grins and touches my hand.

"Why are you here, Jonas?" I glance at Camille, who gazes at me with a serious look in her eyes.

That's when I remember Camille is stronger than she appears.

She didn't fall into a love match with Odin—she orchestrated it, in order to gain control of her island.

And now she has the ear of Abigail. Camille is more influential than anyone gives her credit for.

"If you don't mind my asking," Camille adds without a trace of apology.

"I was going to ask, but haven't gotten around to it yet," Abigail chimes in with her easy smile. "I have to admit, it was a surprise seeing you get out of that car the first night."

"I heard some of the things your father said about my time on the show." Odin frowns as he places his fork and knife across the empty bowl. "I can't imagine he's very pleased with your being here."

I drop my head. I should have expected this, prepared something. "I don't need my father's blessing to live my life," I say. "But as it turns out, he agreed with my decision." I turn to Abigail. "To find love. Isn't that why we're all here? At least, most of us."

She frowns, and the seed has dropped. I overheard Ashton talking to Rupert about some stupid bet one night, and while I don't know the details, I do know that Ashton wouldn't want Abigail to hear about it.

Especially if he's beginning to fall for her, if that is possible for someone like Ashton Carrington.

"I've always been intrigued by reality shows," I finish. This isn't exactly the truth, but it's close enough.

I've always thought that those who let themselves perform for the cameras in the guise of falling in love were idiots.

Love is a lot of things, but not worth humiliating yourself for. Which is why I've been so careful about what I say in front of the cameras. One of whom is standing to my right and has been filming the entire meal.

Every bite, every swallow. Every word we say will be played out for the viewers.

I need to look good for the cameras.

"I think finding love is difficult," I venture. "At times impossible for someone in my position. You have to agree, cousin."

"I do. I did." Odin shares a fond look at his wife.

All of his family members have someone, and two of them are married. So it's not impossible.

And it's not something I'm opposed to.

I might have ulterior motives—at least my father has—for coming on this show, but something good might come out of it.

I glance at Abigail and wonder if she could be the one.

29

Abigail

D INNER WAS A NICE surprise.

The surprise was how well Jonas could cook, but also the moments between him and Odin. I know a little of the backstory of the king and his brother, thanks to Bo, and I wonder if Jonas inviting Odin and Camille to dine with us will help repair the years of bitterness between the cousins.

I like it after dinner, when Jonas and I go for a walk along the beach.

He takes my hand right away, which I suspect is for the cameras. Jonas doesn't strike me as someone who goes in for much PDA.

"You're an amazing cook," I tell him.

"Thank you."

I wonder how many times he's heard that because it seems to roll off him, like it's an everyday experience. Or maybe he expects it.

"How was tonight in comparison to your other dates?"

His question is another surprise. "I don't compare them." The wind has picked up, and a wave rolls against the shore, threatening to splash me.

I tell myself that's why I pull away from Jonas.

"Sure you do," he presses.

"I try not to. You are all different, so what's the point of comparing?"

"What about how you feel toward us?"

He's pushing, and I don't appreciate being pushed, especially not about something I'm not comfortable talking about. "Are you looking for validation, or something?"

"Maybe," he surprises me by saying. "I'd like to be convinced you want to be here with me. I feel it, but I'm not sure you do."

His honesty tugs me back toward him. "I want to be here."

"But you're not sure about me. I get it—you know the family. You've heard the history. Things are not smooth and easy within the royal families."

"You seem to be getting along with Odin. That's a good sign."

"That the cousins can be friends? I'm not here for that."

"Are you sure about that?" I challenge.

Jonas stiffens. "That might be an added bonus."

"It's okay to admit it."

"Is it, though? For years, I hated Odin and the others for their family dinners. We heard so much about them, but the few occasions when I was there, there was so much noise. Inside jokes. They seem to love *teasing* each other."

I've only been to a few of the family dinners at the castle, and while I loved watching the interactions within the family, it can be a lot to an outsider. But my loyalty lies with the family, so I would never admit that to anyone, not even Jonas. "The family is very comfortable with each other. It makes them special."

"It made me jealous," Jonas admits. "I don't have that. I didn't have anything to make me stand out. Honestly, I think that was what got me into cooking. A way to stand out during family dinners." He gives a wary glance. "That might be a stretch."

"Maybe not. It's an interesting way to look at it."

"Is this what these dates are like? Therapy sessions?"

I laugh. "It is what most of the dates have been like. Most," I muse. "Not all."

"You're really peeling back the layers."

"I'm trying to. I don't have all that much time to get to know you, and I have to make the most of it."

"You don't have to make the most with everyone," he says slyly, and I laugh.

My insides warm under his glance. How could I have thought his good looks were cookie cutter? The Erickson blue eyes are rimmed with a green in this light and one of the corners of his lips turn up more than the other.

There is much more to him than I first expected to find.

"Let's hear something about you," Jonas instructs.

"I don't normally start spewing secrets on command. You need to ask nicely."

"Peel back the layers?"

"Exactly."

For a moment I wonder if Jonas is able to do that.

"How long have you been friends with the latest royal wife?"

My guard snaps back. "Her name is Hettie Crow, and she's worthy to be a queen, not just a princess." It's my go-to response when someone brings up Hettie.

Most don't think she's worthy of anything.

We continue walking, and Jonas continues to press. "I take it from that tone you've been friends for a while."

I tell myself to relax, that Jonas is just trying to get to know me. And he knows Hettie is a big part of my life, so why should he want to know more about her as well? "Our mothers met at the hospital when we were born. She's been my best friend forever."

"How do you feel about her marrying into the royal family? Truthfully."

"How do you feel?" I can't help but shoot back. "Because that tone suggests you're not a fan."

Jonas shrugs. "Additions to the royal family mean I'm one more step removed from the throne. Not much I can do to change that."

"Do you feel that way about Tema?"

My icy tone finally has him glancing over. "I sense you're as close to her as you are to her mother."

"I've helped raise her for the past eight years, so yes, I am quite attached."

"Ah." For the first time tonight, a wedge opens between us. "I've never met her. Do you know there's an Instagram page dedicated to her? @fansoftheprincess. Lyra must hate that."

I inhale sharply at the mention of Lyra. "I don't think Lyra is upset about her lack of social media coverage."

"I think you're upset with me," Jonas muses. "You're very loyal," he adds, like it's a surprise to him.

"I am."

"I'm not used to that."

"No? Not to your family?" He snorts a response. "Friends?"

"Are around depending on what I can do for them." Jonas's tone is matter-of-fact, but it jars something inside of me. I've known Bo for so long, and I know what being born into the royal family has been like for him. It seems like it's been just as much of a challenge for Jonas, just in a different way.

"That makes me sad," I tell him. "That you think that, not that it's the way it is."

Jonas lifts a shoulder. He still holds my hand, but there seems to be a disconnect between us. I never wanted that. "It's the way it is. In my world, anyway," he admits.

"Maybe you need a new world."

"That's what I'm here for, isn't it?" He tugs me to a stop. The moon rests low on the horizon, the sky a mixture of blues and purples—the colours of the sunset have faded, but the moon still hasn't risen. The screech of a seagull adds to the gentle lull of the waves against the shore.

"This would be a perfect spot for me to kiss you," Jonas muses.

"It would." I keep walking. "It's too convenient."

Jonas sounds confused. "You don't like convenience?"

"Not when I'm the convenient one."

"I never said that."

"No. You didn't."

"But someone did."

"Do you really want to be king?" I demand.

Jonas chokes a laugh. "You want to change the subject, we'll change the subject. But you're not making it easy to peel back your layers."

"There's too much about you I'd still like to know." That I need to know. Because I'm not enjoying this walk with Jonas. We started out well, but now...

He spreads his arms. "Ask away."

"I just did. Do you really want to be king?"

We walk in silence for a few moments. Maybe I shouldn't have asked. Maybe I should go back and ask him about his interest in cooking.

But no—I need to know these things. I need to know all the things, at least as much as I can, so I can make the decision at the end of this.

Or the end of the night.

I'm still on the fence about Jonas.

On one hand—prince. He's an actual prince, and I've read too many fairy tales not to be excited at the thought of being in love with a man with a crown.

But I'm also best friends with a real-life princess, and Hettie's life has never been a fairy tale. She's found her happily ever after with Bo, but there are days that I know she wished she had married a regular guy.

Jonas hums a moment before he speaks. "About being the king. Would you think badly of me if I said I did? Because that is treason."

"I've been to the dungeons in the castle. I don't think you'll be sent there for saying what's on your mind."

"Do you always say what's on your mind?"

"I'd like to say yes, but no. I care too much about what other people think."

"You need to stop doing that."

I laugh. "Easier said than done."

"It might take some practice, but you'll get there. Like now, I could easily blow you off and not tell you what I really think."

"Is that a good idea?"

"Probably not. So yes, I'd like to be king someday. I would like to have the power in Laandia, and I would like to do what I wanted to do. But that's not going to happen unless one of those shooting stars that the new observatory looks for hits the castle. And it's not a star but a small planet, and takes out the whole family. And my father and my brother just happen to be visiting. That is the only way I'd be king." He chuckles drily. "And that's never going to happen because my father vowed never to step foot in the castle after Odin got married."

"I'd actually prefer the family not be taken out by a small planet..."

"I'd rather it didn't happen either. But when you're told at a young age that you're *thisclose* to having a say in the kingdom, and never get there, it's a hard thing to get over."

Sympathy. It's a new emotion for me to feel for Jonas, but it's there. Yes, growing up in a royal family isn't always easy, but considering that Jonas is part of the family, and yet so removed—it must be so difficult for him.

And what I've learned about him suggests he will never admit how hard it is for him.

"You can still have a say." I soften my tone. "You could work with King Magnus. With Kalle."

Jonas is quiet for a long moment, long enough for the moon to appear in the sky. "I could," he admits That might be a possibility someday. Are we finished talking about me?"

"I'm not sure." I pause in the shade of a tree. "Do you think this would be a good spot for me to kiss you?"

Jonas smiles. "I do, indeed."

30

Tanner

MY DATE WITH ABIGAIL is today.

I need to make an effort with her, to show her that there's interest or I'm going home. After yesterday at the hotel, I can sense her confusion.

If I can't get through to her, she's going to send me home. It's as simple as that. I see her connection to Rand. I heard about her date with Ashton. Jonas went to such trouble for his date.

Dylan went home this morning, which wasn't a surprise to anyone. Jonas did not.

I watched his face when he came out of his room and saw the flash of surprise. I'm convinced he expected a yellow rose to be waiting on the floor for him. He expected to be going home.

I wonder what happened on his date.

I wonder what happens on all the dates, and I don't think it's helping me.

When I played hockey, I always watched replays of the games, going over moves of the other teams, specific players that I would be going up against. I found out as much information as I could, and that improved my game.

But that's not helping here.

I listen to the others talk about their dates, both good and bad. I ask questions, trying to learn as much as I can about what Abigail likes and doesn't like.

When Dylan got the yellow rose, I asked him what he thought went wrong.

"Nothing," he said, a resigned expression on his handsome face. "It just wasn't there. She's great, but something was missing between us, and there's nothing I could do."

Chemistry. A connection. Something that draws you to a person, and binds you. I've heard about it, but I don't think I've ever felt it. And if I don't have it with Abigail, that's it. I'm going home.

And then I'm going to have to do it all over again, but this time as The Suitor.

I'm not sure I'm ready for that. Or that I want to.

I've been thinking about this date since Abigail announced the change in format, wondering about what she would like to do. What would impress her.

And then I stopped, remembering what Abigail had said that the date was supposed to about what *we* like to do. So I started again.

If I were home, back in Halifax, what would I want to do with a woman I had just started dating? Yes, I'd want to impress her, but it would need to be something I was comfortable with, so I could be myself. Be confident.

That led me to the uncomfortable realization that I hadn't felt confident in a very long time.

I sat with that for a while.

"Whales, huh?"

Abigail stands beside me on the boat, hands gripping the railing as she stares out onto the water. The sun sparkles on the waves.

Once I adjusted my way of thinking, focusing on what I would like to do, it was a no-brainer. We were on Saint Pierre, an archipelago in the mouth of the Gulf of St. Lawrence.

There is so much marine life around me, and I want to go out and find it.

Ria helped me book a whale-watching excursion, and now that we're out on the boat, Abigail seems as excited as I am to be here.

I adjust my sunglasses and look down at her.

I told her to be ready for an afternoon on the water, and she dressed for the part—jeans just the right side of tight, and a thick waffle button-up that's more jacket than shirt. She pulled her hair back into a ponytail, wears sunglasses, and a big smile.

It might be worth missing a whale if I can keep looking at her.

"It's the water, really," I tell her. "Anything in it."

She cocks her head and looks up at me. "But you play hockey instead of swimming."

I gesture to my physique with a grin. "Do I look like a swimmer?"

"Not really. You look—" She bites her lip to hide the smile. There's no hiding how she's looking at me, though. "You look... no. Not a swimmer, I guess." I can't hide my smirk. "I don't know many swimmers."

"And you know hockey players?"

She turns back to the water, and I study her profile. Cute nose. Full lips...

Nice lips. Soft, with the upper lip just a touch fuller than the bottom. A rosy pink colour, when she's not wearing lipstick, or some slick gloss.

I would say they are kissable lips.

At least they look like they may be. I think I'm the last to find out. At least I hope so.

I'm the only one who hasn't kissed her yet. The realization rocks me more than the boat does, and I almost miss her next words.

"My brothers still play," Abigail is saying. "Not at your level, mind you."

There's so much assumption about my playing here, and I've done nothing to dissuade them. My name on the screen will have *hockey player* after it in bold. That's it. That's still my identity. "My level isn't that special these days," I admit.

If I'm going to talk to anyone about it, it's going to have to be Abigail.

And the way she turns to me, her expression open and interested, makes me think that she'll listen. That she might understand what it's like to go from hockey's next thing to nothing.

"What happened? How did you go from wannabe whale watcher to hockey player?"

My heart does an odd stutter. Somehow, Abigail has picked up on life before hockey. She's heard me mention marine life more than hat tricks and penalty boxes. "Former," I say in a gruff voice.

Abigail blows off the distinction. "You still play, so you're still a hockey player."

Playing in a beer league is so different from being a third-round draft pick, but it's nice that she groups them together.

"I wanted to be a marine biologist," I confess, expecting an expression of surprise. I'm not disappointed. "I took courses and summer camps at Dalhousie University when I was in high school. I was all about finding the whales and understanding them. Hockey was there, but it was a distant second."

"And then?"

I'm glad she asks. I'm really glad because everyone assumes I dropped my first love for a chance in the NHL.

"And then I got my first concussion and failed my biology exam. It messed up my average, and I missed a summer course. That summer, I grew four inches, gained about fifty pounds in muscle because I took out my mad at the gym. When I started hockey again in the fall, something changed."

"I asked Kalle about you," Abigail confesses with a small smile. "He remembers you. He said you're very talented."

"I was. Past tense." I pause. "Concussions."

"The bane of professional athletes." Abigail stares out onto the water. I told my story, and she didn't run.

I told part of it anyway, and now I'm left with the nagging regret of not saying more. Of telling her more about myself. She says that's what she wants, but once again, I'm falling short.

"So what happened?" she finally asks, turning back to me.

"I had seven concussions in four years."

"No, not that. What happened during that summer when something changed? Was it just a growth spurt? An angry teenager?"

I catch my breath. "No one asks that."

"I ask that." She glances up with a smile. "You ready to dig deep?"

I can't see her dark eyes under the sunglasses, but I want to. I want to see how deep she wants to go, because she might not like what she finds.

"I got big, and I got strong," I begin. "And I liked feeling like that. The team—my coaches—they were impressed. I guess it made me a better hockey player, but nobody was looking at my skill level. It was just my size, because it made me a target. An enforcer, so to speak." I swallow. "I became the goon on the team. I played defense, and I defended my team to the best of my ability. There were a lot of fights. I took a lot of hits."

Abigail's mouth twists with sympathy. "The concussions."

"It got so bad that I spent more time in the penalty box than playing. And I spent more time on concussion watch than either."

"I can't see you as a fighter," she muses. "I know hockey players, and you're not like that."

"The first time I broke a guy's nose, I cried in the locker room after the game," I admit. "The coaches hated that. They told me to man up. They said that with my size, I could really help the team. Be a team player." I smile ruefully at the waves because I don't want to see how Abigail is reacting. "They said it like I wasn't a team player before. I loved hockey, but I never wanted to be the tough guy hockey player. I wanted to be a marine biologist who played hockey."

Abigail presses my arm, then slides her hand over mine, gripping the rail.

"I kept it up as long as I could and then finally the doctor refused to clear me to play, and then it was over. I was out, and forgotten by the end of the day."

"They wouldn't have forgotten you."

I remember the sting of unread messages. "They did."

"Tanner."

Her soft voice stings too, because I don't want pity. I don't know what I want, but I have too many people feeling sorry for me because my hockey career is over. But she's not finished... and she's not pitying me.

"They didn't appreciate you, and that's wrong. You gave them everything and suffered for it, and for them to give up on you? Disgusting."

"It was my choice to play the game like that," I argue.

"Because you were trying to help your team. You just—" She stopped and a shadow crosses over her face.

"What's wrong?"

She shakes her head. "I just had a thought..."

"Which you can share with me. Goes both ways."

She huffs a laugh. "I guess. I just thought that I spent a lot of time trying to help others... and maybe I suffered for it too."

"When you helped raise Tema?"

She looks at me sharply. "That wasn't suffering."

"Of course not, but you were there for it all. And... I bet you never really felt appreciated, did you?"

It's only a guess, but I know how it feels.

"Hettie has never said thank you," she whispers.

I flip my hand and thread my fingers with hers. "That must hurt."

"I never really thought about it," she admits. "But now I wonder if she somehow blames me for leaving, even though it was her idea. I just made it sound like an adventure so she wouldn't be so scared."

"You were trying to help."

"And so were you, and I just hijacked your story." She gives a shaky laugh. "Back to you. What do you do now?"

"I coach," I say, enjoying the feel of our fingers entwined. "I have a U12 Double A team, and I help out with a girls' team as well."

"I love girls playing hockey," she says, and I take a deep breath. I did it. I was open and vulnerable, and nothing happened. Nothing bad, anyway.

"Me too. My sister plays in the women's league."

"That's so cool."

"Did you never want to play?"

Abigail shakes her head. "I got tired of all the attention my brothers got from my parents. They were always running the boys to games and practices, and I couldn't add to that. I played soccer for a while, but Hettie persuaded me to stop that."

"How did she do that?"

"Started dating Bo. Hanging out with them was more fun than running around a soccer field."

"And Spencer?"

"And Spencer." There's nothing in her tone that conveys what she's feeling.

Or how she feels.

"You must like kids if you're coaching," she says.

Subject changed. Got it.

"I do. I'd love to have a few of my own."

"A few?" she asks and I shrug. "What about you? Is this the digging deep part of the date?"

"I do want kids," she says slowly. "But—"

Before she could continue, shouts are heard on the port side of the boat. I tug her hand and hurry over, just in time to see a pod of humpbacks breach close to the boat.

Abigail gasps at the sight—and laughs when the splash reaches us.

People are pushing back and forth, trying to see the whales and back away from the water. I tuck Abigail under my arm to keep her safe.

She looks up, and her face is glowing. "That was so amazing! I've never seen them so close. It was like—"

I kiss her.

I have no idea why then, when there are whales—my favourite mammal—so close, but her expression and her happiness... It wasn't the perfect moment I was waiting for, but it was pretty good.

I cup her cheek with my hand and lean in. I don't ask, I don't give warning, I just do.

What I've wanted to do since I first saw her.

And I think she's wanted it too, because when my lips brush against hers, she smiles.

"Hi," she breathes against my mouth.

"Hi," I say.

"Finally." And she takes the back of my head and pulls me down to her, mouth seeking the connection we are both searching for.

With that simple kiss, the shock of electricity between is there. It's there, and it's growing and building and...

We keep kissing.

31

Abigail

TANNER KISSES ME.

Tanner is kissing me.

Soft lips tasting of salt, strong hands cupping my face. Tanner kisses with purpose, like he's been waiting and watching and studying what I like from a kiss.

But how would he know that? Maybe this is just how he kisses all the time.

Bodies press around us, cries and cheers from the whale watchers, and I wonder if there is another pod of whales.

But I don't stop kissing him.

Tanner's lips move with the perfect amount of pressure. He shifts, one of his hands stroking down my back to slip under the hem of my shirt to splay against my lower back. I press against him, rising on my tiptoes to plunge my fingers into his hair.

I've wanted to do this since the first night. Even after seeing the quick expression of annoyance as he walked toward me, I still wondered what it would be like to kiss Tanner.

And now I finally get to kiss him, and I'm not about to stop.

But then more than one small body ricochets off me, throwing me off balance, and I pull away from Tanner. It's not a great way to end such a kiss.

"They're *kissing*," a loud voice cries.

"Yes, stop watching them," says another.

When I glance around, there's an audience of four kids looking at us. "Whales." Tanner points as another humpback rises from the water.

"Oooh," the kids cry and head for the railing.

I rest my forehead against Tanner's shoulder. "You okay?" He tilts my chin up with a finger.

Inwardly I cheer, because I think he's going to kiss me again, and I'm good with that.

He doesn't. But the smile on his face suggests that he wants to.

I manage a nod, smiling at him like he's a rainbow after a storm.

"That wasn't quite the perfect moment I planned on," he admits with a shy smile.

"It was pretty perfect for me," I confess before I can stop myself. Am I supposed to tell him that? Practically confess that it was one of the best kisses I've ever experienced?

Top five, at least.

Top three, considering that before I started as the Suitorette, the list of those kissed wasn't all that long.

"Yeah?" I want to take off Tanner's sunglasses so I can see his eyes. I want to see him looking at me.

"Maybe," I concede, wrenching my gaze away from him and wondering how goofy I look staring at him like that.

He takes my hand and presses a kiss to my wrist.

I'd like to blame the waves for how off-balance I suddenly am, but no.

Tanner makes me swoon. He gives me butterflies—butterflies that swoon.

I knew that was a possibility when I first met him, but the reality is so much more.

Being this close to him makes my head spin. Things are tingling.

Tingling, like I stuck my finger in a light socket.

It feels a lot better than it sounds.

And it's like he knows it. He leads me back to the railing, and points out pods of whales in the distance before anyone else sees them. And as the boat heads back to shore, he shows me seals on the rocks and rattles off a list of seabirds flying overhead.

I'm not the only one listening to him. We have quite a crowd surrounding us by the time we're back at the dock.

"Was that okay?" he asks as we disembark.

"The whales or the...?"

"Oh. Ah." A flush rises from his neck. "I should have asked for permission."

"You didn't need to. Then. That was... nice."

"That's always what a guy wants to hear after he kisses a girl," he says ruefully.

I laugh. "My brain is a little jumbled right now."

"From the boat?"

I look at his lips. The lips that jumbled my brain. Tanner has always interested me. Intrigued me. There's no doubt I'm attracted to him, but he's always...

"I didn't think you were interested," I admit.

"I didn't think *you* could be interested," he confesses. "I don't know how you feel about Spencer."

I laugh. "Spencer who?"

Tanner takes my hand. "Am I losing you when we get back to the marina? Or could we—could we maybe go for a walk?"

"We could, and I'd like that."

It's like Tanner has changed before my eyes. I saw him as a nice guy, a fun date. I knew he was close to Lyra. And honestly, I didn't think he was that into me.

That kiss told me differently.

"You're really good with kids," I say as a family rushes by waving their thanks for the mini-show-and-tell.

"I like kids. They're fun. There's no pretending with them. They say what they think. Like Tema."

There's an ache in my chest at the mention of her name. I haven't spoken to her in days. I haven't seen her in longer. "Tema definitely does."

"That kid," he marvels. "You seem really close."

It feels strange that the men don't know what Tema means to me. I haven't wanted to bring her up, instead focusing on getting to know them, rather than share what is truly important to me.

I think I've been afraid of what they would think. What they would say about my being so obsessed with someone else's child.

Tema is more than that, and I'm not obsessed.

I have been accused of that, though.

"I was in the delivery room with Hettie," I say, hesitating. "I don't know how much you know about the royal family."

"I know Kalle. I'm a bit of a fan," he admits. "And then what Lyra told me."

Lyra. We need to talk about her, too.

But me first. "I left Battle Harbour with Hettie after the queen died. We didn't know she was pregnant until weeks later. Hettie's been my best friend since we were born. Our mothers were best friends, and my Mom kind of stepped in when her mom left—" I shouldn't say any more since that part isn't my story to tell. "I helped her raise Tema," I finish instead.

"You love her." It's a statement. No judging, just matter of fact.

"She's my world," I agree. "And I know that's not good, because she's not mine, but she feels like it. But now that Hettie is back with Bo, I have to give them space. I have to let them do it together. But it's hard, and I miss her so much…"

Tanner squeezes my hand, and I realize my eyes are full of tears. I wipe them away impatiently. "I'm being silly. Tema isn't mine. Bo deserves time with her."

"Doesn't mean you can't miss her."

"I don't know why I told you that."

"You can tell me anything, Abigail."

I think I really can. But before I get into more of me, there are a few things I need to ask him.

"I know you're not supposed to bring up exes on a date…" I hedge.

"Lyra was never my ex," Tanner says. "If that's where you're going with this."

"She kind of was."

Tanner shakes his head. "She wasn't, because as soon as Spencer showed up, he was all that mattered to her. Sorry to say that."

"I knew when we got together there was this thing between them. An unbelievable chemistry." I wince at the word. Of course Spencer had chemistry with Lyra, and not me. "I just thought maybe he would forget it. Or I could help him forget—which is insane, because Lyra is... she's a princess. She's beautiful and famous, and I was an idiot to think I could ever compete."

"No," Tanner argues. "Don't say that. You could give anyone a run for their money, Abigail, princess or no princess. Spencer was..."

"Don't say he was an idiot, because then I'll know you're just trying to make me feel better." I manage a laugh. "And I don't need to feel better because I'm over him. I was over when I said goodbye to him. I'm happy for him, that he finally made it work with Lyra." I take a deep breath. "It's just... it's embarrassing. You know."

"I do know, but I'm telling you that you don't have to be. Spencer—Spencer is a very smart man, and he had a history with Lyra. That's why she picked him. And that's why he wanted to make it work. Not that you were lacking anything."

"Just a crown."

"Lyra is a princess. That's true. But she's also a strong-willed woman used to getting what she wants. She's never had privacy or lived on her own without her family's interference."

"She actually lived on her own in Chicago," I point out.

"I did not know that. There is so much I didn't know about her, and probably more that I never would. Because she was closed up. She was... like this."

Tanner stops on the sidewalk and begins to button my shirt.

I threw a green button-up over my T-shirt this morning, thick cotton against the chill of being on the water. I kept it on, sleeves rolled up, but left it open.

It's spotted with water.

For a man with such big hands, Tanner has a lot of dexterity when it comes to little buttons. I have no idea what he's doing, but I'm willing to see it through.

He finishes with the button under my chin. "This is Lyra," he explains. "Buttoned up. Maybe Spencer can get through, but I think it's because he knows her so well, and has for so long. She wasn't open with us. Not really. And how can you be vulnerable with someone if they're not doing the same?"

"I don't know if I've been vulnerable with the others," I whisper.

"I don't care if you have." Tanner is busy unbuttoning my shirt. Here on the sidewalk of the sleepy downtown area, Tanner is undoing my shirt.

It's a surprisingly intimate gesture, more than if we were in a room alone together.

A bedroom.

And Johnny is filming all of it.

"This is you," he says as he finishes, pushing my shirt open, big hands on my waist. "You're open and honest, and *you*. Lyra is who she thinks she needs to be. But you've always been you. Loyal friend, caring mother, sexiest girl with glasses I've ever seen—"

I kiss him then, and it's even better than the first time.

32

Basher

TANNER IS LATE GETTING back from his date with Abigail.

It doesn't matter much to me—there are a few hours between dates, so it's not like he's infringing on my time. But it's getting close to my showtime.

Everyone is waiting for him to get back now.

For me, Tanner has been one of the front-runners since the beginning. And it's not because Abigail has shown a preference for him over the rest of us, but it's because he's such a good dude.

If I can't have her, I want Tanner to get her. Especially if he gets her over Jonas.

But I still want to shoot my shot.

"He's late." Rand is in the lobby with me, staring down the road leading to the hotel.

I nod.

"Maybe something happened to the boat," he worries.

"Do you want something to happen to the boat?" I counter.

"Of course not."

"Then don't even say it. The universe hears all."

"Do you actually believe that?" Ashton drawls in his *don't care* way. He's mixing drinks at the lobby bar—something to keep busy without looking like he cares about Tanner's date.

He cares, more than he lets on.

We all do, which is why we're waiting.

Not sure where Jonas is, nor do I really care.

There's always a guy other guys don't get along with, and this time it's Jonas. He's not exactly the villain for the season, but he's nobody's favourite.

I really hope he's not Abigail's.

There are five of us left. She has to have a favourite by now.

Really hope it's not the prince.

"I said I was going to play drums, and look what I do for a living."

Rand looks at Ashton with a shrug. I like these guys. I spend a lot of time with the male species, and as a species, there's a lot to say for them.

We wait, each of us thinking the same thing—Lyra gave up halfway through to be with Spencer. What if Abigail does the same thing? What if she never comes back from her date with Tanner?

"I see a car," Rand says finally, relief evident in his voice.

It stops in front of the hotel, and we watch as Tanner gets out—and then Abigail.

They look happy together, and more than a little damp.

No one says a word as they walk in, holding hands. Smiling, shooting little glances at each other, like they've got a secret.

This is the first time Abigail has come back to the hotel after a date. Does she look like that after her dates with all the guys?

I have the last one-on-one date. Abigail is going to have to make some cuts after tonight, and seeing her with Tanner brings it all home.

It doesn't feel nice.

But still, we rally as Abigail comes in, surrounding her, forcing her to let go of Tanner to hug Rand, then Ashton. Tanner stays beside her, his face a mask of emotions: happiness, jealousy, the odd scowl as Ashton gives Abigail a kiss, fondness... and more?

I've gotten to know him pretty well, and Tanner looks more at peace with himself now than he has since he got there.

Must have been a pretty good date.

But still, it feels nice to have Abigail's gaze searching for me. "Basher," she cries.

"Hey, pretty lady." I push through for a hug.

She smells fishy. I can deal with fishy.

"We're late getting back," she says apologetically, still with her arms around me.

Around me—no one else.

"I thought I'd see if you're ready and if you could come with me to Camille's while I get changed," she invites.

"Maybe a shower," Tanner mutters, still hovering beside her.

She sniffs and grins at him. "Maybe. Do you mind? Camille wants to meet you."

"Sure. Is she a fan?"

"It's more like she's never met anyone in a band before. Other than the king, of course."

"I'm ready when you are."

I say goodbye to the others, and look away as the happy expression on Tanner's face slips into bitter resignation.

I know how he feels because I've felt it every time someone leaves with Abigail.

I doubt Camille has ever heard of the Water Rhinos.

I've been in the band for over ten years now, after starting it with my buddy Slater in high school. It's been a ride—highs and lows—and we're riding a high right now, getting ready for a tour.

The rest of the guys were supportive of my coming on the show, but I know they all think I should have stayed back in the city to practice. To work on songs.

I told them I need a little love to make better songs, and no one could argue with that. I just hope I find love so it's not all for nothing.

Even if I don't find love, I can now say I'm on friendly terms with the royal family of Laandia.

Camille is sweet with her questions about the songs and playing in big stadiums. And Odin joins us, bringing me a pint of meady goodness, the king's own honey mead recipe.

I like hanging out with regular folks.

Not that they are really regular—Odin is a prince and Lady Camille runs the country. But I've met princes before and heads of countries and compared to some of them, Odin and Camille are really regular.

I don't get too much time with them because Abigail is a quick-change artist. We're out the door in no time.

Part of me wants to invite Camille and Odin to join us, but I am the last date, which means this might be the only time I have to spend with Abigail. I'm not wasting it.

"Where are you taking me?" she asks as I help her into the SUV.

"I'm taking you to a baseball game."

She looks surprised. "We're not supposed to leave the island."

"There's baseball on the island. I made sure of that."

Lady Camille and one of the producers helped me find a game for that night. And it's a good game—the pitcher has a wicked eighty-mile slider that skims the corners of the plate.

"Baseball, huh?" We settle in our lawn chairs with a cooler between us under the shade of a few scraggly trees.

The rest of those at the game—parents and a few girl-friends—keep their distance, but I can tell they're watching every move we make.

Maybe that's why I don't touch her as much as I want to.

Abigail draws as much attention as the camera guys. A few of the women wave at her, one of them yells something about Jonas, and everyone at the field ignores me.

Abigail is the famous one here, and I don't mind one bit.

"Baseball," I confirm, my two fingers spread like I'm about to throw a splitter.

"Did you play?"

"I still do," I admit. "There's a team of musicians that plays out of Toronto. I throw with them when I'm home."

I've surprised her. I like that. "That's a different side of you."

"I don't play twenty-four/seven. The drums, that is."

"How long have you been playing?" Abigail wants to know.

"My mother bought me my first drum kit when I was seven. My dad signed me up for baseball camp that same summer. That's when they got the divorce and both wanted to buy my love."

"Your mother won?"

"She was less of a dick than my father back then. I'm good with both of them now, but my mother..."

"I can see you as a mama's boy. In a good way," she adds.

"Is that usually a bad thing?"

"For some guys, it most definitely is." She laughs. "Are you close to her?"

"If close means she comes to every gig within a three-hour radius, and I talk to her every day, then sure, I guess I'm close to her."

She likes that. Most women do, but there haven't been many who I share my closeness with my mother. "I think that's a good thing. The way you treat your mother is supposed to be an indication of how you'd treat your wife."

"Well, I've never wanted a wife before, but I think I'd treat her pretty well."

Abigail waves at the cooler between us, at the silicon glasses filled with wine, the mini charcuterie board. "I'd say you're off to a great start. Why haven't you ever wanted a wife before?"

"Haven't met the right woman, I suppose?"

"And I'm sure you've met your fair share?"

"That's a personal question, isn't it?" I tease, and Abigail pushes at my shoulder.

"Getting personal is the whole idea here, Basher. What's your real name?"

I rear back, pretending to be offended. "You don't think my parents would have named me Basher?"

"They'd be an interesting sort of parents if they did."

I hum in my throat thinking of my parents. "They were. Interesting. They were madly in love for five years, had me, and then almost immediately fell out of love. But they stayed together, making all three of us miserable for two more years, until my father met the woman who would become his second wife, and the best step-mother a guy could ever have."

"Did your mother ever remarry?" Abigail hands me a hunk of salami from the plate and takes one for herself.

"Three times. None of them ever stuck. She likes to say that her best relationship is with me."

"Sweet, but isn't that a bit of pressure?"

"Not for my mother."

"You are a mama's boy."

"Proud to admit it."

"So why did you come on the show?" Abigail asks.

"You don't beat around the bush much, do you?"

"I have four weeks to figure out which of you is going to be my happily ever after. Would you beat around the bush?"

For the first time, I think about how much pressure this must be for her. Not only becoming the Suitorette with basically no notice, but trying to figure out what might be the rest of her life in only four weeks.

I've been trying to figure out mine for years and no luck yet.

The band wasn't ever supposed to be forever. It wasn't even supposed to be a real thing. I started playing with Slater and his brother when we were in high school, and things got real when we won the battle of the bands for the local radio station.

It wasn't an instant success, but it was a success. And we kept getting more and more of it.

With the success came the girls.

I never thought of them as my happily ever after, if that's what Abigail wants to call it. But they were fun, and I enjoyed my time with them.

"I've had my name down for a while now," I admit. "About five years ago, someone from the show reached out to see if any of us were interested."

"The other guys in the band?"

"Slater was a hard no. He's got trust issues. Mick thought about it for a hot minute, but then I said yes and he lost his chance."

"It only took you a hot minute to agree? Did you know Princess Lyra would be the Suitorette?"

"Oh, this was before her time. I said yes, but then "Don't Do Me Like That" exploded and we suddenly had all these gigs lined up. I couldn't say yes to the show because it'd let the other guys down."

"I can see you not wanting to do that," Abigail murmurs and my insides warm. I like that she thinks that.

"Second time they called me was for Chrissa's season."

"That's when Grayson was on," she says excitedly. "We watched that one."

"That time my mom was sick, and I said no go."

"I'm sorry about that. Is she all right?"

"Beat breast cancer two times and she's doing great now. Third time was Esme's season—"

"Odin was on that one. Briefly," she adds with a grin.

I give her an admiring smile. "You're quite the fan. I've watched a few episodes, but I'm not rattling off who's been on it like you are. I had to say no that time because we were recording an album, and I wrote three of the songs for that, so I wasn't missing it. So when they called this time, nothing was getting in my way. And I wasn't letting Lyra going home spoil my fun."

"Did you—? Were you—?"

"Did I like her?" I was expecting this but didn't give any thought to what I should say. The truth slides out easily, though. "Course I did. I think you like her or really don't. Did I see us ending up together?" I shrug ruefully. "I had a brief fantasy about it the first few nights and then, no. We had fun; we would have had fun, but the spark wasn't there."

Abigail leans forward. "What do you need for the spark to be there?"

I mull that over. "Nobody's ever asked me that."

"Do you have a type?"

"I like women," I tell her with a grin.

She laughs. I like her laugh. I like the way she listens, those big brown eyes fixed on me like I'm the centre of her world at the moment.

I like the way she looks, period.

"I like a woman with a brain," I decide. "Who can think for herself. Some of the girls I meet when I'm with the band—let's just say if I told them the sky was pink and the moon was out during the day, they would be all, of course it is, Basher, you're so cute. I mean, I am pretty cute." I preen, and she laughs again.

"You are very cute," she agrees.

"So you think I'm your type?" I ask with another grin.

"If you look at who's left, there's no way I could even have a type. You're all so different."

"But I'm your favourite, aren't I?" I tease.

She touches my glass with hers. "I'm having a very good time tonight," she assures me.

I'll have to make do with that.

33

Abigail

IT'S THE PERFECT END to a very nice day.

I kept Basher for the last date as a treat to myself. I knew I liked him—my collection of Water Rhino CDs is testament to that—and the fangirl inside of me would have been too excited at giving him the first date.

And it's obvious what still happens to the man who gets the first date rose, even though the producers have said over and over that there's no curse.

As much as I had been looking forward to my date with Basher, I'd never in a million years imagine that he would take me to a baseball game.

But it's kind of perfect.

"I have to say, you smell much better." Basher nudges my shoulder as he reaches for the popcorn.

"Tanner got most of the wave."

"Then it's good I'm not here with him."

"Tanner might be more likely to go to a hockey game."

I didn't want to bring him up. I've sat through—how long? When I check the scoreboard, I realize the game is in the third inning.

I've lasted three innings without saying his name.

Tanner, Tanner, Tanner.

Tanner kissed me. A lot. We were late getting back to the hotel because we found a sunny spot outside of town that was deserted.

We kissed a lot, and I can't stop thinking about it. About him.

And how I went on the date thinking there was nothing there and found the possibility of everything.

I'd like to see Ria and Rue say there's no chemistry between me and Tanner now.

But it's not fair to be thinking of him now, so I pull myself back to Basher.

"How is everyone getting along at the hotel?" That's not talking about Tanner, but if Basher happens to bring him up...

"It's a good group of guys," Basher reassures me. "Only been a few pissing contests, excuse my French."

"Anything I should be aware of?"

"Nothing that I want to waste my time talking about. I'll tell you anything you want to know about the guys in the house, but I'd rather talk about you and me."

That should be the right answer, but I'm still looking for more about Tanner.

After today, I feel starved, desperate to know more about him. I can ask him, but when? There are five men left, and I need to give them all equal time.

And now it's Basher's time. "What do you want to talk about?" I ask.

"Would you want to stay in Laandia after this?" Basher wants to know.

"After what, exactly?"

"After we fall madly in love and I put a ring on it."

I laugh with delight. "Is that your plan?"

He picks up my hand and brings it to his lips, dropping the softest kiss ever on the knuckle of my ring finger. "It is."

My laughter dies, and my heart stutters. The way Basher looks at me—

"I'm falling for you, Abigail. I'll just come right out and say it."

He's falling for me. I knew going in that was a possibility—of more than one man having feelings for me, but I honestly didn't expect it.

A rock star, a hockey player and a prince...

And I'm not sure what to do about it.

Is it possible for me to care about more than one man at a time?

I touch his cheek. "Basher... what's your real name?"

He still holds my hand. "You don't think my mama would have named me Basher?"

"That would have been predicting the future."

"Richard," he admits. "I went by Rich, but a lot of times, I was Dick Doyle. So, yeah, I was into Basher."

"I like it. It suits you."

"You suit me too."

He's so open about how he's feeling. I never would have imagined that. "How do you see it working?"

"Aha!" Basher grins with delight, and the sight of it makes me smile. He's not as handsome as Dylan nor does he have the model-good-looks of Ashton, but he's cute.

Basher is cute. Especially given how happy he looks. "I've got a chance," he cheers, and heads turn our way. And then someone hits a double, and the attention shifts back to the field.

"Of course you do. So logistically..."

"I need a place in Toronto to be near the band," he says matter-of-factly. No arguments or concessions, but this is his career, and that of his bandmates. He can't just think of himself. "But when I'm on tour or recording or writing, I can be anywhere," he adds.

"And how often is that?"

"Not going to lie, it gets pretty intense when we're putting an album together. But we're not doing that every day. Would you want to stay in Battle Harbour? With your folks? With Tema?"

"I can't imagine not being close to her," I admit. "I know it sounds silly because I'm not her mother—"

"But you helped raise her. I know the story. Just because you didn't give birth to her doesn't mean you can't love her like she's your own."

"I do," I whisper. "I didn't think anyone here would get that."

"Anyone who cares about you can see how much she means to you. I think that must give Tanner a leg up on the rest of us, seeing as he's totally smitten with the little miss."

"That was because of the pool day. He was so good to her."

"I like kids. I can be good to her, too."

I smile at him. "I'm sure you can be."

"The being good with kids will help T win over the ladies when he's the Suitor."

"When he's... what?"

There's a roaring sound in my ears, and it takes a moment to realize one of the players has hit the ball over the fence and the crowd sounds their approval.

Could it be too loud for me to hear what Basher said? Did he really say...? "Tanner is... what...?"

"There's been talk of one of us getting the nod to be the next Suitor," Basher says blithely. "My money is on Tanner."

"He..." My stomach has dropped into my shoes, and I stare at my fingers twisting in my lap, trying to breathe through the surprise.

Shock. Utter dismay.

If Tanner is planning on being the next Suitor, then what was today?

"I didn't know that," I say quietly.

Basher is focused on the field, and doesn't realize anything is wrong.

Everything is wrong.

"Nothing is official, of course," he adds. "You still get your pick. We're all here for that."

"Who has talked about it?" My voice feels far away, and I clear my throat to stop the sensation.

"Everyone. Nobody. Nobody will admit they're interested. Not me," he assures me. "I don't think I could handle picking between all those women."

"That's what I have to do."

Basher pats my knee. "And you're doing a great job."

Am I? Am I really doing a great job if the men are talking about what's going to happen after this is over? Contingency plans?

Being the Suitor—which means not being with me.

Tanner has a contingency plan.

I have a hard time pulling my mind back onto the baseball game.

34

Grayson

ABIGAIL BURSTS INTO CAMILLE'S after her date with Basher.

Ria was on pickup duty, and she trails after her with the wide-eyed expression that I've come to know means something is wrong.

I sigh and take a last sip of the very nice French wine that Camille poured for me. Odin is away tonight, and I shared dinner with Camille. She's been regaling me with the history of Saint Pierre. I'm not much into history, but it's pretty interesting.

Story time is over now.

I meet Abigail at the kitchen door. "Who did you pick as the next Suitor?" she demands.

My heart sinks because this isn't the face of a woman back from a successful date. There's no softness in her eyes, no smile on her face, none of the sweet *did that really happen* expressions that I've come to recognize when a woman has feelings for a man.

Or the other way around.

It's too bad. I like Basher. I would have given him three-to-one odds of ending up with her.

I glance at Rue, who joins us from the office we've been using. She shifts her gaze away from me. I'm on my own for this one.

Rue has become overly friendly with Abigail. I don't blame her—I like Abigail too. She's fun, friendly and much more easy-going than Princess Lyra. Or so I thought. But we're—I'm—responsible for this show, and I have advertisers and people above me who want me to keep to the format, and Rue being friends with Abigail means one less person on my side as the bad guy.

"We haven't made that decision yet," I tell her. "It shouldn't mean anything to you."

"Of course it does," Abigail argues. "What if they decide they want to be the Suitor more than they want to be with me?"

"Do you really think they would?" Camille follows me from the kitchen. She is also Abigail's friend, and I like to think she's my friend too. She might be on my side.

Not that it's going to come to picking sides.

"I don't know." Abigail huffs a sigh as she toes off her sneakers. "I barely know them."

"You should be getting to know them," Ria points out. "We're getting some really good footage. And the chemistry with Tanner was off the charts."

That slows Abigail, but not enough.

"That doesn't mean I know who's going to pick me in the end," she protests. "And if they have a choice between me and their own show?"

Does she honestly think any of those men would put their own show before her?

Okay, I've seen this before. Archie, the last Suitor, had a melt-down with a week left to go, convinced that none of the women wanted to be with him at the end.

He was wrong—the final two women both wanted him at the end.

But Archie ultimately chose wrong—it was only four months before the woman he picked and proposed to eventually broke up with him.

I'm not about to share that with Abigail.

"You're going to pick them," I share instead. "This is your show, Abigail. Your choice. I'm just doing my job preparing for the next show."

Other than Princess Lyra and Abigail, we've always picked the next Suitor or Suitorette from the previous show. Fans have already been introduced to them, and are hopefully invested.

Plus, they know the drill. They are already used to kissing on camera and that makes my job a lot easier.

"But if they know about your preparations, it might make them not pick me back." She's worried and scared of ending alone. I've been there during my time on the show.

It doesn't mean it's not good TV. I discreetly nod at Ria, who picks up her phone and starts filming.

"Are you worried about that?" I ask in a gentle tone. "The man you chose not picking you?"

"I'm not talking on camera," she snaps.

"I know it's difficult," I soothe. "But it's a great time to be vulnerable. We haven't talked about your uncertainty about the process."

"This isn't an uncertainty, it's me regretting ever signing up for this." Abigail looks around, looking for an escape. We've met her in the front hall—accosted, some will say. Camille must be on the same wavelength because she motions for Abigail to come into the kitchen.

It's a good kitchen, a spacious yet homey kitchen. And there's wine.

Camille pours a glass, and Abigail settles at the table.

I nod for Ria to keep filming and take the seat across from Abigail. "Do you really regret giving love another try?" I ask.

She puffs out a breath and wraps her hands around the glass. She's a pretty woman, not stunning or classically beautiful, but her face shows all of her feelings, which is perfect for this show.

The best was when we caught her reaction when Jake Crow stepped out of the car. With that look, it's not surprising that he was sent home after the first date.

"I just got dumped by Spencer," Abigail says in a low voice. "And I've opened myself up for it to happen again—and this time, even more people will get to see and talk about it."

There's embarrassment there, and real worry, but thankfully no sadness. Abigail said she was over Spencer, but it had been a real concern, having her step in so quickly after their breakup.

It takes time getting over a love. We were lucky that none of the men had developed serious feelings for Lyra during her time on the show.

I had some long talks with the men about that too.

"What happened with Basher?" I ask, gentling my voice as best I can. "Did he say something to upset you?"

Abigail shrugs as she stares into her wine. "He said he was falling for me, but will that even be enough to want to be with me at the end?"

"You have to trust them."

"Like I trusted Spencer?" Abigail looks over at Rue. "Can you not show that? I don't want to seem more pathetic than I already do."

"No one thinks you're pathetic," Rue promises. "The men adore you. There's so much excitement with them, so much more than when it was Lyra."

"I don't know why," she grumbles.

"Because they all feel they have a chance with you. There's no frontrunner, so they're all in it. And regardless of what you think, they're in it to win it. Win you."

"All of them?

"All of them," I assure her. "I know this is tough. I know it's the ultimate leap of faith, but you have to trust them. It won't work if you don't."

She doesn't respond. "Are there at least a few of them that you feel that you can continue with? That you might trust; or at least begin to?"

"Maybe." She meets my eyes with so much uncertainty that I feel for her. "Do I have to send more home? Because right now I don't know who. It's hard to be sure of them. What if who I want decides they want their own show more than me?"

The plan was to narrow it to four men tonight and give out the rose, sending one home tomorrow. Another day, and we'll need to organize family visits.

"Tell you what," I say, improvising faster than I even have before, even when I was pitching for the majors. "One more group date tomorrow and then you'll decide. You can have time with them all and make your decision on which four to keep."

Abigail nods. "Thank you."

I glance at Camille. "And we'll bring Camille and Odin along for moral support."

"Can Hettie come too? And Bo?"

Rue raises her eyebrows when I look at her. "We'll need another day to arrange for family visits," she says in a low voice. "Why don't we use them as family until we get to the final two?"

When I see Abigail's expression, there's no way I would say no to her. "We'll make it a royal family event," I promise.

35

Abigail

GRAYSON TAKES PITY ON me and lets me have a last group date before I pick the final three.

It's perfect timing because the downtown area of Saint Pierre is being transformed for an island-wide party to celebrate the end of the capelin roll. There will be drinking and dancing and fresh lobster rolls.

I am very excited about the lobster rolls. I haven't had a good one since I moved away.

And I'm focused on the food because I have no idea which of the men I should pick. Or send home. There are five left—one more than there should be.

I'll eventually have to narrow it down to two—an insurmountable task.

I like them all, in different ways. I feel like I've had breakthroughs with Ashton and Jonas. Tanner. There are strong connections with Rand and Basher.

But I don't know if any of the connections are strong enough. If they would pick me in the end.

And that's my problem.

"You're playing it safe," Hettie says as we get ready for the party.

As promised, Grayson invited Hettie and Bo to join us tonight, and I've never been so happy to see my best friend. I might be analyzing our friendship, and finding things that I've not thought of before, but that doesn't mean Hettie still isn't my best friend.

And Tema, but Camille has taken her and Bo to her bird sanctuary on the other island. They'll be back for the party, and I know Tema is already working on how to stay longer at the party than the hour Hettie allotted.

I want to see Tema so badly, but I also don't want to be up-staged by a nine-year-old princess.

Being upstaged by Lyra is bad enough.

"How else should I play it?" I demand, turning to look at Hettie as makeup artist Hazel draws a cat line, resulting in a scroll of black eyeliner on my cheek. "Sorry."

"A little warning would be nice."

"My bad." I sit perfectly still as Hazel cleans me up and draws two perfect lines, but my mind can't be restrained. *Ashton, Jonas, Basher. Tanner. Rand.*

Who wants to be the Suitor more than they want to be with me?

"What is your heart telling you?" Hettie demands, going through the racks of clothes. Every once in a while, she'll pull out a hanger to admire a dress or shirt.

"I don't trust my heart because my head is telling me no one will want me in the end."

It sounds worse when I admit it out loud.

"Tell your head to shut up," Hazel mutters under her breath.

"Yes, that," Hettie agrees. "And add one of those words that Tema isn't allowed to say with it."

I slump in the chair, staring at Hettie's reflection. She has always been there for me. We've been doing everything together. I was there when she gave birth. But her life with Bo is separate.

And my life—if I have a life with one of these men—won't have anything to do with her.

That will be something else I'll have to get used to. It all seems like so much.

"Tell me who to pick," I beg.

Hettie laughs. "Not on your life. I'm not having you come back in six months and tell me I picked the wrong one for you."

"Please."

Hettie's smile fades when she realizes I'm serious. "Abigail. Come on. You can do this. You know yourself better than anyone. And you know these men."

"But Spencer..."

"This has nothing to do with Spencer. You told me you were over him."

"I was. I am."

"You took a chance with Spencer when you knew it was never going to work out. You took a chance because you thought it would be a way we could stay together. You and Spencer, me and Bo... You could live at the castle, see Tema all the time. Nothing would have to change."

"There's a lot that has changed," I admit. Was that the only reason I was with Spencer?

Probably.

More than probably.

I've been lonely for so long, with only Hettie and Tema in Vancouver. I missed my family, my friends. Dating. I never let myself fall for anyone because a relationship would get in the way of taking care of Tema. How could I follow Hettie back to Battle Harbour—because that's where I knew she'd eventually end up—if I had ties to Vancouver?

Were Hettie and Tema my excuses for being... what? Scared?

I did give up a lot for them—but I gained a lot as well.

"I let you give up your life for me," Hettie whispers as if she can read my mind. "I dragged you with me, and I dragged you home. And that was wrong of me."

The only sound is Hazel blowing on her brush. Hettie stares at my reflection. I know this is a conversation that needed to be had, but I didn't mean *now*.

"You didn't drag me anywhere. I wanted to go with you," I tell her automatically. I don't know what surprises me more—that the conversation is happening, or that Hettie brought it up.

She shakes her head. "I've been thinking about this. And I've been talking about it with Bo and his therapist. And I never realized—"

Hettie puts her hands on my shoulders, squeezing tightly. In the reflection of the mirror, I can see tears filling her eyes. "Hettie, no."

"Abigail, yes. It needs to be said. You helped me raise my kid, and now that Bo is in the picture, what happens next? Eight years of being a mom, and now what? What happens to you?" I reach up and grab one of her hands. "I'm so sorry."

"Please don't cry," Hazel says between gritted teeth. "The eyes are perfect."

I laugh, trying to blink away the tears. Hearing Hettie say that—yes. That's how I feel, only I didn't think I was allowed to feel like that. I thought I should be happy for Hettie and Tema to have Bo in their life, not resentful that he's taken my spot.

But that's exactly what I am.

"Abs, I know I can't make up for everything you've done for me. Given up for me. But just know, I will do everything in my power to make sure you stay in Tema's life."

For Hazel's sake, I blink away the wash of tears. "She's not mine."

"But she thinks she is, and I'm so okay with that. And so is Bo. It doesn't matter who you're with, she will always be yours. Okay?"

I nod. Hazel swipes a cotton pad under my eye to blot the wetness that has escaped. "Okay. But that still doesn't help me pick who to keep."

"You know."

"I really don't!"

"You will after tonight. And Abigail? I need to thank you. I should have done it years ago. Thank you... for everything you've ever done for me. I know it's been a lot."

I hug her then, and Hazel has to redo most of my eye makeup.

36

Rand

THE DOWNTOWN OF SAINT Pierre has been transformed—the street closed, and picnic tables fill out where parked cars once were. People walk down the street, and lines have already formed at the brewery, the pub, and the stand set up for lobster rolls.

We came together, but once the SUV dropped us off, the men scatter, all wanting to be the first to find Abigail.

Every man for himself.

I stop for a pint because this is a night that feels like I need liquid courage. Abigail will send one man home tomorrow. If I get a pink rose tomorrow morning, I'll be so close to being one of the final three.

I really want to stay.

I catch sight of Jonas in the crowd walking with Ashton. My competition. None of us know who Abigail prefers, but my heart sinks when I think of the two of them.

A prince and a billionaire.

Tanner stands a head taller than the rest of the line at the pub. A former hockey player.

A crash of cymbals grabs my attention—Basher has found himself on the stage, settling behind the drum kit with a grin. A rock star.

I'm a teacher, hanging on to this pint like it's a lifeline.

But I'm still here. Abigail must like me enough because I'm still here.

She's here.

A group passes through the sawhorses blocking the street, and then I see her.

White jeans, cut off at the ankle and hugging her just so. White top, held together by tiny little straps, dipping and fluttering in the breeze. Her hair is loose and curly, and she's not wearing her glasses.

Things tighten inside me, even more when she sees me and waves.

I start toward here. Am I the first to see her? Will I be the first to have her to myself? Will I—?

And then I see who she's with.

Half the Laandian royal family has arrived: Lady Camille and Prince Oden because this is her town, but it's Prince Bo, with little Princess Tema on his shoulders, that has my steps slowing. His wife, Princess Hettie, Abigail's best friend. And Prince Gunnar with two dark-haired women who look familiar, and I'd probably know their names if I checked an Instagram post on the royals.

They are all here, and Abigail is in the middle of the group because these are her people. I'm going to meet the princes of Laandia if I walk over to her right now.

I keep walking. They may not be my people, but I really want Abigail to be my person at the end of this.

It makes me catch my breath at the thought of this.

I started this for my sister, but I'm here because of me. Lyra was—Lyra was something, but Abigail is something else. I can see it with her, the hazy future finally taking shape. A life with a partner of my own, someone I respect and admire. Someone I like to spend my days laughing with, my nights loving.

I could love Abigail. I'm not there yet, but it's close, like dangling your toes over the diving board, needing to take one final step.

Or waiting to be pushed.

"Rand!" The expression on Abigail's face when she sees me is everything. It's meeting your best friend for brunch, seeing your past crush in a crowd. It says she likes me, maybe as much as I like her.

Maybe more than like.

It's more than like for me, only I haven't used the right words for it.

I care. I'm crushing on her. I'm interested, fascinated, slightly obsessed.

I'm not in love, but it's close. So close.

"Hey." There may be royals surrounding her, but I give Abigail my full attention like they don't matter because she is the queen of my heart.

It sounds cheesy, even in my own head.

"You look great." I touch her hip, leaning down to kiss her cheek. But Abigail moves her head so that my lips meet hers. And then she hugs me.

She just kissed me in front of the royal family, and now she's in my arms, and she smells incredible.

"It's good to see you," she says in a husky voice.

It's been three days. But still. "I missed you," I tell her, which is the truth. I just didn't know how much.

Abigail laughs, and I don't expect her to reciprocate that. She told us she would keep her feelings to herself until the end. And it's not quite the end.

I've made it this far.

She pulls back with a smile on her face. "Meet Hettie," she says.

37

Basher

I SEE ABIGAIL COME in, but I don't go to her.

I'll make my own entrance, one that's a little loud.

"You good?" Alan asks from behind the mic.

"Yep." And then I hit the kick pedal and give him a beat.

I'll enjoy the party soon, but I'm happy here, behind the drum kit. It's not mine, but I get to borrow it for a bit.

The guitar starts and I'm off.

It's easy to keep a good beat for the band, and I throw in enough of my own stuff for the guitarist to look back with appreciation. And the crowd cheers when, after the first set, Alan takes a break to introduce me.

He asks if I want to sit in for a few more songs, and of course I say I do.

I see Abigail standing in the crowd with Rand. I recognize a couple of the Laandian princes with her, but I honestly don't know which one is which. They're talking and laughing. Rand looks comfortable.

Good for him.

When the band starts playing one of their old classics, Lady Camille leads the charge to the dance floor set up in the middle of the street. And then Ashton is there, tugging Abigail to join the crowd, while Rand shakes his head.

Abigail goes with Ashton.

Ashton has some moves.

Maybe I shouldn't be behind the drums right now.

38

Ashton

I DON'T REMEMBER THE last time I danced.

We go to clubs a lot, but I stick to the tables or the bar area.

When we were younger—pre-puberty young—I used to dance with my sister. Fenella used to make up routines and beg me to perform in front of her mirror. This was before TikTok blew up, and I stopped performing when Fen started filming us.

I've no doubt I would have ended up as some meme if there were evidence of that out there.

Fenella takes credit for my moves. I do have some good ones, but my sister had nothing to do with it.

After a few minutes of awkwardly moving side to side, Abigail throws herself into the music like she doesn't have a care in the world.

She's not *that* great, but I like her enthusiasm.

Most of the women I dance with are too conscious of the other dancers and those watching to be comfortable in their skin. Who are watching, what they're thinking. What they're going to post about it, because any woman who shows up on a dance floor with me is going to have their personal history dissected online.

Which is why I rarely dance.

But when this episode will be televised, Abigail will already have been dissected ad nauseam. People will be looking at her, not me. My role as a dance partner might only be a brief moment in the episode.

I'm fine with that.

I'd rather watch Abigail than be the centre of attention.

I like the way she dances. Enthusiastically. Energetically. And yes, it's sexy.

Do I want to end up with Abigail at the end? It's a given I want to end up in the last three, but is that because of the bet with Milo or Abigail?

I like Abigail. I truly do. She's a normal, regular woman—at least she will be until The Suitorette comes out, because I suspect the show will make her a star. But right now, she's not worried about followers or fame. No one is sponsoring what she wears, drinks, drives. She works for her own money.

She wants to be a teacher, of all things.

How would a teacher fit into my life?

Granted, my sister has embraced the quiet life, finding love with a barista, and settling down in small town Battle Harbour. But am I ready to follow suit?

Because if I end up with Abigail, my life will change.

Her life will have to change as well, but I have my suspicions that Abigail would adapt to change better than I could.

Am I willing to change for a woman I like, but not yet love? I don't even know if I'm capable of love. It certainly hasn't happened before.

My shoulders are grabbed from behind, yanking me out of my musings and back to the present, where Abigail is still throwing herself around the dance floor with Camille. Prince Gunnar of Laandia has joined us.

"Ash," Gunnar bellows, trying to be heard above the music, because Basher is killing it on the drums. "Can't believe she hasn't kicked you out yet."

"I must be doing something right," I tell him, switching the smile into a smirk.

Ashton Carrington smirks more than he smiles. That has been posted numerous times.

"You having a good time?" Gunnar demands.

"I am," I say with more than a little surprise. I've known Gunnar for years, so there's no pretending I dance in the streets of small towns on a regular basis.

"Good." He slaps my shoulder and begins to move beside me. Gunnar is an okay dancer, but can't compare to me. "Camille told me about this, so we wanted to show up for her. Didn't expect to see you."

"Lucky you," I manage, but I've caught onto the *we*.

We being Gunnar's girlfriend Stella, who slips into the group dancing with Abigail and Camille.

And Stella's little sister, Sophie.

39

Jonas

I CUT IN WHEN Ashton is dancing with Abigail, and I'm happy to do it.

They looked all together too cozy, and it's time for me to stake my claim. Especially since more of my cousins have arrived.

Bo and Gunnar... Odin, of course. Why are they all here? Tonight of all nights. I need some time with Abigail.

I need to tell her how I feel so she knows to keep me around for the next rounds of dates.

I want to be here with her, but my cousins are about to spoil everything.

Like always.

I hold Abigail in my arms as we waltz around the dance floor, but I'm not paying attention to her, instead focusing on my cousins.

They're not even wearing their crowns, and they still can't pass for anything but royalty. It's good that Kalle isn't here—

"Jonas?" Abigail taps on my shoulder. "What are you staring at?"

"I..." For the first time, I stammer on my reply, and I hate that. I also hate that I hear my father's voice in my head.

This is a good thing they're here. They can see you with her, how well you fit in.

I'd like to tell my father's voice to be quiet.

I want to stay with Abigail and enjoy her company. Not try to broker peace between my cousins in order for my father to gain power over his family. Somehow.

I don't want that at all.

Maybe I do want Abigail.

She's still looking at me with concern. "Lyra is here," I manage.

I saw her dark head approach the others, and I wanted to give Abigail a heads up.

"What?" Her eyes snap as she stops mid-step.

"Over there with the rest of them."

Abigail is pretty when she smiles, but when she's angry? There's a spark in her that I quite like. "Why is she here?"

Unfortunately, if she's this mad with Lyra, it might not help my plan to reunite the families. "Abigail, don't—"

"I'm going to talk to her." And Abigail breaks the hold and storms off, leaving me alone on the dance floor.

40

Abigail

"WHAT ARE YOU DOING here?" I demand without pre-amble and not many manners.

Even without the heels, Lyra has always been taller than me, and I hate how she looks down at me. "I don't often say no to a party," she says in her low drawl.

"It's *my* party," I hiss.

Spencer isn't here with her, and I'm glad. I'm not ready to talk to Spencer right now.

And for once, the cameras aren't on me.

Lyra frowns, her blue eyes chilling as she recognizes that something is amiss. "I wasn't aware that you had usurped my sister-in-law as prefect of Saint Pierre. A lot must have happened since I left."

"A lot *has* happened."

"That's what I said. Did I miss something?" She has the gall to look confused. "I thought we were okay."

"After you took my boyfriend."

"After I gave you a chance at *twelve* boyfriends," she points out.

"Giving me a chance with your leftovers?"

"That's rude."

I fist my hands at my sides. "It's the truth."

Lyra frowns, crossing her arms. "I don't see it like that. The truth is that none of those five men left have given me more than a passing glance tonight. Including Ashton, which is his loss because Fenella sent him a care package. Those are *your* men, Abigail, for you to do as you see fit with them. It's not like they're possessions, but they're more yours than they were ever mine."

Hearing her say those words takes some of the wind out of my sails. "They were half in love with you," I still insist.

Lyra scrunches up her face. "I never got that vibe. Not from those guys. Especially not Jonas." She mock shivers. "What's up with this? I didn't think lack of self-confidence was ever your thing."

"It's not my thing. I have plenty of self-confidence."

"You sure about that? Look, Abigail, I like you. Get Spencer out of the picture, and I think we could have been friends. I like the bond you've got with Tema, what you did for Bo."

"What did I do for Bo?"

"You took care of Hettie. And you never bad-mouthed him when they were apart, which I can say about none of my friends."

"Bo has always been my friend too."

"I know, and I respect that. And I can see how it would have been if you ended up with Spencer. It would have been—"

"Please don't say convenient," I say through gritted teeth.

Lyra grins. "Bit of a trigger word for you?"

I don't smile in return.

I don't know what I'm doing, confronting Lyra about something she had no part of. If I'm to be angry at someone, it should be Spencer.

But there's no point, because the only thing he's done is follow his heart. It's no one's fault that it didn't lead him to me.

Not that it would have been a great romance. I've always thought friends to lovers was the way to go, but you have to make sure there's a big jump, not the slow, gentle slide that isn't noticeable until the line has been passed.

"Is this a bit of a jealous thing?" Lyra asks bluntly.

"I'm not jealous of you."

"You should be because I'm jealous of you."

I rear back in shock. "Why on earth would you be jealous of me?"

"I love my family and I love my life, but sometimes I wish I could just start again somewhere else. Like you did. And then you came back, but instead of sliding into your old life, you made it clear you had a new one in mind. That's why I thought you'd be perfect to take over for me. Another fresh start for you. You could take charge and pick what—and who—you wanted."

"You could have done that."

Lyra shakes her head. "I've been in love with Spencer for my entire life, only I never let myself understand what love felt like, so I had no clue. Watching my brothers fall in love showed me what I could have too, if I were brave enough to go for it. So—be brave. Go after what you want."

"What if they don't want me?" The question pops out of my mouth without a conscious thought about who I am asking. Because how could I have been so angry with Lyra two minutes ago, and now I'm letting her give me a pep talk?

If that is what this is.

Lyra frowns again. "Is that what this is? That's stupid."

"I don't think it's stupid. Any of those men would make an amazing Suitor, and who's saying they don't want that more than they want me?"

She laughs. She *laughs*. "Can you hear yourself? Are you listening to this utter bull—"

I do listen. And I don't like it.

I've never doubted my self-worth. Never suffered from low self-esteem. So why am I on the cusp of ruining things because I'm scared of not being wanted?

There's no way Spencer could have done that to me.

Because it's not about Spencer.

41

Tanner

I NOTICE ABIGAIL OFF to the side with Lyra, and neither of them looks happy.

I've never asked Abigail about her relationship with Lyra. I assume, given her closeness with the Laandian royal family, there is one, but right now, it looks like it might be a little volatile.

I've never asked her how she felt coming on the show, taking over from Lyra, after Lyra basically took her boyfriend.

Why did I never ask her that?

I asked her other things, I told her about my dark secrets, but knowing why she came on the show should have been a priority.

I also never told her about my reasons for it either. It doesn't take a lot of insight to figure out I didn't want to talk about it.

Before I change my mind—and before Basher gets to her, because the way he was looking at Jonas dancing with Abigail suggests he'll be off the stage and on the dance floor with her very soon—I head over to Abigail.

"Ladies," I announce myself. Both heads turn to me.

Lyra's expression softens, like she's glad to see me. We *did* have a connection. It wasn't just me.

Only she had a stronger one with Spencer.

"Tanner," she says with a smile. A real one. I like that I know her real from her fake.

I could give her a hug. I probably should. But I slip my arm around Abigail instead. "You okay?" I murmur.

"Peachy." The word snaps into the air.

"Johnny is a little enamoured with Basher playing, but as soon as he stops, that camera is going to be fixed right here on the two of you," I tell them. "I don't know much about the show, but I can only bet that's going to be the highlight of one of those *What happens next week* teasers."

I can feel Abigail's body relax, and I'd really like if it was because of me.

It's a surprise how much I'd like it to be me.

"Thanks for the warning," Abigail says grudgingly.

"Johnny likes Basher?" Lyra asks with delight.

"Everyone likes Basher," I correct. "He's a great guy."

"So are you." There's a wistfulness in Lyra's voice that is new, and I know where this is leading even before she opens her mouth. "Tanner, I should—"

I think the next word is going to be *apologize*, but I don't want to hear it. Not now. "Lyra, I'd love to catch up with you, but I came over to ask Abigail if she'd dance with me." I glance down at Abigail, at how her eyes widen with surprise, and yes, happiness. "What do you say? Can your feet take anymore?"

She takes the hand I offer. "As long as you're not planning on stepping on them, I'm great."

Before we walk away, she turns back to Lyra.

My date, she mouths.

Lyra holds up her hands.

Winding our way between groups of talking, laughing townspeople, I lead Abigail to the dance floor. "Do I want to know what that was about?"

"Things needed to be said," is all Abigail says as her hands reach up to my shoulders.

Grade school dancing, I decide as I wrap my arms around her waist and we begin to sway, is much more my style than the fancy footwork Jonas tried with her.

"You shot down Princess Lyra," Abigail adds, with more than a little glee in her voice.

"I'm here for you, not Princess Lyra. It's your date."

"That's what I told her."

She giggles softly and leans closer, and I breathe in her scent. Fruit and candy, I decide. Sweet, but not overly so.

Her mouth is shiny from her lip gloss, and I take that as encouragement that she hasn't kissed anyone yet.

Not that she's going to kiss me.

I want her to kiss me.

During every interaction I've had with Abigail, the thought of me being the next Suitor has been in the back of my mind, and I'm beginning to resent it. I haven't agreed to anything, and it already takes up too much of my mental energy.

Should I? Shouldn't I? What would happen? What would it be like?

It's apparent before my date with Abigail yesterday that it has gotten in the way. It's hard to be in the moment with someone, like I want to be with Abigail, when you've got a back-up plan swirling around your head.

I've got my head on the right way now.

I've never had a backup plan, and that was always a criticism after hockey ended. But here is a second option laid out for me. But I find, as I sway to the music, holding Abigail in my arms, that I don't want it. I don't want a second option.

I don't want the back-up plan.

And realizing that makes everything so much clearer.

There's one option I want, and she's just moved closer, our bodies only a breath apart. I lean down, resting my chin against the top of her head.

I have no idea what this song is, but I hope it lasts forever.

"Tanner." Caught up in my thoughts and how good it feels to hold her, I suspect it's not the first time Abigail has said my name.

I straighten, a smile on my face. "Abigail. I haven't told you how happy I am to see you."

"Are you?"

My smile fades a bit. "Of course. And I wanted to talk to you... I feel like I need to explain a few things."

"Such as?"

"The first night we met. I was—"

Abigail shakes her head. "You don't have to explain anything. You were hesitant about meeting me. It's understandable."

"I *wanted* to meet you. I was supposed to go last, but Jonas messed it up at the last minute."

"Jonas...?" Her brows knit together.

"He threw me off my game. I'm really sorry about that."

Her face softens. "It's okay."

"It's not. It was a first impression, and I blew it. And then, when I saw you at the hotel when you came to pick up Dylan..."

"You did seem to get away from me as soon as you could."

"Because I'd been running, and it was hot, and I was sweaty—"

Abigail laughs. "You were very sweaty," she agrees.

"It was running down places that it shouldn't be running..." I confess and she laughs again, this time a true belly laugh. "I wanted to hug you, but it wouldn't have been nice for you and I didn't think you'd be up for waiting for me to shower and change, so I just got out of there. And got Dylan for you, so the others couldn't have more time with you. Petty, I know."

"Honest," she argues.

"I'll always be honest with you," I promise, but my smile fades when I notice her expression becomes serious.

"And tonight? Do you have anything you want to admit about tonight?" she asks in a quiet voice.

Fear, like I'm standing in front of a concussion doctor, fills me, and I blank on anything else I've wanted to apologize for.

"I heard they asked you to be the next Suitor."

I didn't see that coming, but I should have. It's a small island, and an even smaller group filming the show. "Oh, that," I manage. "They mentioned it might be a possibility."

Her lips tighten, but what I focus on is the sadness in her eyes. "Yes, that. Is that something you want?"

I push a curl behind her ear. I like Abigail with her glasses, but it's easier to see her eyes without them. There have been a lot of emotions crossing those dark eyes tonight, and I've been able to read them all.

I want to know more. I want to be able to decipher all her feelings.

I shake my head. "I don't want that." I want her. And these last few days of thinking about it... even if I didn't have her, I don't think I'd want to be the star of a circus like this.

As I realize that, everything becomes lighter. I don't know where this will end up with Abigail, but I need to take my shot. I want a chance with her, and having a back-up plan isn't helping.

I can figure things out on my own.

"What do you want?" she asks in a low voice.

As close as I've gotten to Abigail in the last few weeks, I just realize that I've never told her how I feel. I've shown her, or at least I thought I have.

Or maybe, this close to the end, Abigail needs more confirmation.

"I want you," I tell her.

She catches her breath. "And if I don't pick you in the end, would you—"

I smile because she can't hide the flicker of hope in her eyes. "I'll still want you. And I suppose I'll have to get over you while you go about your life, because I do want you to be happy. But I also want to be the one who makes you happy. I want it to be you and me at the end." I lean down again, my mouth close to her ear. Johnny is back on the job and zooming in on this moment like the good cameraman he is.

I really wish I could have this moment without any witnesses.

"I'm mostly in love with you," I say to Abigail.

She makes a sound in her throat—a hum, or a muffled laugh. "Mostly? What does that mean?"

"It means that if you kiss me now, I'll be all the way in."

I feel the curve of her lips as she presses them against mine, and it tips me over the edge.

And tonight, it's a good place to be.

42

Ashton

THE NEXT MORNING IS the last day roses are given out.

At least the ones left at the door of our hotel rooms.

I see why the show does it this way. I *have* watched The Bachelor—a little embarrassed to admit that, so let's blame my sister's influence—and the way they do it on that show looks painful. The men and women lined up waiting to be picked, like a middle school gym class, the camera focusing on every smile or wince, waiting for fat tears to roll down faces.

This way—the Suitorette way—is much more civilized. We open the door at a scheduled time, check out the colour of the rose on the floor, do the, *ah, that's too bad* comments, and say goodbye to whoever is leaving.

It's hard to get upset since whoever leaves opens the playing field for the rest of us.

Last night, the five of us made inane small talk during the drive back to the hotel from the street party. No one mentioned roses. Five of us are left but at least one will be leaving today. My opinion yesterday was that Tanner was the underdog, but the way he was canoodling with Abigail by the end of the night, it seemed like he's pulled it together.

No one mentions that either.

Grayson told us yesterday that it's up to Abigail to decide how many men she wants for the last round of dates. They are good ones—the one-on-one dates which may lead to an overnight. I heard Rue say something about family being involved as well, seeing as time is limited because it's only half a season.

It's obvious we all have a connection with Abigail, and I can't figure out the front-runner. Each of our names has been top of the whiteboard on different occasions.

As I get camera ready, I have no clue who is going home.

Maybe she'll give out three yellow roses and leave only two of us left.

Maybe she'll keep all five of us for another few days, narrowing it down after each date.

Nothing Abigail does surprises me. She's really making this season her own.

All I know is that I don't want to be the one sent home.

It's not just the bet with Milo, although that's a part of it. I like Abigail. I'm not in love with her, but I like her. I like being around her.

I like that she's comfortable around me. The real me. The one I keep to myself.

I never thought a regular girl would think I would be worth the trouble, at least not a regular girl not in it for the fame and fortune that may well come from dating Ashton Carrington.

Abigail helped me see that I have more options other than the insipid influencer/model/pseudo-celebrity types who flock to me, thinking only of what I could do for them.

No one has ever seen me like Abigail sees me. Or if they have, no one has called me out on it.

I don't want to go home. I'm not ready to leave this little reality world bubble.

"Two minutes!" comes the call from the hallway.

I check myself in the mirror, running a hand through my hair because it's a little too perfect.

I can't let them see that I'm trying so hard. Or that I really want this.

Do I really want Abigail?

She's cool; she's cute. I like how she listens to me. But do I want to marry her?

Probably not, if my mind flits back to the party last night. At the jolt I got from the simple sight of Sophie Laz standing there in her yellow sundress.

Definitely shouldn't be thinking of Abigail in the long run if Sophie is still stuck in my thoughts. Not that there's any possibility of anything with Sophie.

My life would eat her alive.

I hear a door open and wait another thirty seconds. Schooling my expression into blank nonchalance, I open the door.

There's a yellow rose on the floor.

It's me.

*

Grayson tells me Abigail will stop by in an hour to speak to me. Before then, I'm supposed to pack up and say my goodbyes.

I'm surprised it was me. But not that surprised.

I'm upset—but not that upset.

I'm annoyed I lost the bet, though.

The others pile into the room with me as I start throwing things onto the bed.

"I can't believe it's you." It's the fourth time Rand says that, like he might actually mean it. Rand's a good guy—a little too earnest and totally innocent about so many things, but I can see women thinking he's sweet. Respectful, dependable, honest.

I bet he's good at communicating. At being vulnerable.

All the things I'm not.

Tanner and Basher are like that too, so Abigail must have a type.

Although I can't figure out how Jonas is still here. I can't see Abigail fangirling the crown—not that Jonas has much of one.

He has a baby crown.

He's more like me than I'm me, so how does he get to stay if she's kicking me out? That baby crown?

That annoys me too.

"You all wanted it to be me," I tell him, carefully folding my shorts. Three buttons done, arms and shoulders tucked, fold three times and into the packing cube for shirts.

If there's one household chore I'm good at, it's packing.

Not that it's much of a household chore.

"If I'm gone, that's a lot less competition for you," I add.

I'm not entirely joking.

"She only picked one to go home," Tanner muses. "Wonder what that means."

"She can't decide between the rest of us. But you, Carrington, seem to be expendable." I can't stand that sneer in Jonas's voice. The little prince is bearable for the most part, but once in a while, a little slime slips out.

"And I still can't figure out how she's kept you around so long," I retort. No one says anything, but I can tell the others agree. They just don't want to say it themselves.

Maybe Jonas himself agrees. If he has a shred of self-awareness, he might.

The smug expression matches his sneer, and there's a little more slime slipping out. "I'm still here, going into the important dates," he says.

"All of them are important dates," Rand argues. "We don't have much time with her."

"Did you do something to upset her last night?" Basher asks.

I shrug and move on to my pants and shorts. "Got me."

Ever since I saw that flash of yellow, I wondered if Abigail noticed me watching Sophie.

Probably not, since I barely looked at her.

But when I did, she kind of seared herself into my mind.

Tanner thumps my shoulder. "It does suck that you're leaving," he admits.

"Does that mean you're going to miss me, big boy?" I tease. I like Tanner. Big and brawny, but with more brains than anyone realizes. Out of everyone, I want him to win. At the start, I'd have said he had it in the bag, but things have been different lately between him and Abigail.

Although they seemed to have patched things up last night.

And he's still here, while I am packing to go home.

I decide then not to go home. I'll go to Battle Harbour, keeping a low profile that Grayson, and our contracts, insists on. I can hang out with Fenella for a bit and wait for this to be over.

"Yeah." Tanner grins. "It's cool having you around."

"Don't worry that pretty head of yours. I won't be going far. I'll want to stay close to pick up the pieces for our prince when he doesn't win." I flash a smile at Jonas.

"I'll point out that you're the one packing here," he says in that patronizing voice.

I hate that he's right. I am the one going home.

43

Abigail

I'VE NEVER BEEN SO aware of the cameras as when I arrive at the hotel to talk to Ashton. At the microphone strapped to the small of my back. Even the assistants are hovering.

Are they here just to watch me say goodbye to Ashton, or is there another reason? I've never had this much of an audience, even that first date on the beach.

Ashton sits on the couch in the hotel lobby, looking as cool as ever. His expression is inscrutable, dark blue eyes narrowing as he watches me approach. I can't read what he's thinking, but I can imagine.

The yellow rose dangles from his fingers.

"I'm sorry about that," I apologize as I sit down beside him.

His smile is his usual smirk, but there's something missing from it. "Forgive me if I don't believe you. If you were truly sorry, then you would have kept me around."

I widen my eyes because Ashton sounds... serious. "Are you upset?" I whisper.

"Of course I am," Ashton drawls. "You're sending me packing before Jonas. Guess you've got a thing for crowns."

"Ashton…" *This may be more difficult than I expected.* I thought Ashton would be flip and glib and make some snarky comment and we'd say goodbye as friends.

"It's cool." He waves his hand, but his tone suggests things are far from cool. "I knew it wasn't going to be me and you at the end."

"I—"

I thought about it.

And I really did. Every time I was with Ashton, I forced myself to wonder *what if*. What if he was at the end with a shiny, sparkling ring? I pictured it with each of the men, and some were easier than others to put myself there.

Ashton wasn't easy to imagine. Because after I pictured *him* being there at the end—which was relatively simple—I started thinking about his life.

About how I might fit into his life. And that's when things derailed.

Because I couldn't go there. If Ashton was just Ashton and not *Ashton Carrington, billionaire*, things might have been different. I care about him.

I don't love him—not yet. But I don't know what might have happened if I gave him one last chance. The friendship is there—I seriously like him. What if he wasn't who he is? What if I weren't the Suitorette? What would have happened if we met randomly on the street?

Nothing at all, I concluded. Because he will always be Ashton Carrington, and if I wasn't the Suitorette, there would be no reason for us to have met in the first place.

"I didn't know how to fit into your life," I finally say.

"Oh, I think you could figure out how to fit in anywhere," he counters with a lazy smile.

This isn't going to be easy at all. I push down the self-doubt, and trust my instinct. "We have very different lives. Bank accounts. Maybe too different."

"So you don't like me because I have a big bank account. That's refreshing."

I stare at the rose in his hand. "I never said I didn't like you."

"You didn't like me *enough*," he corrects.

"What about you?" I demand. "You never once told me how you felt. You didn't even hint at it."

And he didn't. The other four—and a few of the early men—told me that they cared. That they were falling for me. Ashton talked about his family one time, and that was the deepest we got. There was never any mention of feelings.

There were dances and dresses and a few really good kisses, but that's it.

And at this point in the process, I need more than that.

"You shouldn't worry about the difference in bank accounts." The insouciance in his voice that he arrived with is back, and better than ever. "There would be an iron-tight prenup. My father would make sure of that."

"I don't care about the money."

"Everyone cares about the money."

"Sure, maybe I would care if *you* had billions. But right now it's your father's money."

Ashton's face tightens. "And someday it will be mine."

"Is that how you see it? You're expecting to be given this gift."

He snorts, and I give a start. "If you think being a billionaire is a gift, you're watching the wrong movies." There's a harshness in his tone that I've never heard before. I don't like it. "My father is dedicated to his business, to the extent of his family. He never shuts it off—his phone never shuts off. He has three assistants who know him better than his own children."

The bitterness in his voice—Oh, Ashton. We never got into this. "Is that the life you want?" I ask gently.

"No. No, it's not. But there's no out for me. That's who I am—Preston Carrington's son."

I press his knee. "You're also *you*. Ashton Carrington. Who is nothing like his father."

"I don't think you've gotten to know me enough to say that."

"Whose fault is that?"

Ashton leans away from me. "Touche."

I don't like this side of him. Cold, cocky. A poor loser. If he keeps this up, I'll stop thinking of what if and forget about the regret. I'll...

Which is exactly what Ashton is trying to make me do.

"Have you ever been in love?" I ask, tempering my voice.

"I think you know the answer to that," he says with a dry chuckle. "Since you know me so well."

I take a breath. "I hope you fall in love someday, Ashton. Someday soon. Because that's what I'm trying to do. I'd like a partner, someone I can rely on, someone I can trust."

"And you can't see me like that. Thanks."

"The thing is, I *do*. I did. I imagined it all, Ashton, all of it with you. But the problem for me—other than the radically different lifestyles and that iron-clad pre-nup that I might have had an issue with—"

"I thought you didn't care about the money?" he interrupts.

"I don't. But I don't like planning for divorce before I even say I do."

He smiles ruefully. "Welcome to my world."

"That's the thing. It isn't my world. I don't think I would be a good fit, but never think—" I reach for his hand. "Never think I didn't want it. I think you would be an amazing choice to be at the end of this with. But I don't think *you* think that. You need to learn to love yourself before you take a chance and fall in love."

His quick inhale tells me I've reached him. "You don't think I love myself?"

"I don't think you like yourself very much sometimes."

The mask slips at that, and he sits quietly beside me for a long moment, rolling the stem of the rose between his fingers.

I'm not sure what else to say to him other than goodbye. And right now, I'm still having difficulty with that.

But he finally does it for me. "Thank you," Ashton says, handing me the rose.

"For what?"

"For keeping me as long as you did. I'm sure you'll hear about this, but I want you to hear it from me: I came on the show as a dare. Milo bet me I couldn't make the top three. Looks like he won." He holds up four fingers.

I did not know that, but it doesn't surprise me. I knew there would have to be a good reason for Ashton to join the show, more than just a chance at a princess. "Is that why you're so upset you're leaving?"

Ashton looks at the ocean. "I would have liked the chance to be the driver, but I'll figure it out another way. Lyra kept me around because we were friends. I told her she could *confide* in me, that she should keep me around until it got too weird. It was fun with her."

"It's not fun with me?"

He chuckles and turns to me, taking my chin in his hand. "Not at all." He leans in and brushes his lips against mine, sending a shock through me.

What did I do?

"You're the best person for this show," he says in a soft voice. "I wish you a lifetime of love with the best man. Which isn't Jonas." He winks. "Don't let him fool you."

"Sour grapes?" I manage.

"Maybe a little. But seriously, he's not cool to the other guys, and that says a lot. Maybe he's given you the sad little boy story, but I'm telling you, it's not the real him. Be smart."

I nod. "I will be. I wish a lifetime of love for you, too. You just have to be brave enough to go and get it."

"Oh, I'm nothing if not brave." He taps my nose with a finger. "Be good. See you soon."

And then Ashton Carrington leaves the hotel.

44

Basher

I FIND ABIGAIL ON the couch in the lobby.

I knew Ashton had waited for her there, and I wanted to give them a chance to say their goodbyes. Ashton wasn't happy about being sent home, but who would be?

For him, I think it was mostly embarrassment, and I can't blame him for that either.

But Ashton has left, and Abigail sits alone, staring out the doors to the ocean.

"Abigail?" She starts at the sound of my voice. "Okay to talk for a sec?"

"Sure." She arranges her expression into a smile. This must be difficult for her. What would it be like to develop feelings for different people and have to send them away one by one? Does she still have feelings for Ashton?

Does she have feelings for *me*?

"Everything okay?" she asks as I settle beside her. Johnny unobtrusively picks up his camera.

"I should be asking you that. You look sad."

"I am," she admits. "I said goodbye to Ashton. It wasn't easy."

"I think it was better for him that you wanted to explain in person," I tell her. "If that makes it any easier for you."

Abigail scrunches her nose. "Depends if he liked what I said, I guess. But you're not here to talk about Ashton. Are you?"

"No. He's a good guy despite what his life must be like, but no. Not here about Ashton."

"About you?"

Abigail sent Charlie home because he told her about Duke being here for the wrong reasons. Does she actually think I'm here to talk trash about someone else? "All me."

But how do I say it?

My fingers fidget, tapping incessantly, and I wish for my sticks to hold. I reach over and take Abigail's hand.

"I'm sending myself home," I say, in the gentlest voice I can manage.

I do feel a little bit happy about her shocked expression. "What?"

There's disappointment in that word, and I'm happy about that as well. But I hope I'm imagining that tiny bit of relief.

"I'm leaving," I tell her. "Before you tell me to go."

"But I wasn't going to—"

"Yet," I interrupt. "We both know I'm not going to be one of the final two. You deserve to be with one of those three guys. I'm falling for you, Abigail, but they have fallen. They're all in. And I'd put money that you're all in with them too. At least two of them, anyway."

"Basher." Abigail's smile is sweet, and regretful. She's not telling me to stay, though, so I know this is the right move.

"This has been a blast," I assure her. "I'd do it again in a heartbeat, even knowing I don't get the girl."

"You'll get the girl. A girl."

"But it won't be you." I bring her hand to my mouth and press my lips against her knuckles, once, twice, holding it there until I let go. "And so I will take my leave so you don't have to worry about kicking me out next round."

"But, Basher..."

I stand up, smiling down at her. "Be good. But not too good." I wink. "See you around."

And then I walk away, wondering if I have time to catch the ferry out of here with Ashton.

45

Abigail

B ASHER JUST... LEFT?

He sent himself home.

What the *heck*? Who does that?

Apparently Basher does.

After a few moments of quiet reflection on the couch—which Johnny films—I head through the hotel to the pool, wondering if I'll run into anyone else who will be sending themselves home.

Last night I had five. Now I have three. Who knows how many I'll lose before the end of today?

I can't help but feel a little bitter about the whole thing. And scared, because what if I did the wrong thing by sending Ashton home? Or what if Basher was the one and I'm left with my second and third choices?

He wasn't. I know that, so there's no point heading into a spiral about something I know not to be true. Basher was cute and so much fun. He almost got the yellow rose this morning along with Ashton, but I held back because I wanted to see what happened when I kissed him again.

I didn't send him home because I wanted to kiss him again. I'm not proud of that, but it's the truth. We really never got a good kiss, and I thought I deserved to see what he had.

I will never tell anyone that.

Except Hettie, because I told her last night. She's the one who convinced me it was okay to just give out the one rose and take the kiss from Basher.

I brought Hettie and Tema to the hotel with me this morning, both for support and because Tema wanted to go swimming. I thought it would have been easier with Ashton—that he would have agreed with my decision. Sure, fine, you're right, we're not meant to be together. Let's be friends.

I *think* we ended up there, but I'm not sure. I'll be going back through our conversation, but now I'm a little flustered by Basher's sudden departure.

The bright sun has me reaching for my sunglasses when I get to the pool area.

Hettie sits by the edge watching Tema swim. I'm the one who convinced her that Tema needed swimming lessons, and I'm the one who took her to Mommy and Me classes when she was just a baby because Hettie couldn't handle letting her out of her arms in the water.

I never told anyone in that group that I wasn't Tema's mother. I had one hour, once a week, that I could pretend that beautiful baby was all mine.

It probably wasn't healthy, and maybe a bit stalkerish, but I had been running on five hours of sleep a night between full and part-time jobs, starting classes, and helping Hettie with the night feedings, so I wasn't feeling all that healthy back then.

But the main point is, Tema is, at nine, already an amazing swimmer, so strong and graceful in the water. It's a toss-up whether she'll go into synchronized or become a competitive swimmer. Or even just get a job as a lifeguard in the summers when she's older.

I did that, and Hettie gives me credit for how great she is in the water.

It's not Tema I watch, though.

Tanner stands waist deep in the pool. I watch as he crouches to let a laughing Tema stand on his joined hands. When she's steady, he pushes her up and out of the water. She's airborne for a few seconds before she curves her body and slices back into the deep end in a very pretty dive.

Synchro, then.

I clap my hands, and Hettie turns, along with Rand, who is sitting in the shade of an umbrella. I was so focused on Tanner that I missed him there, because Tanner is...

He was a hockey player, and he still looks like it. Skating does very nice things to a body.

I know this. I've seen him in a bathing suit. I've seen that bare chest with the sprinkling of hair—not too much, not too little. The muscles etched into his torso. The long legs, and thick thighs and...

I swallow and focus on the smile on his face instead.

On how happy he seems to see me.

Because Tanner is in the water, and Tema is not about to let him get away from her, Rand gets to me first. He is also smiling, and looks especially pleased that I'm there, but there's not the catch in my heart that I get from Tanner.

That's a bittersweet realization.

"Hey." Rand always goes for the hug rather than the kiss, and I've always appreciated that. "How did it go with Ashton?"

"It went." One thing I've tried to do is not talk about the other men when I'm with one of them. I don't want to waste their time, and I honestly don't know how much they report back. But this is different, because it indirectly affects Rand too. "Basher left too."

"What?" This is news to Rand, so maybe they don't report back as much as I thought.

"He found me just after Ashton left, said there wasn't the same connection with him as I have with you—with the others—and sent himself home."

"He never said anything about that," Rand declares, leading me across to the pool. "Tanner, did you know Basher wanted out?" he calls.

Tanner scrunches his face with confusion, and it's so cute that I smile to see it. I have it bad for these boys today.

Definitely one of these boys.

"Why?"

"He thought he was going next and wanted to make it easy on me," I admit.

"Was he?" Rand asks quietly.

I glance at Hettie, who, well aware of my kissing situation with Basher, tries to hide her smile. "Well, maybe."

"So you shouldn't be too upset," Hettie says. "You can focus on the three who are still here."

"I haven't seen Jonas in a while, so maybe it's just two," Rand jokes.

Jonas. Rand. And Tanner.

Three men. I have to choose one.

I thought picking between twelve men was bad, but one out of three is infinitely worse.

Tanner says something to Tema, and wades through the water to where I stand by the edge. Kicking off my shoes, I sit beside Hettie and kick my feet into the water so I'm at his level.

"Hi," Tanner says in a quiet rumble, his gaze fixed on me.

I think of the feel of those lips on mine last night. "Hi," I say, not bothering trying to hide my smile.

"That's too bad about Basher." He shrugs ruefully. "It is, but not really."

"I know. It had to be done, but it felt…" I didn't like how it felt, but I'm not about to talk to them about it. "Anyway, looks like you're having fun being a giant pool toy."

"She commanded me to swim with her," Tanner says.

I look at Hettie with horror. "Did she really?" That's the fear of both of us—Tema is Princess Tema of Laandia and that kind of power and privilege could easily go to a nine-year-old's head.

"She asked me politely, and then she knighted me with a pool noodle, so then I had to do whatever she wanted." He smiles at Hettie. "She's an incredible swimmer."

Hettie points at me. "That is all Abigail's doing."

"Tanner, watch to see if my legs are straight," Tema calls before she ducks under to do a handstand.

Her legs are not straight, and Tanner wades back to correct her.

"She adores him," Hettie says under her breath.

"It's definitely mutual."

Hettie makes a check mark with her finger.

There was a list last night.

After the street party, I sat with Rue and Grayson and did the debrief. I needed at least one man to send home, and after the fun I had with all of them, it really felt like I was throwing one of them under a bus.

Hettie joined us, and when my hesitation was frustrating everyone, told me to make a list, because that's what I do.

Ria helped decide on the categories: attraction, connection, ease of the future, things in common, and kissing, to Grayson's dismay.

Ashton lost out on the future, and things in common. I wanted one more chance for kissing with Basher, which is why I only gave out one yellow rose.

Basher is still gone. No kiss for me.

"Two-minute warning, Tema," Hettie calls as Tema surfaces.

"Are you heading back?" Rand asks.

She nods. "Gunnar already left with Stella and Sophie and Lyra. And Bo wants to go to his place in Wabush for a few days, so we're headed there."

By the time Hettie gets back to Battle Harbour, this will all be over. I'll have made my decision. I might have found love.

Or I might be setting myself up for heartbreak if who I pick doesn't pick me back.

There's an uneasiness at the fact Hettie won't be around for that. She's always been there for the important decisions.

That might be because all the important decisions so far have been about her.

I have given up a lot for her and Tema, and while I don't regret it at all, it's time for me to come up with decisions that are mine. I need to make this one on my own.

Tema splashes to the side of the pool. "Say goodbye to Abigail," Hettie instructs.

Her face falls. "I don't know who you're picking," Tema pouts.

I don't know who I'm picking. But I lean forward. "You'll be the first I tell," I promise in a loud whisper.

"Maybe the second?" Hettie says under her breath, and Tanner laughs.

"She should definitely tell the princess first," he says, and Tema hugs his arm.

"Exactly, Sir Tanner."

Tanner beams, and all I can think is this man needs to spend more time with children because he is so good with them. "I'm Sir Tanner."

"Yes, you are."

Tema gets out of the water, and Rand gets her a towel. Hettie moves to supervise the drying off, leaving Tanner with me.

I try not to stare at the droplets on his chest. "Bad morning?" he asks.

"Wasn't the best," I admit. "But it had to be done."

"I'm glad it didn't happen to me. Thanks for that."

"Thanks for still wanting to be here."

"There's nowhere I'd rather be." He leans against the pool edge, strong arms on either side of my legs to cage me in. "Want to hang out today? Am I allowed to ask that?"

"Probably not."

"I'd still like to."

So would I. There's nothing more I would like to do but stay here with Tanner, enjoying the sun and the water, and maybe have him throw me around a little like he did with Tema.

That realization trips my heart.

I think that should go on the list.

"The powers that be will have work for me," I tell him ruefully. "I'll have to smile."

"And you're so bad at smiling." He brings his fingers to my lips and presses one against them. "It's one of my favourite things about you."

"It's nice to have something to smile about."

"Could I take that to mean me?"

"You should definitely take it to mean you, Sir Tanner." Before I can change my mind, and realize this isn't a good idea in front of an audience, I lean down to press my lips onto his.

It's only a moment, but I'd like it to last a lot longer.

That should go on the list too.

46

Rand

I get the first one-on-one date. These are the big ones because they may lead to an overnight stay.

Where we stay somewhere overnight. Together.

After I saw Abigail with Tanner this morning, I really thought it could be him.

I like Tanner. And if I wasn't in the running for her heart, I would like Tanner with Abigail. So as much as I like the guy, I need to figure out how to beat him.

We're still in charge of our own dates, so I ask Ria to organize a trip to Camille's bird sanctuary.

The next day, we leave right after lunch, meeting at the tiny runway to catch a flight over to the next island.

Abigail is dressed casually in cut-offs and a Green Day T-shirt, trading her purple frames for a pair of sunglasses that take up most of her face. She's got a unique style that I admire, mainly because it's so different from mine. I live in my khakis and polo shirts.

My sister used to tell me I was a grown-up version of Brian from The Breakfast Club.

I've never had the anxiety that the character did, but other than that, there are a lot of similarities. Smart; socially awkward at times.

I've always called myself a geek, but luckily, I've never been shoved into a locker.

But I've got the girl to myself today, and there's one in three chance that I end up as the last man standing.

Abigail motions me to the window of the plane. "Seals," she bubbles. "They never get old for me."

I really like her excitement. She's complex, but it's easy to make her happy.

I think I can make her happy.

Thoughts like that have been popping into my head for the last few days. I'm thinking of the future, and I'm thinking about what it would be like to have Abigail in my life on a full-time basis.

I'm not sure how she would feel about moving to Oshawa, though.

I know without asking that she will want to remain close to Tema, but I can't leave my sister. She relies on me, but it's more than that. She's a big part of my friend group.

I wouldn't want to leave my friends, because when you grow up more than a little socially awkward, it's not always easy to make more of them.

But what if Abigail doesn't want to leave Laandia? She got just back, so she might want to stay. What do we do then?

It's easier to look at the seals down below.

"Those are where the puffin nests are," Abigail points out as the plane banks for landing.

"Did you know that Saint Pierre was a big deal during Prohibition?" I ask.

"I did!" Abigail bounces her shoulders. "Al Capone used to stay at the hotel."

Finally, I've met someone who matches me in worthless trivia. "The same hotel we're staying at?"

"Maybe? I read it was Hotel Robert, but I think yours has gone through a lot of names, so it might be."

I nod. "I'll find out. Because it's a puzzle, and I like to solve them."

People are puzzles too, ones I'm not that good at solving. At least Abigail is easy and open, although there are a few things that I sense she doesn't want to talk about—the other men, and her past relationship with Spencer.

I don't blame her for not wanting to bring up the other men with me, because that would be uncomfortable for us both. I'm not in a rush to bring up past relationships because that means I'd have to share as well.

That could be something we could talk about tonight, out of sight of the cameras.

It's an easy landing, and an open Jeep waits at the airport for us. The Jeep is ancient, and it's a tight fit with Abigail and me, Johnny with his camera, and Ria to make sure we all behave, along with the driver. It might have been easier to walk.

Camille meets us at the rescue centre and gives us a tour.

I'm not sure what the relationship between Camille and Abigail was before the show started, but they are clearly friends now. Because of Abigail's closeness to Princess Hettie, I assumed she was close with the rest of the royal family as well.

But I saw her with Lyra last night, and it was clear there's not a lot of closeness there. It's obvious there's a warm friendship between Camille and Abigail. It's not Abigail and Hettie, but the two chat like old friends. And instead of feeling left out of their chatter, I'm right there in the middle of it because Abigail won't let go of my hand.

I like holding her hand.

We're there for the afternoon, and I learn more about birds and the Maritimes than I ever expected to. Camile has done an amazing job with the sanctuary.

I run through a beach full of seagulls with Abigail to give Johnny something fun to film.

After the flight back, where Camille joins us, I drop them off and head back to the hotel to change. Abigail is meeting me back here for a romantic dinner by the water and then…

I'm not sure what … will entail.

In other seasons, the Suitorette has had the opportunity for private time after dinner, getting the key to a special suite to spend the night, without the intrusion of the cameras. Grayson explained that we should take the time to talk about anything personal we don't want broadcast on the show. He said that most of the Suitorettes make up their minds based on what happens in the suite.

"Go for intimate, but that doesn't always mean physical," he told us. "This might be the last time for you to be vulnerable with each other, and that's a lot more important than making out all night."

Which is true, but no one should be knocking an all-night make-out session.

We had a romantic dinner at the hotel, but neither of us ate much. It's difficult when the cameras are fixed on you, plus both of us were talking a lot. The words kept tumbling out and over each other, but I couldn't tell you what was said. I talked about my sister a lot; Abigail told me about Laandia and how it felt coming back home.

Dinner was over all too soon, but not before Abigail picked up a card left on the table.

A suite in the hotel has been arranged for you, should you want to continue your night and deepen your connection.

"Do you want to have a sleepover?" Abigail asks with a grin.

"I do," I tell her automatically.

Do I want to? Absolutely.

Am I nervous about this and also feel awkward about how it's arranged for us? Also yes.

But I'm not about to turn down the opportunity.

By the time we get to the room, Abigail has picked up on my nerves. Or maybe she has nerves of her own, because she is quiet as we explore the luxury suite, standing on the balcony and staring out over the waves.

It was a relief to say goodnight to Johnny and the camera, but shutting the door on him means that this is the first time I'm totally alone with Abigail.

It's not all that comfortable.

"They left us snacks," I say, pointing to the fruit and cheese tray on the table.

"Great. I never eat during the dinners. I'm always afraid they'll get a picture of me eating with my mouth open."

"Do you often eat with your mouth open?"

"I've been known to," she replies with a grin. "Is that a deal-breaker?"

"I'd have to find out just how open your mouth is when you're eating."

The laughter breaks some of the tension. We eat crackers loaded with soft Brie and sharp cheddar, toss grapes to each other. Tell embarrassing dinner stories.

And then, things go quiet again.

"I thought this would be…" Abigail begins. "I didn't know what this would be like."

"Do you want to play Scrabble?"

Abigail looks at me with astonishment. "It would relax us," I say quickly. "It relaxes me. No pressure, because if you would rather—"

I see the relief in her expression, and if I weren't so overwhelmed at the thought of what tonight could mean, I would be overthinking that look on her face. "I would love to play Scrabble. But—"

I grab my bag by the door. "I carry a travel game. I have chess too."

"Scrabble. I play with Tema. She's improving her vocabulary."

"I've noticed she has an excellent vocabulary for an eight-year-old."

"Nine. Her birthday was in June."

I set up the board on the coffee table, and Abigail brings the snacks. We eat cheese and drink champagne and play Scrabble.

She starts with *bezoar*, which we playfully argue about until I discover that we're both Harry Potter fans, so I give it to her. I counter with *heart*.

The second game has me laying down *romance*, which is good because I use all my tiles, but brings up the uncertainty that maybe we should be doing something else.

"Best two out of three?" she asks after she wins the second game. I took the first game.

"Definitely."

I may be making a mistake in reading the room, but it seems like Abigail is happy with our game playing.

"Have you ever been in love?" Abigail asks as we pick tiles. I look up in surprise. "You had *romance* and *break* as words."

"You had *heart* and *pain*, so you tell me." She smiles as she drops her gaze. "You were in love with Spencer. Anyone else?"

She shakes her head. "I never really took the time to fall in love. And with Spencer, it was a friendship that became more."

"Sometimes those are the best ones."

Another shake of her head as she lays down the word *wander*. "It was convenient," she admits. "That wasn't the best."

"No. That could be like settling, which is never good."

"What about you? What's your sad love story?"

"How do you know it's sad?"

"Every love story has a sad ending, or you'd be still together. And you wouldn't be here on the show."

"And not here with you, so maybe it's a happy ending."

"Do you believe in no regrets, because the path gets to where you are in life?"

"Lyra didn't believe in regrets."

The name slips out before I can stop myself.

Abigail winces. "Were you in love with her?" she asks, trying for casual.

"I didn't know her well enough to fall in love with her," I tell her honestly. And I didn't. There might have been the beginning of feelings for me, but I never even got the opportunity to tell her about my sister.

"She was too busy with Spencer." Her voice is steady, without a trace of bitterness. Either she's a good pretender, or she's really over him.

"She had deeper connections with some of the other guys," I admit. "She and Ashton had something interesting. Tanner. Jon, but he left. He wasn't really into the whole reality show deal."

Her eyebrows raise. "Tanner and Lyra?"

I think I may have thrown him under the bus. "I'm not sure how strong the connection was. She did spend a lot of time with Spencer."

That might have made it worse.

"Why did you stay? You didn't know me, so you can't say that."

"I want to fall in love," I admit. "I've been in love once, and you're right—it didn't end well. She said I needed to get over my guilt about my sister's accident and stop focusing on her so much because I wasn't giving her enough attention."

"Ouch. I hope you told her to try thinking of other people for once."

"I do focus on my sister, and I probably wasn't giving her enough attention. Which was funny, because I felt like I was ob- sessed with her. I spent all this energy wondering if she was happy, what I could do to make her happier. How I could make her love me more."

"That doesn't sound like a healthy relationship."

"Oh, it wasn't. And I know that now, which is the only reason I'm telling you this. I can learn from my mistakes."

"That's good to know. I think I can too. I won't let myself settle for anyone. And I..." she pauses. "I have to start living for me. I need to make myself a priority."

"I get the feeling you weren't really doing that."

"I don't think I knew how. I've looked after Hettie for so long, and I didn't realize I didn't need to. She's perfectly capable of standing on her own two feet, especially now that she's back with Bo. I want to be a part of Tema's life, but I don't need to be there for Hettie as much as I was." She looks at me with surprise. "I think I just realized that."

"That's a good thing."

"I think it is. Thanks."

"For what."

Abigail laughs. "The Scrabble really helped."

47

Abigail

I WAKE UP BESIDE Rand, both of us still in our clothes and lying on top of the blankets.

Nothing happened.

A lot happened: I kicked his butt in the third game of Scrabble and declared myself the champion. But more than that, talking to him gave me the clarity I've been missing.

Only I didn't know I was missing it.

My head feels clearer, and I never realized it was so cluttered. I've always put people before me—not only Hettie, but my brothers. My parents. Growing up, I tried to take up less space, so they didn't have worry about me and could focus on my brothers.

I lay awake for a long time thinking about that last night.

I know now that I didn't need to do that. And they shouldn't have let me.

I still may not know what to do about the three men remaining, but I'm going to focus on what *I* want. Where I want to be, not what is convenient for others.

I don't want to be selfish, but I need to think of myself.

I can make decisions for myself, maybe for the first time.

"Good morning." Rand smiles with his lips tightly pressed together because—always a gentleman—he's aware of morning breath.

I angle my chin down so he doesn't get blasted with mine. "Morning."

"They're coming with the cameras soon," he reminds me.

I grimace. They want to film the morning after. Rand suggested leaving out the Scrabble so they can see that, leaving not much mystery about what we did—or didn't do— last night.

He's such a good guy.

Rand sits up. His hair is mussed even more than his linen shorts, lines from the pillow etched on his face. "What are the chances they'll bring coffee when they come?"

He's the first man I've ever slept beside, other than Spencer. We used to have sleepovers at my place in high school as a way for Hettie and Bo to have more time together. They would take my bed, and Spencer and I would make a nest on the floor with pillows and blankets. We would whisper together, trying not to laugh at the kissing sounds from above.

For the first time, I wonder if Spencer and I will be able to restart the friendship. Just friends, like we were always meant to be.

That's different. I'll give Rand credit for that.

"I hope we can always be friends," I say.

Rand freezes mid-stretch, and I realize what I've said.

"Friends?" he asks.

He does a good job keeping his voice steady.

"I mean..."

He turns to face me, shuffling back to put more distance between us. His smile is rueful.

He knows.

"You mean you want to be friends," he says. "This is the yellow rose moment."

"Rand... I'm sorry."

And I am. He's such a good man—honest and kind and sweet. I have fun with him, and I do feel a connection... but I don't think it's enough.

He shakes his head. "Don't be. I had such a good time with you last night. I'm glad you didn't say anything so I could have this." He sweeps his hand between us. "Waking up with you."

If I said this last night, neither one of us would be in this bed right now. I would have headed back to Camille's and Rand would have gone back to the hotel. He'd be gone by now.

But I didn't want to say anything last night. And I didn't mean to say anything now. It just... slipped out. But now that it's out there, the word *friends* hanging between us like a clothesline, it feels right.

I should have said something last night. I don't want to lead Rand on.

"Last night was amazing. And so... helpful."

He chuckles. "That's what I want to be. The helpful friend."

"Rand..."

"It's okay, Abigail. It's been good between us, but it's missing something for you. I get it."

"You think...?"

"I think we could have a chance, but I'm not the one making the decisions here."

A knock on the door sounds. "I'm going to ask them to give us a minute."

"No need, especially if they brought coffee. You made your decision, and I respect it. I respect you."

"Thank you."

He gets up to answer the door and throws a sad smile at me. "Doesn't mean I have to like it."

The cameras arrive and put us to work pretending that we woke up. They ask both of us to change into sleep attire, so I guess having us in our clothes from yesterday spoils the mystery of *did-we-or-didn't-we*.

Again, we didn't.

But then we have to film where I tell him I wouldn't be picking him in the end. That I thought it was time for him to go home.

It's so hard to do again. I manage to find better words to soften the blow—and it is a blow for Rand. I knew it would be. That's why I wasn't going to say anything... until I did.

It's better that way, but it still hurts. For me as well as Rand.

I cry.

It takes a couple of hours to finish, and by that time all I want to do is run from the cameras. From Rand's hurt expression—he tries to be stoic, but I can tell he's upset.

There's absolutely nothing I can do about that.

I have to make the choice that's right for me.

48

Rand

I DIDN'T EXPECT TO be sent home after last night.

I knew it was a possibility, especially since there was... limited... physical activity. But we have—had—a connection. At least I thought we did.

"Are you surprised?" Grayson asks after they let Abigail go. They told me they wanted to get my reactions, any insight about the process.

Talking about it helps.

Talking about it on camera does not.

"I am... but no. I really like Abigail. I care about her. I'm falling—was falling for her, and I honestly thought we could have a future. We've got the same ideals and values. We're both teachers." I laugh. "Although that might not be a good thing." I sigh. "We had a good friendship."

"That's important to you?"

"I thought it was. But looking back, I think the friendship took centre stage. The big earth-shaking moments of falling in love weren't there. And I think it's okay if you ease in, because it's not the intensity that keeps you going."

"That's what you believe?"

"I do." I pause. "I did. But I don't think Abigail does. I think she wants the big—" I press my fingers together and then push them apart. "I think she wants the big boom. And I really hope she gets it." I stare out the window at the waves. "This has been my first time in the Maritimes. It's a beautiful place."

"Do you think you'll come back?"

How long will it take for the thought of Saint Pierre to lose the bittersweet tang, like a perfectly nice cup of tea with an espresso bean dropped in? Where I met the girl, and lost the girl, and met another girl, only to lose her too.

"I think so," I manage. "Someday."

49

Abigail

I TAKE THE STAIRS down to the lobby after they finish filming me. I'm hollowed out, wrung dry from last night, from this morning.

I didn't mean to tell Rand then.

But I didn't know when else I was going to tell him.

There are three men—now only two—left. By this point in the process, I should know who I want and be narrowing it down to the last two.

I guess that's what I did.

Would Rand have made it to the final two if I hadn't been swept away in a haze of friendship?

He might have, depending on how the next few days go. But deep down, I know I wasn't going to pick Rand unless I needed a safety net. Because Rand was the safe bet. I would be happy with him, but I might have been settling.

That's not fair to Rand, and it's not fair to me. It was good, but it was missing something. A spark that would have ignited something more, something that would have been more than comfortable and convenient.

That's not what I want. If I've learned anything, it's that I want a spark. Fire.

More heat.

And I don't want to slide into anything again. I want that *hold-your-breath* moment when I see him. I want that heady feeling when you make the leap into the pool.

I want to leap. I'm ready for a leap.

I left Rand in the suite with Ria and Johnny and Grayson, to tell his side of our story.

All I want to do is have a few hours to decompress. My date with Jonas isn't until tomorrow, and I like how they give a day in between. I'm sure the men are impatient to have it over, after being sequestered here in the hotel for—

Tanner.

Halfway down the stairs, I see him coming through the doors, sweaty and disheveled, like he's been running. I'm not staring—really—but I can't turn away as he lifts the hem of his shirt to wipe at his face, giving me a glorious view of muscles and abs and Tanner torso.

"Hi," I call, my voice sounding a little strangled from the attempt to look away.

Thirst trap. I understand what that means now.

"Abigail."

His smile is wide and welcoming, and he snags a bottle of water from the cooler by the desk before meeting me at the bottom of the staircase.

"Hey," he says. "I'd hug you, but I'm a little sweaty. Again." He opens the bottle and drinks, and I wonder if he knows just how attractive he is. Tall and broad—on skates, he would have been a menace to the opposing team, but here, standing taller than I am, even if I'm two steps above him...

He makes my stomach tighten. He makes my knees weak. He makes me smile.

"We have to stop meeting like this," he adds.

"Uh... yeah." Yes, he is sweaty. Yes, I would still like a hug.

"How was your date?" Tanner asks and my smile fades.

One of the most surreal aspects of this experience—and there are so many—is how it feels being the sole guests in the hotel.

It's open for us. People work here for us.

Granted, I don't think they've had the grand reopening after the renovations, but it still feels strange to have the run of the place.

But not as strange as Tanner asking how my date with Rand was. Granted, it's more like a colleague asking how my weekend was rather than a bestie wanting all the details, but still—strange. Awkward.

And because of this, I sit down on the stairs.

"Do you really want to know?"

Tanner slumps beside me. "Not really, but I think it's better to know, then to let my imagination run wild."

I get that. When I heard Spencer came on the show, I concocted so many scenarios between him and Lyra. The first week, I drove myself crazy thinking about what they might have been doing.

I'm sure the reality was far tamer.

"I don't know what I'm allowed to tell you," I admit.

"You don't have to tell me anything." He tries to smooth his expression, but there's a worry furrow between his brows. "It's none of my business."

"It's kind of your business," I counter. I touch his knee, still radiating heat like he's a furnace. If I tell him Rand is going home, that tells him he just made the final two. Am I allowed to say that? Is that against my contract or something?

No one is here, but I glance around the lobby like Grayson will pop up and drag me away before I can say anything.

"Yeah." His shoulders hunch and he blows out his breath in a frustrated gust.

I think my bumping into him just ruined his day.

I don't like that.

I don't like that when I leave him, he's going to imagine everything that might have happened with me and Rand, and it will twist in his stomach like a snake.

I don't want that for him, especially after our moment by the pool the other day

"I can tell you what *didn't* happen," I say softly before I can stop myself.

When Tanner looks up, I open my eyes as wide as I can.

It takes him a moment to get it. "Oh. *Oh.*" The relief on his face is instantaneous, and kind of cute. It's a little disloyal to Rand, but it's not like he's going to tell the others something happened when it really didn't. That's not Rand.

"Okay..." He's really trying not to smile, which makes *me* smile. "I'm not sure what to say to that."

"Maybe don't say anything at all."

"Yeah." He takes a deep breath, and I hide my smile. I don't want him to worry, but I can't help the relief that washes over *me* that he *was* worried.

This is all so weird.

"What did you do last night?" I've always wanted to ask what the men do here when they're not with me.

"Hung out in my room. They don't let us watch TV, but we can stream stuff."

"What did you watch?"

Tanner looks like I've caught him with a stash of candy during training. "I finished the third season of The Morning Show."

"Really? I wouldn't have thought you'd be into that." No sports, no rough-and-tumble action, but a drama with strong women in the leads?

Tanner is more than sports and rough-and-tumble action.

"I've always had a thing for Reese Witherspoon," he admits and I laugh.

Then it fades. "Were you in love with Lyra?" My question is direct, abrupt, and maybe not the best timing.

Tanner looks at me with surprise. "I... I don't know. I don't think so," he stammers.

"I shouldn't ask —"

The plastic bottle creaks and cracks as he squeezes it. "Yes. You should. You definitely should. I cared about her." He gathers his thoughts, and I wonder if he's filtering words so I won't be hurt. "But it wasn't love. It was more than like, but not love. And it might never have turned into love. But I did like her."

I nod. Did I need to know that? Yes, because the last barrier between us melts away.

"But she's gone, and you're here. And I feel very differently about you."

I feel dizzy, and my smile keeps widening. I shouldn't be smiling because Tanner came here to find love with Lyra, and it didn't work out.

That shouldn't be a good thing.

But it is, because it means he's still here with me.

I move closer, wanting to tuck myself against his warmth, but... still sweaty. "How do you feel about me?" I ask, letting an odd, flirtatious tone in. It's like opening an old door, and I have to tug on it.

And it creaks.

Tanner smiles at the attempt, but he's all seriousness. "I think you know how I feel about you. At least I hope you do."

I nod. Hearing this is good, but it adds to the mess I need to sort out. Rand told me how he felt, and I didn't share my feelings. I can't share now.

But I want to.

I want to stop the furrow from deepening between Tanner's eyes. I want him to stop imagining the worst.

Not yet. I can't say anything yet.

Tanner realizes I'm not going to share and finishes the water in a last gulp. "So. Date with Jonas tomorrow?"

I nod. "And then you, with a day in between."

"I don't know if I can wait that long." He's serious, but not creepy serious.

I promised myself that I wouldn't tell more than one man how I feel about them until I know how this is going to end up. And I don't know—it's as if the end is visible, but not clear. I still need to decide some things, figure out the real direction my heart is pointing. And I think I owe it to all the men to give them equal chances.

But there is a reason I kept Tanner for the last.

"I saved you for the last, because I'm the most certain about you," I tell Tanner. "At least I am, now that I've got the Lyra stuff out of the way."

"You should be certain about me." Tanner moves closer, cups my cheek. "I'm all the way there, Abigail. I'm not just falling for you—I'm falling in love. I see a future with you, and I really hope you see it too."

I bite my lip so I don't say anything. Because I want to. I want to say a lot.

Instead, I lean in, sweat or no sweat. Rand, or no Rand. And I kiss Tanner right there on the stairs.

The two of us alone in the lobby, with cameras off filming Rand talking about my date with him, and how he feels about me.

I don't think about that.

I think about Tanner, how his lips feel moving against mine. His arm, steady at my back, his fingers caught in messy curls.

How he shifts, deepens the kiss. How I want to crawl into his lap and hang on, staying there as long as I can.

I kiss him like the kisses can tell him what he deserves to know. What I'm not able to tell him.

Yet.

And then I leave him, because I have to plan for my next date with Jonas.

50

Jonas

THEY LEFT IT UP to me to plan the date with Abigail, but they won't let me do anything I want to do. I suggested flying her to Boston, to Toronto, even St. John's, but they said no.

I'm not used to the word no. And I don't like it.

Because I can't do anything I want to, I decide to spend the day at the beach with her. I saw how happy she was during the fish roll, so I know she likes it.

I plan a little picnic with wine and cheese—surprisingly, Saint Pierre has a nice selection of both—and the assistant packs it in a basket for me.

As I wait for my ride, another of the assistants comes to find me. "We had a message from your brother, Prince Mathias."

"Because you confiscated my phone," I say coolly. I'm a prince of Laandia and they took my phone like I'm a fifth-grader cheating on a test.

"Yes, well those are the rules, which you were told going in." She tries to match my tone, but obviously can't.

I think her name is Rue.

"Prince Mathias informed us that he will be arriving on the four o'clock ferry and would like to join you for dinner," Assistant

Rue continues. "We've already made arrangements for your dinner with Abigail."

"What? He's coming?"

"On the four o'clock ferry."

"But what about dinner with Abigail? This was my one night with her."

"And your brother will be joining you for dinner. It's a great way to introduce family. After dinner—" Is it my imagination, or is she looking down her nose at me? "That's all on you."

"Thank you," I say to dismiss her, because no one needs to witness how that little change has sent me reeling.

Mathias is... he's my older brother. That's all I should have to say about that, but there's so much more.

He thinks our father should be king. We both do, but it's more with Mathias because if our father had received the crown from his father, then Mathias would be the Crown Prince, first in line for the throne.

Instead, Magnus is king, and Kalle is first in line.

It's how it is, but no one needs to be happy about that.

But Mathias is coming here, ostensibly to give me his opinion of Abigail. I don't need it, or really want it, but my big brother thinks he knows more than anyone else.

The car arrives for me, and I stop thinking about my brother because Abigail is in the back seat waiting for me.

I like her more than I expected to.

She's... refreshing. Not like any of the other women I've dated, who made it clear that they were looking to elevate their status by beginning a relationship with me.

I understood that mentality because, before Abigail, I looked for women who could do something for me, whether it guaranteed media coverage, an introduction to someone, or to gather information on businesses or people I was interested in.

Yes, I have used women. I don't regret it because they use me too.

Abigail isn't like that. At least if she is, she's very good at hiding it, maybe better than anyone I've ever seen.

"Hi," she says cheerfully as I climb into the SUV.

I can't help but notice the dark circles under her eyes, and the sight of them leaves me with an unsettled feeling in my stomach.

They have us separated in the hotel now, secluded so we can't talk about the overnight dates.

We also don't know who is still here. At least I don't.

I know Ashton left, and Basher followed. I don't know the reason for this, because he didn't get a yellow rose. No clue if it was his decision, or Abigail told him to go, nor do I really care.

I didn't come here to make friends.

With Basher and Ashton gone, that leaves only three of us. I've got a one in three chance to be the last man standing.

I don't say anything as I get in the car; instead I lean in to claim a kiss. We've kissed before, but this is impromptu, and not being filmed, so I take advantage of it. Abigail isn't pulling away, so I deepen the kiss, my hand twining in her curls to cradle her head.

As soon as her hand finds my arm, I pull back. "Hello," I say in a husky voice.

"Hi," she manages, a little breathless.

From my kiss, I think smugly. "You already said that."

"I... yes." It's nice to see her smile is even brighter than when I got in the car.

"Ready for a beach day?" I ask her, moving back to buckle my seat belt. As soon as it's locked, I reach for her hand.

"Yes," she says, looking at the way our fingers lace together.

"No fish today," I warn.

"I love the capelin roll," she tells me.

"I... do not," I say regretfully.

"Do you spend a lot of time outside?"

"I like to ski. And we have a cottage in Ontario. I spend time outside when I'm there. Are you an outdoor person?" I ask, almost as an afterthought.

"Enough, I guess."

We're spending the day outside. I hope that's enough for her.

We arrive at the spot I picked for us. The fish are gone, save for the odd carcass that didn't make it back into the water and is now picked apart by the birds, but the smell lingers.

I'm not used to being close to the ocean, since the family home is on the other side of Laandia. There's no fishing there, only forests.

I'm also not big on trees.

We walk along the shore, covered with tiny pebbles, so I keep my shoes on. Abigail seems to want to know more about me, asking how I spend my time in Toronto.

I tell her about the theatres, the museums, the club where I play squash. The society I'm part of. The nightlife.

"You like living there?" she asks.

"I do."

"Would you consider coming back to Laandia?"

"Is that what you expect?" I counter.

It's taken Abigail this long to ask about relocating. I don't know if that's a good thing she's asking about it now, or if she's looking to rule me out because I want to stay in Toronto.

Which I do. It's far enough from my family. I have friends there. I'm established.

"I'm not sure," Abigail admits. "I'm at a cross-road right now. Or maybe it's more one of those big highways in the city where there are all these lanes, and ways to get off and on."

"Have you ever seen one of those highways?"

"I have but Vancouver traffic wasn't as bad as Toronto. From what I've heard."

"So you're saying there are options as to where you end up?"

"I always thought I'd want to stay close to Battle Harbour, but now...now I'm not too sure. That might not be the best for me. I'm trying to put myself first."

"I think that's a good idea. You're not tied to Battle Harbour. To the castle." I can't keep the bitterness out of my tone, at the thought of losing her because she needs to be close to the family.

It's good that she puts herself first, but I hope I'm more of a priority than cousin Bo and his wife and child.

I can offer her more than they can.

It's true that some of the resentfulness toward my cousins has dimmed with the time I've spent with them. It's starting to wash away, like the rolling bodies of fish, but there's still some bitterness that lingers like the smell.

I consider the topic closed by the time we head back for the picnic. I've made my arguments for moving to Ontario, and Abigail seems excited at the thought.

But as I lay out the food, and pour her wine, she seems distracted.

"You seem to have a lot on your mind," I say when she doesn't respond to my smile as I hand her a cracker topped with Brie.

"It's..." She bites her lip as she searches for the words. "It's a lot," she finishes.

I take it to mean being on the show. We're nearing the end, and she needs to make the hard decisions. It's what she signed up for, but she had to know it would end like this.

There can only be one at the end, and I hope she guarded her heart.

I hope she narrowed her choice at the beginning, or else this might be very difficult. It always is when emotions are involved.

Which is why I prefer leaving emotions off the table.

It must be a lot, finding the words to send the other men home.

I've never once considered that it will be me that she will need to find the words for.

I haven't paid that much attention to Abigail's connections with the other men, but I can't imagine what they have is stronger than the one I have with her.

Plus, I can offer her so much more than anyone else here.

"You mean sending the others home?" I ask.

Abigail seems confused at the question. "Sending the others?"

"Well, yes. It must be a lot. What to say and how to say it."

She nods, dropping her chin to study the ant who has braved the picnic blanket in search of a snack.

I squash it with my thumb.

When Abigail looks up, her expression has shuttered, like she's bracing herself. "You've never told me how you feel about me, Jonas."

Where did that come from? We were talking about the other men. Sending the other men home.

"Shouldn't I have that information before I decide to send anyone home?" she continues. "About all of you?"

"What have they said?" I demand.

"This is about you and me. I've spoken to the others. All except... you."

For the first time since I arrived, unease gives a twist. "I'm not one to discuss emotions. Especially on camera." I flick my gaze to where the cameraman is filming all of this.

I want to tell him to put it down, to stop.

"But that's the whole point of the show. To be vulnerable. To be open and honest."

"What do you want to be open and honest about?"

"I've been waiting for *you* to do that," she admits.

"Me? I told you about my family. Cooking. What else—?"

She rests her chin in her hands with a sad smile. "Have you ever been in love, Jonas? Have you ever told a woman you love them?"

"I... no," I confess.

"Do you think that love is important in a relationship?"

"I think there's a lot that matters in a relationship. Trust, and respect, and communication."

"But not love?"

I realize now that I've dug myself into a hole. Abigail wants me to confess my love for her, and I... can't.

I've never done that because I've never been in love. I've been with women I respect and admire. No one I've really trusted. I've kept my distance, and it's worked out for the best.

But the way Abigail is looking at me, I wonder if she sees that as a detriment, and not something to be proud of.

"Love is..." For once, I'm at a loss. How to you describe the importance of something I've never known?

"It is," she finishes, nodding like she understands it completely.

Maybe she does. Maybe her relationship with Spencer had been more than just for show. It could have gone deeper than I realized.

That I could understand.

I never asked her about it because I didn't think I needed to.

I lift a shoulder. I feel like I've taken a wrong turn and there's no way for me to right my course.

I need a work-around. I need to be open and honest—like Abigail wants—or this is going to turn very badly, very quickly. "Abigail, you need to know that I come from a family that doesn't emphasize the importance of love."

For the first time, there's an emptiness as I say it.

My parents may have loved each other once, but it's about how they tolerate each other now. My sister is engaged to an Italian duke, and she loves her new villa more than him. And even my brother Mathias—he wanted to marry Edie England not because he loved her but because he had some old-fashioned view about he could save her from working as a bar manager.

And also, steal her away from cousin Kalle. Mathias wanted Edie before Kalle woke up and realized he did.

Kalle and Edie are now planning a royal wedding, so Mathias lost out on that plan.

Love has never been on my radar. Ever.

But now...

"If you were going to propose to me," Abigail begins, toying with the edge of the blanket. "*If*. What would you say?"

I take a deep breath. I have thought about this because I assumed I would make it to the end. I spent many nights crafting the perfect proposal.

All the words seem to have vanished now.

"I would say I could make you happy," I begin, mind racing, trying to remember the bullet points. "That I could see my future, and you are a big part of it. That I want to share my life with you, share my privilege and position, and how it could open doors for you, for whatever you wanted to do."

Abigail bites her lip, her attention on the waves.

It's not exactly how I thought she'd react. I must have forgotten more than I thought.

"Do you know what I want to do?" she asks, instead of reacting to my practice proposal.

"Teaching," I say, because I do remember the things she had mentioned about herself. "But I thought you would change your mind."

She sucks in a breath. "You thought... really?"

"It's a fine position, but for someone of my status? There are better uses of your position."

"Because a teacher and a prince doesn't make sense?"

"No, thinking that you would have to work doesn't make sense. I can take care of you, Abigail." I take her hand and, for once, her fingers don't curve into mine. "Let me take care of you. You looked after Hettie and Bo's daughter for years, and you don't have to do that anymore. Let me."

She finally returns my smile, but something is missing. "That's a sweet offer."

"I mean every word. This is what I want to do for you."

"I've no doubt you do. But I don't need to be looked after." She pulls her hand away. "I'm very capable of looking after myself. I'm very good at it, actually. What I do want is someone to love me. Passionately. Unconditionally. You may be a prince, but I want the fairy tale." She smiles sadly. "And I don't think you can give it to me."

"Fairytales are made up stories," I argue. "What I can give you is so much more. What's love compared to opportunities? Experiences? A life of luxury."

"It's so much more when love is the experience that I'm looking for."

51

Abigail

Jonas doesn't get it.

There is more I say, about how I came on the show to find love, not opportunities. That what he can offer me isn't as important as finding a man who feels the same way about me.

I honestly think I care more about Jonas than he cares about me.

I finally walk away, leaving him on the beach. There will be no dinner with his brother, no overnight date.

Jonas is no longer in the running for my heart because he's not capable of giving his in return.

And that makes me sad for him.

I saw something in him at the beginning—a sliver of vulnerability, a glimpse of the man he could be. That still might be there, but I don't have the time to dig it out.

Nor do I want to.

Rand is gone. Jonas is leaving. That leaves Tanner.

"Is Tanner your choice?" Rue asks me on the drive back to Camille's. "He's the only one left."

A cold hand of fear grips me. One man remaining. What if he doesn't choose me? What if I've narrowed it down to one, and he was the wrong one?

And then I remember the way Tanner smiles at me.

"He is." And the fear is still there, but so is relief that this is almost over.

And happiness that it's Tanner. Excitement.

"When can I tell him?"

"We can push up your date to tomorrow."

"Does he know the others have left? Are leaving?"

Rue shakes her head. "We've separated them with no contact."

"So Tanner has been on his own this whole time without anyone to talk to?"

"It's how we did it this time."

"It's not a good way to do anything." The way he worried about me and Rand— Tanner must be going crazy imagining what was happening between me and Jonas.

"What if I don't want to wait?"

Rue smiles. "Be patient for another day. You'll get him soon. And I'm glad. He was always my first choice."

"What about him being the Suitor?"

"He might have been up for that in the beginning, but last time we talked to him, he didn't want any part of it. And he didn't want you to know that he even considered it. He thought it might upset you."

It did upset me, but I'm not telling Rue that.

I'm too busy making plans.

And the plans don't involve my waiting until tomorrow.

After we get back to Camille's, we do the recap. I tell them in no uncertain terms that Jonas is no longer in the running. Grayson still wants to keep him here so we can push the anticipation for the viewers wondering who I will pick.

I refuse because I don't want to pretend. I also don't think I can act like that with Jonas.

I'm upset with him.

I kept Jonas here, over Ashton, over so many others, because I saw something in him. That something is gone now. He's...

I don't want to even think about what he's missing. Because he's missing out on so much.

I'd rather think of Tanner.

I head to my room, leaving Grayson with Rue and Ria to plan the next day's date.

I don't want another date with Tanner. I just want to be with him. I want to tell him how I feel, and I really hope he feels the same.

I *really* hope he does.

After I go to my room, I sneak back down to find Camille in her office and tell her my plan.

Which is why I now find myself on a bicycle, heading along the road to the hotel.

The island is small, and it's not far from the prefect's house to the hotel, but I make two wrong turns and there are more rolling hills than I expected.

I'm a little sweaty when I finally arrive.

For the first time, there's no welcoming committee to greet me. The hotel is deserted, the lobby empty and echoing.

I have no idea where to find Tanner. If he's even here. He could be out for another run. I wish I had asked Rue about what he's been doing to give me an idea, because I don't want to wander around in case I run into Jonas.

That would... that's about the last thing I want to do right now.

All I can think of is finding Tanner.

That's when I hear the quiet splash.

Please don't let it be Jonas, I beg as I make my way to the pool area.

And it isn't.

Being the Suitorette has been a challenge in so many ways. I've questioned my reasons for being here, done a lot of painful soul-searching, questioned myself. I've second-guessed myself more times than I care to admit.

But when I see Tanner in the pool, water streaming down that chest, there's no second-guessing.

And once he sees me walking toward him, the smile on his face tells me that sharing how I feel with Tanner is going to be the easiest thing I've done since I've been here.

"Abigail," he calls.

It's time for the jump.

And I do.

52

Tanner

"**W**HAT ARE YOU DOING here?" I demand.

Abigail is *here*.

In the pool with me.

She should be with Jonas. They should be on their date, with Jonas doing everything he can to make Abigail believe he cares about her. Is in love with her?

I honestly don't know how Jonas feels about her. I can't imagine how he isn't falling in love with her.

But Jonas is nowhere in sight, and Abigail is in the pool with me. She just stepped over the edge, still in her clothes.

"You've still wearing your shoes," I explain.

"I didn't want to wait," she says. I think for a moment that she's going to hug me, but stops herself.

"Wait for what? Where's Jonas?"

"I told him to go home."

It takes a moment for me to fully comprehend her words. I'm still in awe that she's here—not a lot of women would jump into a pool fully dressed.

And camera-ready, I realize. She wears a black sleeveless romper that would be perfect for a date with Jonas.

She told Jonas to go home.

It takes a moment for me to understand, and another to find my voice. "And Rand?"

"Him too. I don't know if he's left yet, but he's... I told him it was only friendship. I said—"

"I don't care what you said, as long as you didn't tell him you're in love with him," I burst out.

Abigail shakes her head. "I haven't said that to anyone."

Okay, that's a good thing, but...

"I told myself I wasn't going to tell anyone how I felt until I knew for sure," she continues. "And until there was only one man left. The man that I pick."

My heart stops. Literally stops and then starts double speed. If Abigail is here, if Rand and Jonas have left, then I'm... maybe this means...

I stare at Abigail. There are smudges under her eyes from her mascara. As I gently try to thumb away a smear, I notice the tears in her eyes.

Tears... what does that mean?

"Who's that?" I ask in a slow voice. "Who do you pick?"

I'm a little slow at getting there, but I want to make sure.

But then Abigail smiles, and I know. The whole world will know if they see the way she smiles at me.

"You," she says.

She tries to say something else, but I don't let her. I cup her face—with tears streaming down her cheeks, making the smears of mascara worse, that beautiful, beautiful face that I *love*—and I kiss her.

I kiss her with body and soul and as much of my heart I can fit into a kiss.

And she... laughs.

"I have things I need to say," she tries against my lips.

"I have things I need to do," I tell her.

"It's good things," she protests, her hands gripping my arms.

"This is a good thing too. Four weeks." I give her four kisses, one for each week I've waited. "And four before that."

"You didn't even know me."

"I've waited my whole life for you, Abigail. I don't want to wait a moment longer."

"That's what I thought too. That's why I'm in the pool."

She gives in to my persistence, saving everything she wants to say—that I want to say—for later.

After Grayson finds us kissing in the pool.

53

Grayson

IT TAKES TWO DAYS to film the final scene.

When I realized Abigail had snuck out of Camille's, I knew exactly where she went.

So maybe I didn't rush over as quickly as I could have.

Abigail only wanted Tanner, and that was obvious to all. But I still had a show to finish.

We gave them the night together, to talk, to plan. To say all the things they needed to say to each other. The next day, I put on my producer's hat and told them what I needed of them.

Which basically involved some acting, and trying to rein in the happiness that was spilling out of both of them.

I met with both of them individually—which was surprisingly difficult, since they didn't want to leave each other's side—and planned the finale with Rue and Ria, sorting out through the hours of footage to see what we could use to fill in the space the final date would have taken up.

Neither Abigail nor Tanner wanted one last date. They wanted out of the reality bubble to move on into real life together.

I heard mention of Battle Harbour. Of Halifax. I overheard Abigail suggest Tanner join her in teacher's college. I heard talk of the future, of not wanting to wait.

Of wanting to start their life together... *now.*

I had no clue that Abigail was so impatient.

But finally, after one last long night at Camille's, we're here, watching Tanner tell Abigail how he's fallen in love with her.

Abigail tells Tanner she knew it was going to be him the day at the beach. And how she wanted to tell him that she was falling in love with him every time she saw him.

Especially when she saw him coming back from a run.

I let them both plan out what they wanted to say, to make it as seamless as possible. My editing team is first-rate, but they had their work cut out for them to make up for the lack of a final date—until Johnny came to me with the footage he had secretly filmed of Abigail jumping into the pool.

It turned out to be a good season.

And this will only make it better.

I watch with a smile of affection as Tanner drops to one knee. I let them work out what they wanted to say, but we kept this part quiet from Abigail because Tanner wanted her to be surprised.

And I wanted to show that surprise to the viewers.

I helped Tanner decide on the ring.

Abigail drops to her knees before Tanner, and I wince at the possible damage to the dress.

I helped Abigail decide on the dress to wear.

I have no idea how the two of them decided anything without me to help.

It takes another hour of breaking into the hugs and happiness to get the last shots we need of Abigail and Tanner. I finally let them go with my heartfelt good wishes and a promised invitation to the wedding.

There is only one last thing for me before wrapping this season.

"Abigail has found love with Tanner," I say into the camera. "And there is no one wishing her the very best more than the ones who have watched the process from the beginning. Tanner and Abigail might have had a few rocky patches over the last few weeks, but there is no doubt in anyone's mind that they are meant to be together." I gesture off camera. "And I'm not the only one who thinks that." I smile at the man who joins me. "Rand? How do you feel about Abigail finding her happily ever after—and with someone who isn't you?"

We ran through this bit a few times so Rand could find the poise he wanted.

"I'm honestly so happy for them both." Rand's voice even and sincere. "Tanner is a great guy, and Abigail... Abigail is amazing. I wish them all the best, and hope they have a wonderful life together."

"I'm so glad to hear you say that," I say. "And I honestly can't wait to help you find your own happily ever after—as the next Suitor!"

Epilogue

Ashton

I'M HAPPY TO HAVE my phone back.

I don't bother checking the unread texts waiting for me but hit social media first to find out what I've missed. It's been weeks since I've heard anything other than the latest goings-on in Saint Pierre, and that's not all that exciting.

Yes, I had a phone, but other than texting Fenella, I didn't actually look at it much.

It's like I wanted to follow the rules.

So not me.

It's not as though being trapped in the reality-world bubble for weeks has changed me or anything. I'm still me, same as I ever was.

I got dumped. Abigail told me she couldn't see a future with me, and I...

I still don't know what I am yet.

I'd rather go back to reading the drama Lavinia unleashed on Threads, or scroll through pictures of Coral's latest travel adventure on Insta.

Or even watch the waves as Saint Pierre grows smaller behind me.

They said the ferry from Saint Pierre to Newfoundland took an hour and a half, but it feels like it's already been longer than that.

I don't want to watch the town vanish into the Gulf of St Lawrence because the further away I get, the further I am from Abigail.

And that's like salt in the wound.

Abigail told me to leave. She's dead to me.

She's really not.

I managed to get hold of Gunnar as I was boarding the ferry, and he's going to pick me up and fly me to Battle Harbour to see my sister.

I don't have anywhere else I need to be. Or want to go.

I don't even want to be back with Abigail either. She made her decision, and it wasn't me. I'm not one to beg, or even chase a woman. If she doesn't want me, so be it. I'm over it.

It sounds so easy in my head.

In my heart... well, that's another story. A story that's confusing, and hurts a little. There's regret and resentment, and there's a flicker of happiness.

I liked her. I truly liked her.

I never thought that was possible.

But I don't want to think about Abigail, or what I lost out on. I honestly wish her the best.

I hope she's happy... even knowing it'll be with someone other than me. Tanner or Rand...

Someone sits on the bench beside me. Too close; he's actually invading my personal space. But when I glance over—

"Shouldn't you be on a date or something?" I drawl.

Basher grins, his fingers tapping in a silent rhythm. Silent to me, but he can obviously hear it, like a dog can hear different frequencies. "It was never going to work for us," he says ruefully.

His smile is a little sad.

"You don't know that," I tell him, sliding along the bench. Basher's a great guy, but he's seriously too close.

"You saw the way she looked at Tanner," Basher says. "And Rand. And even Jonas. No moony eyes with me."

I sigh. "Same. Although I don't know what moony eyes are. Sounds like a cow."

"More sexy than cow eyes."

"Anything is sexier than a cow," I point out. "So, you just walked out?"

"I told her first."

"Was she upset?"

"...No." Basher winces. "That told me something right there. Sure, she seemed sad, but she didn't tell me not to go."

"At least you got to miss out on her telling you to go," I point out.

"A bit bitter, are we?"

"No." And then I shake my head. "Well, yeah, but it's cool. I know why she did it."

"You have too much money," Basher says as casually as if we're talking about the sky being blue.

"You have money too," I accuse.

Basher slowly holds up nine fingers, one at a time, like he's counting. Billions. I get it.

"She didn't pick me because I'm too cute," he decides. "Also—famous."

"I'm famous too."

"You have more money than fame. I'm more famous than rich. Abigail needs someone normal to fall in love with."

"Someone without a crown," I agree.

"Rand is perfect for her," he says. "But I don't think it will be him."

"No?" Do I care who Abigail ends up with? She didn't pick me, so what business is it of mine?

"Who do you think it'll be?" Basher asks.

"If it's not me, I honestly don't care."

I do care. I may not want to right now, but I do. But it's like I'm still on camera—I'm not about to tell Basher how I really feel.

Mainly because I don't know how I feel. One minute my heart feels too heavy for my chest, and the next I'm jumping with relief at still being unattached.

"Yeah," Basher says heavily. "Same. But I think it'll be Tanner."

"Well, we'll find out in a couple of days if you're a psychic." The thought of Abigail with anyone other than me...

Yeah. We had fun, but I'm good. And I want her to be happy. That should be my concern, not feeling sorry for myself. I've never been in love before, and it was stupid of me to think it was going to happen on a reality show.

"So where you headed?" Basher asks. "The wide world is your oyster. Is that what they say?"

I frown. "Maybe?"

"What's the plan, Stan? Things to do, people to see?"

"What's with all the clichés?"

Basher shrugs. "I kinda don't know what to do now. I've got a couple of weeks before I have to head back to start prepping. I planned on hanging with Abigail and getting to know her better, but now..."

"You think you're going to hang out with me?" It comes across as brusque, rude almost, but Basher's eyes widen at the thought.

"Well... yeah."

"Yeah?"

"Why not? Where we headed?"

"Battle Harbour. Laandia."

Basher stretches out his legs in the seat next to me, hands now tapping on his legs. "Cool. I'm in."

I don't think I asked him. But I don't tell him not to come with me.

Ashton and Basher in Laandia??
Find out more in Babysitting the Grumpy Billionaire!
And there is more Love in Laandia to come—Royal Revelry, coming in 2026. Subscribe my newsletter for the BONUS EPILOGUE that will give you a peak at who's story is coming!!

Thank You!

A HUGE **THANK YOU** to all the readers who wanted *more Laandia*!

When I first started, I only planned for five books in the series. But you made it clear—there are more Laandians whose stories *must* be told. *Royal Replacement* is book six, and I already have three more planned. (I'm not spilling who yet, so don't even ask... but you'll find out soon enough!) After that... well, my lips are sealed.

Fun Facts about Royal Replacement

I had no clue who Abigail would end up with! I'm a mix of plotter and pantser, and for this book, the "pantsing" won. I only knew who the final four men standing would be—and that's who landed on the cover. Writing all the different POVs was such a blast!

I definitely have plans for Basher and the Water Rhinos.

And one last thing: I adore Grayson Grant. (Had to be said!)

And now: Thank you to all my ARC readers to take the time to read my books (and especially those who help me find the typos that slip through! Bernie and Mary – this means you!). If you're not one of those who get early access to my books, I still appreciate you taking the time on me and my books! It's readers like you who give me joy and determination to keep at this gig.

Thank you to those who like my social media posts, and share for me!

Thank you to Dylan for the figures, and to Kaitie for editing.

And finally, thank you to Bachelor Nation for the inspiration!

Happy reading!

Holly xo

READING LIST

Love in Laandia

Royal Rumble
Royal Retelling
Royal Rising
Royal Reluctance
Royal Rebel
Royal Replacement
Royal Revelry

Don't

Don't Tell Me You Love Me
Don't Want to Be Friends
Don't Stop Me Now
Don't They Know It's Christmas

Charlotte Dodd

The Secret Life of Charlotte Dodd
The Missing Files of Charlotte Dodd
The Best Worst First Date Ever
The Hidden Past of Pippa McGovern
The Last Stand of Charlotte Dodd

Suitor Science

Hating the Chemistry Teacher
Falling for The Suitor
Fraternizing with the Ex
Marrying the Billionaire Best Friend
Loving the Wrong Guy
Finding the One

Love & Alliteration

Perfectly Played
Beautifully Baked
Pleasantly Popped

Sisters in a Small Town

Coming Home
Hanging On
Stepping Up

Billionaire Brats

Coffee Break with the Billionaire

Babysitting the Grumpy Billionaire

Unexpecting
Unexpectingly Happily Ever After

Oceanic Dreams – I Saw Him Standing There